Summer of Meteors

Kris Schaale

CATAMOUNT
PRESS

an imprint of Sunbury Press, Inc.
Mechanicsburg, PA USA

CATAMOUNT
PRESS

an imprint of Sunbury Press, Inc.
Mechanicsburg, PA USA

For information about special discounts for bulk purchases, please contact Sunbury Press Orders Dept. at (855) 338-8359 or orders@sunburypress.com.

To request one of our authors for speaking engagements or book signings, please contact Sunbury Press Publicity Dept. at publicity@sunburypress.com.

FIRST CANTAMOUNT PRESS EDITION: September 2025

Set in Adobe Garamond Pro | Interior design by Crystal Devine | Cover art by Kris Schaale. Cover design by Lawrence Knorr | Edited by Jennifer Tedford.

Publisher's Cataloging-in-Publication Data
Names: Schaale, Kris, author.
Title: Summer of meteors / Kris Schaale.
Description: First trade paperback edition. | Mechanicsburg, PA : Cantamount Press, 2025.
Summary: On the brink of the U.S. Civil War, *Summer of Meteors* follows three women from vastly different backgrounds who meet at the Bedford Springs Hotel and become entangled in an Underground Railroad scandal that will forever change their lives. Delving into a pivotal, often overlooked moment in history, the story explores themes of courage, sacrifice, female strength, and the bonds forged in the fight for freedom.
Identifiers: ISBN : 979-8-88819-342-6 (paperback).
Subjects: FICTION / African American & Black | FICTION / Historical / 19th Century / General | FICTION / Historical / 19th Century / American Civil War Era | FICTION / Women.

Designed in the USA
0 1 1 2 3 5 8 13 21 34 55

For the Love of Books!

To all the brave people who fled for their freedom, and to those that risked much to assist them.

Your chants, O year all mottled with evil and good!
  year of forebodings! year of the youth I love!
Year of comets and meteors transient and strange!—lo!
  even here, one equally transient and strange!
As I flit through you hastily, soon to fall and be gone,
  what is this book,
What am I myself but one of your meteors?

—WALT WHITMAN, "YEAR OF METEORS" (1859–60)

— 1 —

Anne

June 1859, Bedford, Pennsylvania

Anne drifted in and out of sleep as the pale blue morning light started seeping into her bedroom window. She lay there, not wanting to move. It was another day facing her life alone.

A terrible racket sounded, jolting her fully awake. Someone was hammering at the front door. Who could be here? She hadn't heard a horse come up the lane. She threw her dress over her head and ran down the stairs, passing her mother-in-law, Agnes, who was grasping her duster around her, alert with alarm. When she opened the door, her breath caught to see a man filling the doorway. It was Constable Smith.

"Mrs. McCoy, I'm sorry to be here so early. I see that I surprised you," he said with some discomfort. "My apologies, ma'am, but unfortunately, I'm here to serve you with this tax notice. You should have gotten earlier notices. Your property is in jeopardy, ma'am."

Anne's hand tightened on the doorframe. "Constable Smith, I *have* gotten notices. This winter was no time to pull together tax money. We're just getting by since I lost my husband." She tried very hard to maintain her composure and not cry.

"I am sorry for your struggles," he blurted out gruffly, "but Jacob's running afoul of the law has put you in this predicament. He should have thought about his family before breaking the law."

Anne was at a loss for how to respond. She had so much to say but couldn't get the words out.

The constable shifted back and forth on his boots for a moment, waiting for her response, and then continued, his voice softening, "I suggest you talk to the magistrate's office about your options prior to the 1857 tax foreclosures becoming final. You could lose your property, ma'am." He paused and looked her up and down. "It's a louse of a man who leaves his wife to the poor farm. A pretty young woman like you might do best to find a new husband."

The heat rose in Anne's cheeks, and her frustration with it. What could she say? Most of the people in town believed that her husband was shot while stealing a horse down in Cumberland Valley. The rumors had ruined his good name. If only she could defend Jacob with the truth of what had happened and stand up for his memory. But the truth was too dangerous. Many other people's freedom and security were at stake.

The constable handed the papers to her, saying quietly, "I wish you the best, Mrs. McCoy. You're not much older than my daughter, and I'd hate to see her in your fix."

Anne watched as he spun on his boot heel and strode down the steps and across the yard to where his ride was tied to the post near the front gate. He untied the horse and swung onto the animal, spurring it forward. Only when he met the dirt road at the bottom of the lane and turned to head north into town did Anne take her eyes off him and stare down at the notice.

* —— * —— *

Later that morning, Anne was hanging up the laundry. Bending down to gather a shirt, clipping one sleeve and then the next, she tried to keep her mind on each small task and breathe in between. Breathing was a chore. The heaviness in her body was almost unbearable. Sometimes, the enormity and pain of life made her feel like she was drowning, like her sadness would drag her right through the thick grass she was standing on and into the earth.

It may be better to sink into the ground. She wished she could lie down next to Jacob and feel his comfort again, as she had for seven years. How could he be gone? Gone from her life, which now she had to figure out alone. How was a widowed Quaker woman of twenty-five going to run a farm and homestead all by herself? How would she pay the bills and care for her child and mother-in-law? The questions in Anne's mind wouldn't stop.

She lifted a pair of her son's small pants from the laundry basket and shook out the wrinkles. The sudden movement jolted her out of the dark reverie. Breathing deeply, she pulled the clothespins from her apron and hung up one leg and then the other. She turned and looked down the hillock where she stood and across the yard into the field below the house. Anne could hear the gushing creek that marked the line between her land and the neighboring farm. The early June rains had stopped, and the brook was roiling and rushing toward town. Her eyes followed the stream up the hill to its source, where two of her cows stood by drinking from the spring as it ran out of the hillside and through the spring house. She loved her beautiful farm. At least there was that.

Anne had been keeping to herself since Jacob died last year. She had managed to distance herself from town, though it was less than a mile to the edge of the borough line. The last time she was there every eye had been on her, whispers following her every move, so it felt easier to stay at the farm and try to get by. But this morning it was clear that the rest of the world would not be so easily shut out. She pulled the tax notice out of her apron pocket and read it again.

1857 Property Tax, 30 acres at 3.33 per acre per annum past due as of Sept 1, 1858. Land deeded to Jacob and Anne McCoy, year bought 1852. $100 owed. Minimum payment: July 30, 1859, $50. Total Sept 1, 1859, $100.

Anne took a deep breath. She had to do something. It was bad enough that Jacob's good name was marred by what the public thought had happened last year. She wouldn't let her family lose everything they had worked so hard for. But how would she find the money? Fifty dollars was more than she made by herself all year. Harvest was in the fall, which would be too late. According to the notice, she had to have half of the taxes owed by the end of July and the other half by the first of September.

Anne sank onto the grass next to her wash basket, looking out at the beautiful pasture toward her neighbor's farm. The late spring trees on the western ridge bordering the Bedford Valley were getting their leaves. The flowering cherries were dropping their petals, which drifted in the wind across the field.

How could she make the taxes owed? The money she and her moth-er-in-law earned together hardly covered the basics like food. Sewing or making butter came to mind. Perhaps she could tutor children. But as she thought through her options, she discounted each one. She only had one cow for butter, and just herself and Agnes to make it. Sewing only got her pennies for a day's work. The school was out of session for the summer, so it would be too late once she could tutor again. Her heart sank.

She could ask her parents for help, but she knew times had been hard the last couple of years, and they had many mouths to feed. Most of her sisters and brothers were still at home on the farm in Quaker Valley.

Tears began to flow down her cheeks. The desire to sink into the ground returned, deep and hollow. Hopelessness seemed to find her almost every day.

Just then, her son, Joshua, burst out of the house onto the porch. "Mamma! There you are! I was looking for you but couldn't find you!"

Anne wiped her tears with her sleeve and smiled to hide her desperation from her little boy as he ran down the slope of the lawn toward the washing line. Joshua, at four years old, was pure joy in human form. He ran straight into Anne, burying himself in her lap.

His eyes and smile were huge as he gushed, "Mamma, I wanted to tell you that I put on my breeches! Grammy said I had to do it for myself today, and she wouldn't help me. I did all the buttons and tied the belt like a big boy!"

"Oh, Josh, what a fine accomplishment! Good for you! You *are* getting to be such a grown-up boy! Mamma is proud of how hard you work to learn to do things yourself," Anne whispered in his little ear, squeezing him to her.

He beamed up at her, and she stood, lifting him with some effort. When had he grown so big? As she held him close to her chest, she felt her heart would burst for loving her dear little man so much. Sometimes it took her breath away how much he looked like Jacob. His twinkling eyes and bright smile were exactly as she remembered her husband's.

Her gaze drifted over his shoulder, landing on the eastern ridges of town. Over Federal Hill and before the backdrop of Evitts Mountain, which was the Bedford Valley's southern end, there was the Bedford Springs Hotel, where the summer season would soon be underway. Housekeeping work would surely be available to prepare for the ladies and gentlemen arriving from many states, north and south, as well as the capital. A tiny flicker of hope flamed inside her.

Tomorrow, she would go to Bedford Springs.

———————

The next day, Anne made her way from her farm up over Juliana Heights and toward the back of Federal Hill. She had taken extra care with her appearance today. Bedford Springs, with its sprawling grounds and richly decorated rooms, was far grander than anything she was used to. She thought about the splendor of the grand old hotel. Wealthy politicians and men of industry spent their summers getting away from the heat and grime of cities like Pittsburgh and the sickness that came with the stinking streets and stifling air of Washington. Much of the growth and industry of Bedford had sprung out of its place in the mountain air. It was at the crossroads of the east-west Great Road between Pittsburgh and Philadelphia and the north-south road between Cumberland, Maryland, where the Baltimore and Ohio Railroad steamed through, and Altoona, where the Pennsylvania Railroad crossed.

Anne McCoy had grown up as Anne Way, a simple Quaker girl, about seven miles west of Bedford in Dunning's Creek. Also referred to as the Quaker Valley, its farmsteads and stores were run by a close community belonging to the Society of Friends. These local Quakers had come west from Philadelphia and Lancaster to find fertile, available land and the religious freedom to live by their own hands and follow their Inner Light, which was God's voice inside them telling them what was true, wise, and God's will. They lived simply and by what their hearts knew to be right.

The Way family worked together to make the farm their life and sustenance. When Anne met Jacob McCoy at a Quaker meeting house gathering about the growing local complications of the Fugitive Slave Act, she admired his passion for helping others. He would help anyone who needed assistance with a broad smile and an easy laugh. Marrying him and leaving Dunning's Creek for Bedford was a big change, but she had followed her heart.

The town of Bedford and the Bedford Springs Hotel were a different world for Anne, but she did her best to stay informed by reading the local paper. The *Bedford Gazette* published political stories and happenings that often put the Bedford Springs at the center of American politics. Last year, the first transatlantic cable was delivered to President James Buchanan from Queen Victoria during his summer stay at Bedford Springs. That was certainly an honor for Bedford and its residents. News from across the ocean! It was a wonder.

A far less honorable moment came two summers ago when the Supreme Court justices met at Bedford Springs to escape the Washington heat and deliberate on the Dred Scott versus Sandford trial. In this infamous case, the court decided that slaves were not U.S. citizens but rather property. This ruling meant that enslaved persons did not have the rights of citizens and that the government had no jurisdiction in deciding on the legality of slavery, making it a state-by-state property issue. The decision caused much prayer and consternation in the Quaker meeting houses across Pennsylvania. For Quakers, it was against God's laws and they believed that every human is equal and worthy of love and justice.

As Anne continued toward the hotel, doubt clouded her determination. Could she work amongst people whose beliefs went against her own? What would her parents think? There was a reason the Quaker community supported themselves and stayed apart. However, she couldn't think of another way to raise the money she needed to keep the farm. As she breathed in the early summer air thick with the smell of honeysuckle, she reset her resolve. She had to protect the farm and her family.

She descended the path down the other side of Federal Hill, recalling that the hill opposite was called Constitution Hill. She knew the names spoke to the strong ties to American politics for which Bedford and the Bedford Springs Hotel were well known. President Buchanan had been spending summers there for many years and lately had used it for his summer executive headquarters. Several other presidents and important politicians also stayed there. The comings and goings of the stagecoaches into Bedford from Cumberland to Bedford Springs kept the roads busy and the town bustling during the summer season.

When Anne reached the top of the hill, she could see the back of the Bedford Springs Hotel below. Elegant and grand, it spread along the front of Federal Hill, running south for hundreds of yards. Closest to

Anne was the newly rebuilt Swiss House and Evitt buildings. Standing three stories high, these long, dormitory-style buildings were crafted of wood and painted white, with porches decorated with fancy spindles and lacelike woodwork. In just a few weeks, guests would sit outside on the rocking chairs enjoying the view and taking in the fine mountain air.

To the south was the Colonial building, which was as imposing as it was elegant. Its giant columns, three stories high, and brick facade were impressive, and its shady front lawns served as a space for horse riding and games of recreation like croquet and badmitten. This building also had broad porches for sitting outside and a grand entrance where guests arrived all day in the summer. Elegantly dressed people would soon stroll across the colonnade to drink the healing mineral waters from the Magnesia Spring. Some guests would come and stay for a month or more, sharing their respite among others of the upper class while making social connections, business deals, and political alliances.

Below her, a coach was wending its way past Naugle's Mill, which stood by the road at the north end of the Springs property. Dust rose from thundering horse hooves as she descended the hill by the miller's house, where the path ended at Springs Road. Pausing to catch her breath, Anne waited for the dirt clouds to settle so she wouldn't be covered with grime when she arrived.

She planned to ask to speak with Mr. Newman, the head cook, whom she had met before when she was selling butter. He had always been kind to her. Her best chance was to apply for a position in housekeeping, as she didn't have other skills or experience in kitchen work. Perhaps he could make a recommendation to the head of the hotel. She didn't know what positions they had available at Bedford Springs, but she could easily do housework for regular pay. How grateful she would be for the opportunity to cover her debts with honest work.

Approaching the servant's entrance at the back of the cookhouse just to the south of the Colonial building, Anne found a young negro boy sitting on a wooden crate, peeling potatoes. Black freemen held many of the kitchen jobs around Bedford. Twelve years earlier, gradual manumission was still the law in Pennsylvania. She couldn't reconcile that while slavery ended in Pennsylvania in 1780, the children of slaves remained bound until they were twenty-eight years old. She could still remember when her neighbor, Jim, had been freed, but his son Jessie was forced to remain enslaved until the law changed in 1847. The North was not that progressive for all its Yankee pronouncements.

"Son, can you tell me where to inquire about getting work at the hotel?" Anne asked the boy.

"Don't know, ma'am, but you might ask Mister Blackburn, the head of house. He's right around the corner with Mister Newman, the cook," the boy said, pointing to the side of the outdoor kitchen.

Anne brushed her hands down the front of her simple cotton dress and apron, hoping to look presentable. She adjusted her bonnet, tucked in a piece of her red hair, which had come loose on her walk, and took a deep breath. Her heart was racing. She must steady herself so she could speak clearly. She headed past the back of the cookhouse and up behind the two men talking, standing still for a moment before they turned to look at her.

"Excuse me, sirs, I am here to speak with someone about working for the coming season. I am Anne McCoy from Bedford, and I have come to inquire if I might get a position in housekeeping." She quickly curtsied, trying her best to show manners.

Mr. Blackburn was a silver-haired gentleman standing more than six feet tall. He wore striped suit pants, a linen shirt, and a tailored waistcoat that spoke of his station at the hotel. He peered down his long aquiline nose at Anne, reviewing her from head to toe with piercing blue eyes.

"What skills might you have besides being a pretty and well-mannered young lady?" Blackburn inquired with a raised eyebrow.

She blushed, a bit flustered, and hesitated to answer.

Mr. Newman kindly intervened. "Blackburn, this here is Anne McCoy. She lives on a nearby farm and provides us with butter when she has it to sell. I am told by the kitchen help that she is a fine young woman and has schooled some of their children. She's been a tutor, too, for some of the well-to-do families in Bedford."

Blackburn raised his other silver eyebrow and cocked his head toward Anne, looking her over some more. "Housekeeping might be a waste for a girl who can read. Can you write? Do you have social manners and know how to sew and iron?"

Anne straightened up a bit. She was proud that she could read and write. She had learned her letters as a young girl because her parents believed in teaching their daughters as well as their sons, which was particular to Quaker families. Many non-Quaker farm women did not have the same educational opportunities as their brothers.

Anne replied, "Yes, sir, I can do all those things. I will do whatever is needed."

Blackburn rubbed his chin and looked closely at her. "I need several well-spoken and well-mannered girls to be ladies' maids. It's only proper that a fine lady have someone to accompany them on walks and at social engagements. You would attend to their needs, take care of their garments, and sometimes write their correspondence or read to them. How would that suit you, Missus McCoy?"

"I think I could do very well in such a position, sir," Anne answered quickly, unable to believe her good fortune.

"Excellent," said Mr. Blackburn. "Miss Harriet Lane will be here in three weeks, and I am in desperate need of finding her a lady's maid. Please come back first thing Monday morning. Your job will be to start preparing her quarters before she arrives. Your pay will be sixty cents per day."

"Yes, sir, thank you," Anne replied and curtseyed.

Mr. Newman smiled and nodded at her, and the men turned away. Anne took her leave and hurried back toward the resort's north side to find the path home. A shaky laugh escaped her, and she glanced heavenward, sending silent thanks. When she got back to the farm she would ask Jacob's mother, Agnes, to help her with her son and the farm while she was at the Springs. Luckily the corn and hay would take care of itself for the summer season, and Agnes could certainly handle the milking. How wonderful to have work that might allow her to meet some interesting people. She loved to learn new things, and serving the visiting ladies might prove exciting.

As she made her way across the sprawling green lawn of the resort, she spotted two men ahead of her on the gravel path. As she got closer, she recognized Elias Rouse, the black barber from town. He was talking to a tall, thin, white man with gray hair and a long beard. She liked Mr. Rouse very much. Her husband had appreciated his efforts at the churches in town, where he helped new black citizens settle into the Bedford area. It was unusual that he would be here at the Bedford Springs rather than at his barber shop.

"Good morning, Mr. Rouse," Anne said in greeting.

"Hello, Missus McCoy. Please let me introduce you to John Smith, who is visiting Bedford and this fine establishment. What brings you out to the Springs on this lovely morning?" replied Rouse as the man with him regarded her with a grave expression.

"I've come for some summer work. Since my husband died, I've found it hard to make ends meet, but I've just secured a lady's maid position starting next week," she explained.

Elias turned to his companion. "Jacob McCoy was an excellent man, Mr. Smith. He assisted in our causes many times here in Bedford Valley."

"I see," said the older gentleman with a smile, his countenance instantly becoming more alert. It was as if a light inside him had turned on. What did his interest in her husband's support mean? Too many people being aware or involved wasn't a good thing.

"I must be going. I hope you both have a blessed day," Anne said as she hurried away. The men were silent, but she could feel their eyes following her.

She crossed the road at the mill and found the break in the greenery that marked the trail home. Her thoughts raced as she climbed up the path that wound through tall maple and oak trees toward Juliana Heights.

So many thoughts crowded her head. Did she know how to press silk and satin? Would she know the proper way to speak to fine ladies? What if she didn't measure up? Hopefully, her lady would be patient. Mr. Blackburn had said "Miss Harriet Lane" was her assignment. She stopped suddenly, her breath catching in her throat. How could she not have recognized the name upon first hearing it? Miss Harriet Lane was President Buchanan's niece—and the First Lady of the United States!

— 2 —

Harriet

Harriet could not wait to leave Washington. The year had been terrible for the president so far, and she was exhausted from trying to keep his spirits up and orchestrate a positive social world at the Executive Mansion.

Just last week, they hosted the Spring State Dinner. The challenge of not seating bitterly opposing congressmen together had become even more complicated by divisions within the existing parties. Though praised in the newspapers for her skills as a hostess, deft handling of seating arrangements, and gracious ability to talk with anyone, Harriet reached her limit and was ready to escape Washington. The humidity was stifling, and so was the political infighting. Today she would begin packing for Bedford Springs. There was much to do to ensure she had the right dresses and accessories for the month-long vacation.

Her three-room suite at the Executive Mansion was hard to navigate with trunks and hat boxes covering so much of the floor. In her dressing room, she couldn't even see the oriental rug anymore from everything strewn about. This packing had to come together, as they were leaving in two days' time. She was usually much more organized this close to the annual trip.

For years, "Hal," as her uncle nicknamed her when she was small, and "Nunc," as she called him, enjoyed their summer holidays at Bedford Springs. Thank goodness they were able to break away this year. Over the past several months, the president had been overwhelmed with events leading up to the midterm elections. The outcome was Uncle Buck's Democratic Party losing the majority in Congress and the emergence of the new Republican Party. The anti-slavery factions of the northern states had fueled these changes. Perhaps this trip would improve his mood.

Her uncle started taking her with him on retreats to the mountains when she finally came of age. She suspected that he put it off as long as possible. Given her precocity and irrepressible spirit—his words, not hers—he was very frank with her about how she sometimes exasperated him. Her uncle loved her dearly, but as a younger girl, she often tried his patience.

The year she turned fifteen, her uncle discovered that she was writing letters to her friend, Henry Johnston, who she had met at Bedford Springs. She had not lived that down. Although she knew it wasn't proper, she had feelings for Henry at a young age. It was the first time she felt those kinds of things for a boy. She now admitted that it *was* indiscreet to correspond with him, but she also believed in her heart that her letters were honest and true. She would never say anything that would compromise her or her uncle's reputation. She remembered the excitement of receiving his letters and reading them repeatedly. Henry had excellent common sense and a good heart. He stayed in her mind to this day.

Uncle Buck had been furious when he discovered her letters and seldom missed an opportunity to remind her of that impropriety. Now she only got to see Henry when their families were both at the Springs. Maybe she would see him this year.

Though she was now twenty-nine, as she packed for the Springs, she felt as giddy as a young girl at the chance to get away and relax. She was pulling her prettiest and lightest gowns out of her dressing closets, and her lady's maid was packing them into the trunks when her uncle arrived at her quarters.

"Getting ready to go, my dear?" he asked, leaning against the frame of her parlor door. At six feet tall, he was still an imposing figure despite being sixty-eight years of age. He gazed around her room and rolled his eyes with a wry smile. Was he going to comment on what a mess it was? Sometimes, his expressions reminded her so much of her mother—his sister. He had the same ability to scold her with warm humor that her mother had long ago. Something about his expressions made her feel that her mother was close, though she had been gone many years.

Harriet darted from her dressing area to her uncle and hugged him. "Oh, Nunc, I am *so* ready to go now, but I still have so much to do before we leave Washington. Tomorrow, we have another dreadful state dinner, and I just can't seem to work out the seating. We must invite Senator Cameron, but I don't want to put him with someone who may stir up trouble. I can't put him with your favored allies either, or there could be a fistfight!"

Buchanan sighed deeply and rubbed his temple with his free hand. His silver hair was a bit shaggy, and the dark circles under his blue eyes told of the long days and sleepless nights of the past several years. This summer retreat was coming just in time.

"That damned Cameron! He devils me in my every waking moment!" he said, the color in his cheeks rising. "He and his cronies are hell-bent on tearing this nation apart with their abolitionist sentiments with no regard for the sanctity of the blessed country as a whole or the Constitution! Ask him not to come if he can't behave himself!"

Senator Simon Cameron had been her uncle's political adversary for many years. They had risen together in Pennsylvania politics and were both been members of the Democratic Party until recently. Given his anti-slavery position and support of the abolitionist movement, Cameron had left the Democratic Party for the new Republican Party. His actions were partly responsible for the Democrats not nominating Buchanan in the 1850 election. Cameron had gone to Richmond and roused anti-Buchanan factions that swung Virginia out of favor for Buchanan. This lost the quorum of southern states that would have put him on the presidential ticket instead of Franklin Pierce. The presidency came his way later, but his bitter rivalry with Simon Cameron was as well known in Washington as in Pennsylvania.

"Now, Nunc, you know we must invite Senator Cameron as it would cause an outrage if we did not. He's the senator from your home state! Perhaps I can put him with the British delegation. He may be diverted with some stimulating conversation about Cuba, never to be seen again all evening," Harriet quipped. She realized that *was* probably the right way to solve the seating issue without risking infighting.

"I don't care what happens to Cameron or where he sits. What I *do* care about is that I came here to discuss our travel plans. We leave on the early morning train to Cumberland in two days to take the noon stagecoach north to Bedford Springs. We have a large party this year, including the widow Eugenia Bass, who will be my guest. She will be bringing her three children and their nursemaid, Janie. I will have four footmen for security, and my secretary, Mr. Jones," he said.

He walked to the front windows and, looking out at the lush front lawn, added, "Your lady's maids have been given time off to see their families. I have taken the liberty of writing to Mr. Blackburn at the Springs and asking him to assign a local woman to you."

"Thank you, Nunc. I'm glad you'll have Mrs. Bass for company. Are you sure her bringing Janie is a good idea, though?" She knew she was raising a sore subject but also felt it was her responsibility to warn her uncle of problems he seemed not to see as plainly as she did. This was a misstep that could bring him bad press and more accusations of favoring slavery.

"Hal . . ." Uncle Buck placed his hand on her shoulder. The familiar touch softened her, but she went on. He was not going to be happy with what she had to say.

"We will be over the Mason-Dixon line, Nunc. The president's party being accompanied by an enslaved person could at best raise some eyebrows and at worst create a scandal. Many Northerners at the hotel may heartily object. Having Janie with our group might be misconstrued as you approving of slavery." She tried to sound conciliatory as she sat on the settee nearby, smoothing her silk skirts. She braced for the long lecture her uncle was sure to give her about the question of slavery that swirled around him and the nation. She'd broached the subject a few times, but he had a way of defending his constitutional views that Harriet felt ill-equipped to counter. Emotional appeals weren't the way into her uncle's sharp mind, which had been too long focused on law and politics.

Buchanan's eyes burned blue, and his jaw set tight. He straightened his back and squared his shoulders. "I am not discussing this with you, Harriet. I support the South's right to make their own choices. Slavery will die its own death by economic necessity without tearing this country apart. I am not in favor of slavery but must preserve the federal union. Mrs. Bass will bring Janie with her as is her choice as a southern landowner from Mississippi."

With that, he turned on his heel and walked out of Harriet's quarters. She heard the main door of the suite slam shut. Her heart sank. That hadn't gone well. Why could he not see that he was setting himself up for political controversy? She was only trying to help.

When it came to the condition of the negro slaves and freemen in the United States, Harriet believed that the time was long overdue for the recognition of every human as a child of God. She believed all people deserved grace, respect, and freedom to live the lives they determined for themselves. One of her first acts as mistress of the White House was to end the practice of employing slaves. These people were not hers to set free and unfortunately had to be sent back to the plantations in Virginia and Maryland where they'd been leased from. She replaced them with paid servants, both black and white.

Her convictions came from her Catholic boarding school education. Nunc sent her to the Georgetown Visitation Convent after her parents both died. Sister Constance, the Mother Superior, repeatedly stated to the girls that "slavery is against God's will." This stance came directly from Pope Gregory XVI, and all the nuns worked hard to impress that viewpoint on their students.

She recalled a story her uncle often told about her. He had been hosting a political dinner at his home in Lancaster as a United States senator. As the guests arrived, many greeted him and asked after his niece. But where *was* little Harriet?

Waiting for the guests to arrive was boring. Harriet had gone out to play. She loved being outside. Along the way, she ran into Old Tabitha, a negro woman down the lane. Tabitha was out gathering up sticks and branches.

"Tabitha, why are you picking up sticks? Do you use them in the baskets you weave?" Harriet asked.

"No, Miss Lane, winter is comin', and I don't have nuff wood put back. I workin' to get kindling. My son needs to go out to get the bigger wood soon," Tabitha said.

Harriet took it upon herself to gather some of the logs they had on the Buchanan woodpile in a wheelbarrow and deliver them to the woman. When the servants finally found her, she was filthy, and her dress was torn. When asked why she had endeavored to haul firewood, Harriet replied, "It's getting cold out quickly this fall, and Tabitha does not have enough wood. She needed my help."

Her uncle told this story as a point of pride as much as to highlight her precocious nature. Where was his pride in helping those who needed him now? He believed the same things she did. She was sure of it. How could he not see the potential political conflicts his guests could cause?

Slavery was wrong. That never changed in her mind since childhood. Her family used to own the general mercantile in Mercersburg, Pennsylvania. As proprietors of the local store that served the whole town, they had been prominent community members who had regular contact with all levels of society. They treated all people fairly and with respect.

Why couldn't her uncle see that he should look for a way to stand up for his values? He treated her like a daughter and trusted her as a confidante, but right now, she failed to get him to see he was dividing the country.

After she'd finished packing the last trunk with her maid, Harriet sat down to write a letter to her best friend, Lily Macalester, about her worries. Lily was the daughter of wealthy Philadelphia industrialist Charles Macalester. Harriet valued her companionship, grit, and independence, which she found to be like her own.

With Lily, she was comfortable discussing anything and knew she would always receive understanding and support. The two wrote to each other at least weekly. Harriet's letters to Lily allowed her to voice her concerns and joys. These missives helped her maintain her even temperament in the whirlwind of the role of acting First Lady.

Harriet Lane
The Executive Mansion
1600 Pennsylvania Avenue, North West
Washington City, District of Columbia
June 28th, 1859

My Dear Lily,

How are you, my friend, and how is your week going? Did the dinner for the Vanderbilts go as planned? I usually wait for your letter before I write one in return, but I needed to write to you

*right now. I so wish you were here. I hope you don't mind me
unburdening myself to you.*

*I had to sit down and write to you as my heart is hurting
over a conversation I just had with Uncle Buck. You know how
he can be; he is so stubborn and set in his opinions. It is hard to
find my voice with him on matters of great importance when our
points of view differ.*

*Of course, I love and respect him as my uncle and now as
the president. He has dedicated his life to what is best for this
country. As you know, he is a strict constitutionalist and believes
that preserving the Union must follow the Constitution's guidance
that the states make their own choices in these matters.*

*As we have talked about many times together, I don't think
he sees that by allowing the South to uphold the institution of
slavery, he is seen as a hypocrite or, even worse, as being in favor
of it! We go around and around on this topic. I am frustrated that
I cannot make headway with him, even though I know how he
objects to slavery. I have told you of his dear nursemaid, Hannah.
She was like a mother to him growing up. He was eventually
able to buy her freedom. He says that, as president, he must think
differently and take action to preserve peace among the states. I
cannot imagine how this will not have disastrous ends.*

*We leave for Bedford Springs in two days. I am sorry to say
that though we will be in Pennsylvania, Uncle Buck is allowing
his companion, a Mrs. Bass from Mississippi, to bring her nursemaid, Janie, to tend to her three children. She is a negro slave.
What will the Northerners at the Springs think?!*

*I am sorry to burden you with my troubles again, but I feel
better having written them out in this letter. I don't know how I
will handle this unfortunate situation, but I am sure we will all
get by and, hopefully, get some much-needed rest. Uncle Buck is
in a terrible state with the stresses of late due to the rising threat
of violence between the states.*

*Did you read that last month Senator Charles Sumner
was assaulted with a cane in the Senate Hall by Congressman
Preston Brooks?! The question of slavery has caused even our*

elected officials in Washington to come to blows! Did you also hear that now the president has declared John Brown an enemy of the nation? There is a $250 price on his head after the horrible bloodshed in Kansas at the Pottawatomie massacre, which was carried out in the name of abolition. The radicals are killing in the name of others' lives. What an appalling contradiction!

May the next few weeks give me and my uncle some rest and relief. How will I do without you at the Springs this year?

Thank you for always being the one I can turn to. I value your friendship, my dear friend.

All my love,

Harriet

Harriet sealed and addressed the envelope, then gazed out the window next to her writing desk. The lawns of the Executive Mansion were finally bright green from the June rains. She would get this sent off today. Perhaps dispatching her worries in the letter to Lily would carry them away.

— 8 —

Juba

As the steam engine chugged its way through the Maryland coun-tryside, Juba took a moment to look out the window at the passing scenery. Watching the lush green farmland roll by, she took a deep breath, feeling her body relax a little, and settled into the plush velvet seat in the presidential coach. The soft blue velvet seats trimmed in gold braid were a comfort.

These rail accommodations were a big change from other train rides she had taken. In the past, she had been forced to sit in the black-only railcar, which had hard wooden benches due to overcrowding. Many of the passengers had to huddle on the floor or sit on their sacks and trunks. A bucket in the corner behind a drape served as a restroom. Treated like cattle—this was the life of black people. If only she could keep these memories from chasing away the moments of peace. She shook her head, trying to push away the angry thoughts.

She checked on her three little charges. The Bass children had fallen asleep all on one bench seat, like a pile of young pups draped over each other. Thank goodness for a break from their constant chatter and move-ment. Ella was the oldest at fourteen, Council, named for Mister Bass, was ten, and little Eugenia was just five, named for Missus and her spit-ting image in miniature.

Children were so much work, but at least she was no longer a field hand. That had been backbreaking work and felt like a long, slow death sentence. She had seen many older field hands who appeared half dead at barely thirty.

As the Maryland towns raced by and gradually gave way to farmland, she saw people working in the fields. An untold number of black people were, like her, trapped in slavery, living their lives at their master's bidding. Everything depended on the master. Were they kind or brutal? Did they at least treat you with basic decency? Missus treated her pretty good, but she'd had her time with a bad overseer and a master who tolerated his fowl treatment of the slaves and looked the other way.

Her heart ached to see bent backs out in those fields. Still burned in her memory were the hot and miserable days working all day with little more food than a cornmeal cake. How could white masters think it was okay to work slaves on so little to eat and only a ladleful of water every few hours? She shook her head, thinking about it. It was exhausting and hopeless for all those souls she watched in the fields—a reason to run if they ever should find the chance.

Just after the master died, Missus discovered that Juba could read and write. The widow saw fit to use her education by giving her a house position. She was glad to be doing inside work, and she liked caring for Missus Bass's young children. Over the past two years working as the children's nursemaid, she felt better than she had in a long time. The previous eight years had been a nightmare.

Her parents were freed in the early 1840s by a decree in their master's last will and testament. They moved to Boston to make a new life in the North. To Juba's mind, the practice of death-decreed manumission was strange. Why wouldn't a white master want to bestow that freedom while they were alive? Sometimes, the heirs wouldn't honor the will, and in that case, people who should have their freedom remained slaves without even knowing that they should have been free. Imagine being free and not even knowing it. Heartbreaking. Or was it worse to be legally free and illegally enslaved? Her life was troubled by these thoughts that she couldn't push away or do anything about.

Juba was born soon after her family arrived in Boston. Most of her early memories were good. She remembered hungry times when one of her parents was out of work or when winter was harsh and food scarce. However, she placed her family as happy, loving, and hardworking. Her mother had been a house slave. Her mistress had taken a liking to her and taught her to read. Her mother then showed Juba how to read and write. Momma understood reading was a way for black people to get ahead in the white people's world. Better jobs went to black people who had these skills.

Everyone knew there was a growing trade in the 1850s for slave catchers. Due to the Fugitive Slave Act, opportunistic men made money by following escaped slaves north. A strong and able field hand was worth close to a thousand dollars. Slave catchers would return the fugitives to their southern masters for a reward, sometimes as high as five hundred dollars. That was the price of someone's life and freedom. Though the North was heavily anti-slavery in general and Boston was full of abolitionists, there was still great danger for free black people there.

Her parents mustn't have been aware that slave catchers were making money by kidnapping free black people. They wouldn't have sent her out on her own if they had known of that danger. At only ten years old, Juba was grabbed off the street. She had been waiting to cross the road with some groceries her mother had sent her to fetch from the corner grocery.

Kicking and screaming, she'd tried to bite the man who had snatched her around the waist. No one close by did anything. She was hit so hard that she was knocked out and woke up much later, far from home. Her head was pounding, her wrists tied, and she was terrified. She often had nightmares of that terror; that moment when she realized she might never see her family again. What had her poor parents thought when she never returned?

Approaching the Mason-Dixon line for the first time since she was taken across it by slave catchers all those years ago, she thought about what her life had been like before her enslavement. Where were her momma and pappa? What were they doing now? Juba thought about them every day. Once again, she had let the sadness sink in and left the quiet moment she had been enjoying. Working her fingers across her forehead to smooth out the tension in her furrowed brow, she took a deep breath and straightened herself in the plush seat.

The Bass children started to stir, and Juba shifted her view away from the window with a sigh. Missus Bass was back in the lounge section of the rail car, sitting with President Buchanan and his niece, Miss Lane. Miss Lane and her uncle were bent close and seemed to be laughing. Missus glanced at them and then looked away, irritated, before standing to come back toward her children.

"Janie, I'd like you to help the children take their lunch now. Get the picnic basket the housemen packed for us. Make sure they eat without making themselves a mess. There will not be time to change their clothes before getting on the stagecoach in Cumberland. I want them looking presentable for their arrival at the train station," instructed Missus.

Why did Missus feel the need to constantly tell her what to do? She always did as she should without any direction. Missus treated her like a child. It was tiresome, and she had to bite her tongue not to object.

"Yes, ma'am. I will put napkins on their collars and laps and instruct them about staying clean. I will wash their messy hands as soon as they are done," Juba replied, ducking her head in deference. It was easier just to get by.

Another constant annoyance and indignity was that her mistress insisted on calling her "Janie" rather than her actual name, Juba. Renaming slaves was common practice. Missus Bass made a point announcing that Juba was "unseemly" and Janie was much more English-sounding, which she said was more appropriate for a house slave. The widow made everyone call her Janie, even the other bondsmen on the farm who had always known her as Juba. She resented it every time someone called her Janie.

✦————◆————✦

Cumberland was a crush of activity and noise when the train arrived at about noon. Finally, the presidential travel party departed safely in their two coaches. What a relief to be in a separate coach with just the children and Mr. Jones, the president's secretary. Sitting with the president made her nervous. A separate wagon with the party's many trunks and sundries followed closely behind.

The carriages lumbered along the rutted dirt road through a wide valley. The children talked incessantly, but the rocking motion of the stagecoach made Juba sleepy.

"There are horses riding up behind us!" cried ten-year-old Council. Juba pulled herself out of half-sleep. Looking out the rear window, she saw a cloud of dust and what appeared to be two riders quickly gaining on them.

The forward stagecoach was a good bit ahead of them, and the president's footmen were ahead of it. What was all the commotion?

"Looks like a couple of riders are coming up on us fast. Maybe they're messengers for the president," said Mr. Jones.

"Stop the stage! Everyone out!" one of the riders ordered as he rode his horse in front of the coach, blocking it so it couldn't pass. Juba could see he had a gun drawn.

"He has a gun! Where is the other coach with the footmen?!" Juba exclaimed.

"Guns! Let me see!" Council jumped forward to get a look. The other two children pressed against the window.

"Oh no, you don't. You sit down now," Juba said, catching the back of his pants and pulling him into his seat.

The second rider joined the first man, jumping off his horse and aiming his rifle at the coach. Both men were dusty and dirty-looking. Neither had shaved nor looked like they'd had a bath in quite a while. Their clothes showed they were not messengers but perhaps thieves. Where on earth were the president's footmen? They were supposed to be their protection!

"I told everyone to get out!" The first man lunged into the stagecoach window and sneered when he saw Juba. "What do we have here?"

"Sir, we are with the president!" Mr. Jones exclaimed.

Finally, two armed security footmen rode up on horseback. They were wearing presidential guard uniforms and had their guns drawn. "What is the meaning of this?" one of them demanded. "You are harassing the president's travel party!"

The two riders put down their weapons slowly and raised their hands.

"The president! We were huntin' a runaway! We thought this here girl was a fugitive," the taller man announced.

The president's men continued talking with the two ruffians, who kept their arms raised, not moving a muscle. Juba couldn't make out the conversation, but she now understood. They were slave catchers. She felt sick. Pressing herself against the seat, she closed her eyes to try to make the sight of them leave her.

"I wouldn't worry, Janie," Mr. Jones said consolingly. "They're getting patted down right now." After a pause, he continued, "Now they're walking back to their horses with their hats still in their hands after paying respects to the president."

Just then, one of the footmen ran back to their carriage to update them. "All is well. Please stay in the coach. The two men were searching for some fugitives who had crossed the border from Maryland and were believed to be traveling this way. They didn't realize they were stopping the president's party." He chuckled and added, "They look quite squeamish and ready to go!"

Remembering her own experience with slave catchers sent a chill down Juba's body even though it was a hot summer's day. When the carriages began to roll forward again, she peered out the window at the rough-looking men standing by the road with their horses. One was tall with curly reddish-brown hair on top of which he had put a dusty bowler hat. He wore a smirk, but she could see he was a bit out of sorts. His companion was shorter and had a heavier build, with blonde hair and a red beard that wasn't all grown in. Frowning and sweaty, they looked shaken, but when they saw Juba looking at them, they leered at her.

Juba sat back against the seat cushion, feeling sick. Memories of being grabbed and hit over the head many years ago took over her thoughts.

Mr. Jones patted her hand. "Are you all right, Miss Janie? Don't you worry about those boys. I've heard that slave catchers roam up and down this valley as it's close to the Mason-Dixon line and a route of the Underground Railroad. Seems stupid to me that they would be down here. Any fugitive that had come this far and made it into Pennsylvania would probably be up in those mountains on either side of us." He pointed to the vista around them. "Up there, they could stay hidden in the daytime. But perhaps they stop and search the wagons coming through in case they're providing assistance."

The valley was a couple of miles across, made up of cleared farmland. The ridges above the valley floor were starting to see new trees growing toward the bottom. Higher up were patches of limestone scrum and dense older forest that hadn't been cut for timber like the trees below.

Was someone hiding up there in those hills and watching them? How must an enslaved person feel to be on their way to freedom? As the stagecoaches and wagon headed north, leaving the slave catchers behind, her heartbeat finally began to slow down. After she settled the children, she sat back, and her breath returned to normal. Yet it was hard to shake the awful feeling in the pit of her stomach after seeing those men.

— 4 —

Anne

The excitement all over the Springs property ahead of President Buchanan's arrival had the hotel staff in a storm of activity. Anne had been working the last three weeks and got paid each Friday. Though she had a long way to go, and each payment felt like just a tiny dent in her debt, she felt a bit of hope, which was a relief. She had helped to prepare the suite of rooms for the president and Miss Lane, who would arrive today and stay for the next month.

How would this go, serving Miss Harriet Lane, the president's niece and acting mistress of the White House? She had been so busy getting things ready for the president's arrival with the rest of the staff that it wasn't until this morning that she awoke before dawn and couldn't stop the tumble of emotions and the racing of her heart. Today was the day she would meet Miss Lane and the president of the United States.

Anne was unsure if a young Quaker woman who had never left Bedford County was up for the task. What if she made a social misstep or didn't know what to say? Mr. Blackburn had reviewed his expectations of service and manners around the president with the staff several times over the last two weeks. That had been helpful, but she felt like she might be sick from worry.

Praying for God's good grace to guide and be with her, she climbed Federal Hill on her way to work that morning. As she reached the crest of the hill, she turned and stopped. The orange sun was rising through the Narrows, where the eastern side of Bedford Valley, Evitts Mountain, was split by the Juniata River cutting through it. The sky was bright pink to the east. The view filled her with hope.

As she arrived at the Evitt building, Anne heard Mr. Blackburn shouting directions to multiple workmen carrying furniture toward the Colonial building.

"Take those tables back to the dining room! And for goodness sake, hurry up, as we haven't much time left to get this lobby ready!" Blackburn directed this to a young man who appeared to be moving as fast as he could with a pedestal table.

She was quite used to this frenzy now. The last three weeks had been a whirlwind of activity as they prepared the resort for the arrival of summer guests and President Buchanan. The musty smell of the closed-up buildings that had sat all winter had been washed away by the clean smell of linseed oil. Fresh air drifted through the open windows, airing out every corner and closet. The scent of lye soap rose from the hardwood floors, which the staff had meticulously scrubbed clean. Dust and mold had been wiped away, and everything was gleaming.

Anne worked hard at the spring cleaning; in particular, she helped Mr. Blackburn make the president's quarters new and grand. With the help of several other housemen, they moved furnishings and replaced the draperies, rugs, and linens with finery "fit for a king," as Mr. Blackburn proclaimed when the transformation was complete. Indeed, the president would be pleased to receive a warm welcome and a beautiful suite awaiting his stay.

Anne had taken extra care to make Miss Harriet Lane's suite pretty and plush. Miss Lane was known in the newspapers for her style, grace, and beauty. Anne tried to keep all that in mind when she was getting her space ready. As a Quaker, she was used to simple and plain furnishings. She had to admit, though, that she loved the comfortable stuffed chairs, sumptuous bedding, and elegant draperies. Miss Lane's rooms had feminine appointments with soft pastel colors and lace. President Buchanan's suite was all red, gold, and blue fabrics.

The day was so busy with the presidential party's impending arrival that Anne didn't realize where the time had gone when suddenly she heard the blowing of a coronet echoing off the valley walls. Far-off sounds of hooves and the grating wheels of stagecoaches and wagons came from the south valley.

Mr. Blackburn shouted orders for all those specifically assigned to the president to gather at the grand portico of the Colonial building to greet the incoming coaches.

"Everyone, ready! Check your uniforms, fix your hair to look your best, and be on the steps at the main entrance in five minutes!"

Anne heard his shouts all through the building and up the staircase.

Taking one last look at herself in the mirror that hung over Miss Lane's dressing table, she smoothed her red curls behind her ears and fixed a few loose strands under her white frilled cap. She swept her hands down her gray cotton uniform to make sure there wasn't visible dust or cobwebs on her skirt. She retied her white apron in the back to make the bow look fresh.

She smiled at her reflection to make herself feel less nervous and whispered aloud, "God be with me today. Please give me the strength to know what to do and what to say. Help me be pleasing to Miss Lane and the president so I can do my job and help my family."

As directed, Anne descended the stairs toward the Colonial building and the grand portico. Right behind her was Thomas Miller, the president's assigned valet. She had been pleased to find someone working here she was familiar with. Thomas was a fellow Quaker she had known from childhood.

He smiled at her and said, "Well, here we go, Miss Anne! We best get over our nerves and head down there before Mr. Blackburn must yell for us again! God bless us all!" He skipped the last two steps at the bottom and sped ahead on long legs.

The wait seemed endless as the staff stood ready. Many squirmed and shifted nervously. Half of those waiting had served the president in past summers and knew what to expect. The others looked pale and frightened. Mr. Blackburn walked along the line of maids and housemen, inspecting them, straightening ties, and dusting off caps.

"Look alive, people, and put smiles on your faces! This is the president of the United States, for God's sake! I want everyone to bow or curtsy as he passes you on the steps. Anne McCoy, I want you on the top step so that I can introduce you to Miss Lane, and you can help her to her rooms." He pointed, and Anne scurried to the spot.

As the carriages pulled in under the tall white pillars of the grand portico, Anne saw the president's silver hair through the coach's window. Facing him was a young woman with a rose-colored silk bonnet with ivory and light green flowers decorating the brim. Below her hat, golden hair was neatly braided and fixed for travel. Anne knew immediately that this must be Miss Harriet Lane, as she had heard tales about her beautiful hair.

The footmen opened the stagecoach door, and the president climbed out first, taking care to duck so as not to hit his head. How tall the silver-haired statesman was! Though getting up in age and a bit heavy in the middle, he moved with a fair amount of vigor. How he comported himself showed his confidence and stature as the most exalted man in the country.

Buchanan turned and reached up into the carriage to help his niece down. Anne observed he did this himself before turning to those in attendance rather than waiting for the footmen to assist her. He did the same for the other woman who followed her. This woman was petite, with jet-black hair and pale skin. She wore a black silk gown trimmed in white lace and a matching bonnet. That must be the widow Bass.

"Welcome, Mr. President! We are ready for your summer stay here at Bedford Springs! I trust your travel was uneventful," announced Mr. Blackburn.

"Yes, yes, fine, Blackburn, other than getting stopped by hooligans in the valley. We are weary of travel and relieved to be here at last," responded Buchanan.

"Yes, sir, we will be happy to get you settled as soon as we can."

"I'd like you to attend to my companions, Blackburn. Of course, you have met my niece, Miss Harriet Lane, as she has been here many summers. And this year, I have the pleasure of bringing the charming Mrs. Eugenia Bass and her three children, who are in the next coach with the help."

Mr. Blackburn bowed his head to both ladies. "Welcome to the Bedford Springs Hotel. We shall make every effort to ensure your stay is restful and comfortable."

He took the cue to start walking the party up the steps toward the staff standing in line, who bowed and curtseyed as the president passed. He nodded in return to each.

At the top of the stairs, Blackburn paused. "Mr. President, I followed the direction in your last correspondence and have assigned this young lady, Anne McCoy, to be Miss Lane's lady's maid for the duration of your stay. I trust you will find her capable of that task, along with providing any support Miss Lane and your party may require."

The president tipped his head to Anne and turned to his niece as Anne gave a deep curtsy of respect.

"I'm so glad to meet you, Anne. I look forward to our time together and getting to know one another," Miss Lane said, offering her hand to Anne.

This was an unexpectedly familiar gesture since Anne was a servant, which was a surprise; she bowed again and took Miss Lane's hand as she did so.

"I'm pleased to serve you, Miss Lane," was all Anne could think was appropriate to reply.

Blackburn reintroduced Thomas Miller, who had been the president's valet last year. He then introduced Lucinda Koontz as the maid assigned to help with the Bass children.

At that, Mrs. Bass cut in. "Oh, that won't be necessary. I brought the children's nursemaid, who is in the next carriage with them. Please make sure she has suitable arrangements in the children's rooms."

Anne looked at the second stagecoach and saw a black woman peering out. She looked nervous. All three children were pressed against the windows, ready to burst out. They probably had been a trial to settle down on the long trip.

Blackburn cut in at this point. "Anne and Thomas, please accompany the president and Miss Lane and help them unpack in their rooms immediately. I am sure they're exhausted from their travels and want to rest and refresh before dinner at seven."

* * *

"What a beautiful suite! This is much more to my liking than the rooms I had last year!" exclaimed Miss Lane, smiling with obvious approval. Anne flushed with pride, though she knew perhaps that wasn't modest.

Miss Lane walked around the rooms, inspecting and touching the new drapes and bedlinens in appreciation. How lovely that the gracious lady noted her work. It certainly was easy to be around the president's niece. This wasn't what she had expected. No sooner had the trunks been carted in than the door closed, and the two were alone.

Miss Lane turned to Anne and said warmly, "Anne, I would very much like it if you called me Miss Harriet when we're alone. I am here to relax and let go of all the burdens and formality that the White House has put upon me, and it would be refreshing for me to feel we are at ease with each other."

Anne was a bit taken aback but quickly dipped her knees and nodded. "Yes, miss, I will try to remember that," she said softly.

Just then, a loud commotion erupted from the rooms next door. Anne and Harriet turned toward the sound. President Buchanan's voice rose, and he seemed quite irritated.

"Oh dear, what in the world is wrong now," exclaimed Harriet. She opened the door to her suite, motioning for Anne to come with her. "Let's see what I can do to calm my uncle down. I worry for his health with his emotional outbursts. His long day of travel isn't helping matters."

They went to the door of the president's suite. The staff set up a grand parlor for him to receive guests. The room contained a large desk for daily correspondence, which would be necessary to keep his work current while he was away. The two women observed several housemen rushing around, moving rugs and furnishings.

"What's going on, Nunc? What are you shouting about?" Miss Harriet asked her uncle. Anne thought it quite endearing that she addressed him with a nickname.

"They have removed my desk! The one I have favored for twenty years! I had that desk brought over from the old Crockford bachelor's quarters when I started staying in this new building with you, Harriet."

The president was clearly agitated, opening and slamming the drawers to the desk which, according to him, was a poor replacement. Thomas, the valet, stood behind him, wringing his hands, terror on his face.

"They have presumed to remove my desk and given me this large oak piece in its place, but it does not suit me at all! Useless! I want my old desk brought back immediately. It fit my shirts just right, and it was the right height for me to sit at for all the endless hours I must spend writing correspondence each day," he exclaimed, quite annoyed.

Thomas turned to Miss Lane and explained, "We have sent housemen up to the garret, miss, to bring down his old desk. Mr. Blackburn refurbished these rooms and thought the grander furniture would be more suited to his position and liking. I see that was not the case. We are so sorry!" After bowing and backing out of the room, he fled down the hall, presumably to help speed the process of correcting the situation.

"Oh, Nunc, please calm down. They thought they were doing you a favor. The staff will correct your issue in short order, and you will have your beloved desk, it seems," Miss Harriet said calmly to her uncle to de-escalate his sour mood.

Anne stood watching it all and was relieved when the president eased himself into a plush wing chair, massaging his forehead with his hand.

"I'm exhausted, Hal. This year and this long day of travel have me at my wit's end. Once they finish bringing my regular desk back, I may rest before dinner," he said.

"I think that is an excellent idea, Nunc," Harriet said.

There was more clamor down the hallway as the housemen worked together to carry the correct desk and its sizeable top cabinet with glass doors. The noise was boisterous, causing President Buchanan to stand quickly. "They had better not damage my desk! Are those ruffians ruining my desk?" The president strode out to the hall to survey the housemen's progress.

"Cameron! What the devil are *you* doing here?!" Buchanan exclaimed from the hall.

A deep baritone voice answered, "Why, Mr. President, how good to see you. I didn't get the honor of speaking with you last week at the state dinner as I was embroiled in stimulating conversation with the ever-engaging minister from Britain. Like yourself, I have come for my summer respite here at the invigorating Bedford Springs. My room is down the hall."

Who was this man talking to the president like that? His tone was chiding if not disrespectful.

The president did not respond but marched back into his suite and slammed the door. Anne suppressed a sigh. It was going to be a long night and perhaps a long summer season.

— 5 —

Harriet

A warm soak in the mineral waters of the Bedford Springs bathhouse was just what Harriet needed. She had been looking forward to it for weeks. Having slept well the previous night and finished her breakfast, she was ready for rest and rejuvenation. She needed a trip to the baths to wash away the taint of Washington's stress.

"Anne, would you please ask Mr. Blackburn to save a spot for me this morning at the spa? I want to spend an hour or two there before lunch today," she said.

After she returned from making the appointment, Anne brushed out Harriet's hair in the suite's dressing area. The windows were open, and a lovely fresh breeze from the porch door caressed Harriet's face. Birds twittered in the trees outside. Anne's fingers were gentle as she eased a comb through her thick wavy hair, easing out the knots from the long journey. She closed her eyes and heaved a sigh. Peace settled through her. After the high-strung and overly anxious servants who attended her at the Executive Mansion, Anne's quiet voice and calm demeanor were such a relief.

"Anne, tell me a bit about yourself. It would comfort me to know more about you," Harriet said.

"I am not sure what to say about myself, Miss Harriet. I recently turned twenty-five years old. I live not far from here on a farm that my late husband, Jacob, and I established. I was raised as a Quaker and I grew up west of Bedford in Dunning's Creek. I have a handsome little boy of four named Joshua."

"Oh my goodness, Anne. You are so young to be a widow. I am so very sorry to hear you endured such a terrible loss." Harriet looked back at Anne in the mirror. Anne was young, but there were shadows under her eyes.

Harriet sat quietly for a moment and considered how to continue the conversation. She was thinking of Anne's situation as a widow, and she thought finding common ground in tragedy might be appropriate to ease the moment's awkwardness. Anne had turned to pick up some hair combs from the dressing table, but she dropped several. Were her hands shaking?

"I have never been married and can't imagine what losing a husband must be like for you, Anne. I can say, though, I understand the pain of losing those most dear to us. I lost my mother when I was nine and not long after that, my father took ill and passed away as well. That is how I came to live with my uncle," she related.

"I am so sorry for your loss, miss. Surely those were hard times for you. How fortunate to have your uncle as your guardian. You seem very close, and I can tell he cares for you like a daughter." Anne gently slid several combs into Harriet's hair to make an elegant updo.

Many years had passed since Harriet had lost her parents. It still hurt to think about that time in her life and she tried not to. She had now been with her uncle almost twice as long as she had been with her mother and father. She missed them, but they were so far back in her life that it felt like a lifetime ago. Anne's loss was more poignant and recent.

"How do you make do as a widow, Anne? Where is your boy while you're working?" she inquired, searching Anne's eyes in the mirror for an indication of her feelings.

"Well, miss, I am here at the Springs to earn money to help support my farm so we can keep it. It has not been easy, and I do worry about losing everything my husband and I built before he died. His mother lives with me and helps care for Joshua while I'm here at work," Anne answered, buttoning the back of Harriet's dress at the collar.

"It must be quite hard to be a woman on your own. I am so glad you found work here and were paired with me, Anne." Harriet continued with a smile, "Tell me about being a Quaker. I have read a little about Quakers and have come to know a few over the years near Lancaster, my permanent home, but I have never had the opportunity to attend a service or learn about your beliefs. What can you share with me?"

"Well, miss, I am not sure what to say as it is all I have ever known and believed. Both my family and my husband's are Quakers. We believe

God's light and wisdom live in every person. And, by every person, we mean regardless of race or background," Anne explained. "We also believe by listening deeply, we can hear God's guidance on what is right. Perhaps you know our church services are spent in silent reflection?"

"Yes, I had heard something about Quakers sitting in silence. I think that is so wise. I enjoy prayer most of all in my religious practice, but my upbringing made it a one-way conversation. I like the idea of listening for a reply."

"Peace is another one of the key tenets Quakers hold dear. We should never harm anyone, even if they harm us. We also believe in integrity. What we do should match what we say we believe. This means acting for peace, for instance," Anne said, and Harriet felt in her bones the strong power and conviction of her softly spoken words.

She sat quietly, thinking about what Anne had said while feeling the calming sensation of the brush gently gliding through the curls by the base of her neck that had been left intentionally loose. She'd not had a conversation quite like this with any of her servants back in Washington. Respect and trust didn't come easily. What a relief this was from the turmoil in her uncle's world.

Harriet looked at their shared reflection in the mirror. Anne had done a lovely job of her hair. Though Harriet's hair was mostly gold, it had quite a bit of rose color in it. Anne had red hair highlighted with gold strands. She seemed uneasy about looking in the mirror with Harriet and glanced away.

Harriet spoke to their reflection, calling out the obvious similarity and laughing. "Why, look at us two girls with ginger in our hair. We are a fine match!"

This brought a timid smile to Anne, who held back a small chuckle.

Harriet added, "See, you're so pretty with a smile, Anne—no need to be shy with me. Soon we'll be headed to the baths, and I will be the one feeling bashful as I take most of my clothing off to climb into the waters. No need for any of that!"

◆━━━ ━━━◆

Later, as Harriet and Anne crossed the shady tree-lined lawn in front of the Evitt and Swiss House buildings to head toward the bathhouse, they came across the tinkling sound of the ornate central fountain. In the middle of the fountain stood a life-size figure of the Greek goddess Hygeia, goddess of good health and cleanliness. Harriet stopped to regard her for a moment, listening to the soothing music of the spray. The goddess's arm was raised, cup in hand, and the stream of water coming from the chalice presumably referenced the healing spring waters for which Bedford Springs was known. Hygeia had a long snake wrapped around her waist and up her arm. This was a classical symbol for medicine and healing. She couldn't help but ponder the incident last night with Senator Cameron in the hall outside her uncle's rooms and how he was a bit of a snake in the grass during what should be an otherwise lovely stay.

"Anne, I am supposed to be relaxing and letting go of stress, but I feel uneasy that some of my uncle's political adversaries are also here at Bedford Springs. I want you to be careful around Senator Cameron. He may try to pry information from you about the members of our party or our plans," Harriet cautioned.

"Is that the gentleman your uncle met in the hall last evening?" Anne asked.

"Yes, he is a longtime opponent of President Buchanan and has a history of trying to undermine him by personal attacks or political intrigues. He has frequented Bedford Springs as long as my uncle has, so it is not unusual for him to be here at the same time. However, with the tension growing among the parties regarding slavery and states' rights, I worry that he may use our summer respite to further his causes," Harriet explained.

They continued to stroll toward the spa, and Anne remained quiet. How much did her lady's maid know of politics given that she lived in this small rural community?

Gushing water could be heard as they neared the spa's stucco and brick building. Outside, a cast-iron pitcher lay on its side, serving as a fountain that spilled clear fresh water into the stone basin below. How lovely. Finally, she would get to enjoy the cleansing relaxation of the spa. As they climbed the stairs to head into the bathhouse, Thomas, her uncle's valet, came running across the lawn behind them.

"What is it, Thomas?" asked Harriet, turning toward the young man. Tall and trim, he was all legs. His brown hair was trimmed close on the sides, but there was a shock of hair on top that flopped over his forehead.

"I'm sorry to bother you, Miss Lane, but I wanted to inform you that the widow's nursemaid, Janie, has a terrible tooth problem. She needs attention right away, miss. I couldn't find the president and the widow to tell them as they were out on a morning walk on Constitution Hill. We need someone to take her into Bedford for care."

"Oh dear. Thank you, Thomas." Harriet turned to Anne. "It seems this visit to the healing waters will not happen after all. We should check on Janie. Anne, I may ask you to go with her into town to get help while I stay with the children. Do you know of a local barber who works with teeth? Thomas, can you arrange a cart and driver?"

"Yes, ma'am, I will go find a wagon to take them into Bedford," the young man answered. He turned and sped toward the stables at the south end of the grounds.

"I would be glad to help, Miss Harriet. Elias Rouse is a well-known and trusted negro barber who, I think, also helps with tooth problems and other minor surgeries. I will show the driver how to get there and accompany Janie," confirmed Anne.

— 6 —

Juba

Juba was soaked with sweat, drifting in and out of sleep as she lay tightly curled on a cot in the Bass children's room. Outside, the door to the porch had been propped open. The air moving past felt good. Even though she was sweating, chills ran through her as the breeze grazed her bare shoulder. Footfalls on the floorboards outside seemed far away and lulled her back into a fitful sleep.

Suddenly, she was back in Boston, and she and her mother were walking down the street. Her mother held her hand and smiled down at her. They were heading toward the market, and her mother was telling her about the items they needed.

"Juba, I'm going to send you over to the bakery side of the market to buy a loaf of brown bread. I will give you a halfpenny, but you make sure to get the change from the lady at the counter." Her mother was warm in explaining, but stern.

Last time, she forgot to wait for the change and a market woman chased her down when she was already with her mother on the other side of the market.

As she stood at the bakery stall, a red-faced white man came up next to her. She didn't know why, but everything in her small body told her to be afraid of this man. She got her change and quickly walked back toward her mother. The man grabbed her arm, pulling her in the other direction. She cried out and screamed for her mother. Terror racked her, and her heart pounded. She realized someone was shaking her shoulder, trying to wake her as she cried out.

"You're okay, Janie. You're all right. It's me, Anne." Anne comforted her softly.

Juba remembered the red-haired young woman she met on her first day at the Springs. In service to Miss Lane, the maid introduced herself and mentioned her love of children and that she was glad to help with the Bass children if needed.

"I don't feel too good, Miss Anne." Juba turned over toward Anne and saw Miss Lane was also there. "I'm sorry to be a burden, Miss Lane. Where are the children?" She tried to sit up, realizing that she was shirking care of the children.

Miss Lane stepped up to the cot and said, "Now don't you worry. Anne's going to take you to get you looked after. I brought you some laudanum from my travel kit." Miss Lane picked up a glass of water from the side table and put a few drops of liquid into it. "Here, drink this for the pain until we can get you some help. Don't you worry about the children. They are with Thomas now and I will watch them and get them back to their mother."

Juba drank the water and winced with the pain it caused passing her bad tooth. She sank back down into the bedding and closed her eyes.

She was on a wagon sitting on the bench with a large man. She was small next to him. A young girl again. When she looked up at him, she saw that he was white. She recognized the overseer from the plantation she had first been sold onto. The overseer was a big man with stringy hair, which grew long over his collar. His jowls hung low next to a deep frown.

When he looked down at her, he smiled, and his light blue eyes crinkled. His look scared her. His teeth were yellow like corn. Her heart raced with fear. Could she jump down from the wagon? She must try. As she leaned out to spring off, he pressed her head down with his wide, meaty hand to hold her to the bench, and she started to scream.

"Janie, Janie! It's okay. Anne and I are here with you." Harriet wiped her forehead with a wet rag and held her hand. She realized it was just another terrible dream.

"Please, Janie. Try to rest. You're okay. We are with you. Soon, the wagon will come to take us for help." Miss Anne was sitting by her side. Both women looked afraid. What had she said while she was dreaming?

Juba managed to drift off again to the sound of Miss Lane and Miss Anne talking in quiet tones. Their calm voices soothed her. They talked about the schedule for the week and which dresses Miss Lane would like the silk brushed and pressed. They talked about the flowers Anne should bring from her farm. Miss Lane was interested in getting some primroses, which smelled lovely and would match the pink gown she wanted to wear the next day.

Juba found herself in the garden at Missus Bass's plantation. She was following the children who were running through the hedge maze. She lost sight of them and began to walk faster to catch up.

The scent of boxwood grew heavier, and she felt it closing in on her. Where were the children? She couldn't find them or even make out the sound of their laughter. The hedge walls were closing in, and she could barely squeeze through. She had a sense that she was in the middle of the hedge. The prickly branches were on all four sides like a green cage. She kept turning, looking for the way out, as the walls got tighter.

She started to yell. "Help me. Set me free. I'm trapped! I can't breathe!"

"Sit her up, sit her up! Oh dear, maybe she's had too much laudanum!" Miss Lane's voice was frantic. Anne held her hand as she came out of her dream and sat her up again, wiping perspiration from her forehead. Juba was gasping for air and was sick on the floor as the two white ladies tended to her. Anne began to clean her up.

* * *

By the time the wagon rolled by Shober's Run, the bubbling creek that ran along the eastern side of the valley past the Springs, and down Richard Street into the town of Bedford, Juba thought she might pass out from the pain. The throbbing in her mouth was blinding. The bumpy ride made her almost wish for death as she lay bundled up in the back of the wagon. Her jaw throbbed, and occasionally, she felt a sharp shooting pain in her tooth. Anne and the white man driving the horses talked loudly over the horse hooves clopping and wheels grinding against the road.

"Mr. Hayes, do you know where Elias Rouse's barbershop is on Pitt Street?" Miss Anne shouted over the street noise.

Why couldn't they be quieter for her sake? Every bump and noise made her head hurt worse. She was shivering, even though it was July, and she was wrapped in wool blankets.

The driver answered, "Yes, ma'am, I believe it is at the west end of Pitt Street, at the base of Gravel Hill."

"Yes, that's right. We should make this left onto John Street and head past the cemetery. We can go down West Street and avoid traffic in town," she instructed him. "Janie, hold on. We will be there in about ten minutes."

Juba tried to divert herself from the pain by thinking about her momma. Whenever she was sad or hopeless, she found focusing on thoughts of her mother helped her get through. She thought about what it would be like to be with her again and feel her warm, soft arms around her. She still remembered her comforting scent. She didn't know if it was the oil her momma put in her hair or some other essence unique to her. When Juba thought of that smell, it was as if her mother was close by. It made her feel better.

She often tried to imagine the day she might be reunited with her mother and father. How would that happen? She wasn't sure, but she kept the image strong. Now that she was above the Mason-Dixon line, she thought about it more clearly. How could she run away and return to Boston? How could she be free again and find her parents?

She thought about what she had heard when they were on the way to Bedford. The slave catchers were there because the valley road was a route for the Underground Railroad. There were stories of people up north who were tied in a long string of kindness. They helped black people escape to Canada. How could she meet those people? If she got to her parents, they could go somewhere safe where they could all be free. Free to not be in bondage or stolen by slave catchers. Free not to be insulted, beaten, or have their lives threatened.

The wagon slowed. Thank goodness. Perhaps she was on her way to relief for her bad tooth. It had been bothering her on and off for many months, and she knew it would have to be pulled out. The wagon stopped, and Juba could hear the driver's voice clearly now. "Miss Anne, you will have to go in and ask Eli Rouse to come lift her out of the wagon. I won't be carryin' no dirty nigger girl," he said with disgust.

Anger flared beyond the excruciating pain in her mouth.

"May God's grace find you, Mr. Hayes! Surely you are disgraced and lost to the darkness talking about another person in such a way!" Anne scolded the man, and Juba heard the maid's shoes marching across the gravel.

Shortly after, the sound of boots crunching on gravel drew closer to the wagon.

"She came with a guest of the president, Mr. Rouse," Anne explained. "I think she has a tooth that needs to come out. She is in terrible pain and can barely sit upright. Miss Lane gave her some laudanum earlier, but I don't know if that is still helping her. I don't think the wagon ride did her much good in her condition."

"Well, let's look at what we have here," said a gentle male voice.

The blanket that Juba had pulled tight over her head to block the blinding daylight was pulled back. A young black man peered down at her with a caring and concerned smile.

"How you doin' today, miss? Miss Anne told me you're in a bit of pain and need some help. I'm Eli Rouse, the local barber, and I've taken care of plenty of bad teeth. All right if I help you inside, girl?" the man inquired kindly.

Juba sat up slowly, and her head started to spin.

Mr. Rouse put his hand on her forehead and said, "Just as I thought— you're burnin' up. Can you stand?"

He shifted her toward the wagon's side and lifted the sideboard off to help her out. Juba swung her feet over the side, but her knees buckled as she tried to plant them on the ground. Luckily, Mr. Rouse caught her fall, and Miss Anne had her arm. Mr. Rouse wasn't tall, but she felt he was strong as he lifted her off the ground and carried her toward his barbershop. The houses on this street were all in a row and close together. They were in town. It was noisy, and there was a lot of dust in the air as carriages passed on the busy street. Juba thought she would be ill but took a deep breath. The last thing she wanted was to be sick on this nice man who was trying to help her.

They entered a whitewashed clapboard house and he carried her through to the shop. The furniture in the main room consisted of shelves, a few mirrors, some wooden benches, and a barber chair. A door led to a smaller back room. She was grateful it was dim inside and that she was out of the heat and sunlight. Mr. Rouse sat her on a chair covered with a light linen cloth. Miss Anne was standing nearby, wringing her hands, having followed them both inside.

"Now let's see what's goin' on here in that mouth of yours, young lady." Mr. Rouse swiveled the chair to face the window at the back of the room. He picked up a mirror on a long metal handle and angled it toward her face, catching the light. Juba took the cue and opened her mouth.

"Oh my, yes, there's the bad tooth," confirmed the barber. "The tooth is split, and there's infection set in. Smell's all I need to know that. I will have to take it out, which should fix most of the problem quick. I'm gonna give you a strong spirit they call ether and put it on this here cloth for you to breathe in," he said.

He turned to pick up a bottle off the shelf next to him and a folded cloth. "Miss Anne here is going to hold your hand so you won't be scared. You won't remember anything after you breathe in the hanky. Are you all right with that?" he asked.

Juba nodded yes, and Miss Anne smiled at her in support. She took her hand. Mr. Rouse covered her nose and mouth with the cloth, which filled her senses, strong but sweet.

When Juba woke up, the light in the room had changed. Gradually, she realized that she was lying down, and though the pain in her mouth hadn't gone away, it was different and not as sharp. There was a wad of cloth in her mouth. The stuffing was making her drool on her arm. Her dress sleeve was all wet, and so was her cheek. She decided to lie still and rest.

She recognized Miss Anne's voice and the voice of Mr. Rouse, the barber who had helped her, drifting in from the next room. She also heard another man speaking.

"Yes, she is a slave. She came with a guest of President Buchanan, serving as a nursemaid for three children. They all came for the summer season," Anne explained.

"Well, that's fine and dandy. The president saw fit to bring an enslaved woman to Bedford! What is he thinking havin' slaves with him? He says he doesn't believe in slavery, but it sure don't look that way." Rouse's voice was quiet but angry.

"Seems to me he's trying to keep his foot on both sides of the line," said the other man, whose voice was deeper than the barber's.

"In any case, I can't help you with what you suggest, Reverend Fidler. I care very much for the fugitives and their plight to be free. It tears my heart out that I can't help right now. My family and Jacob's have always helped whenever we were asked. I just lost Jacob last year for the same and can't risk losing myself or my farm. My boy is depending on me." Anne's voice broke. Why was she so upset and what were they talking about?

"You have a good heart, Anne, and what happened to Jacob is still fresh, but we got to help people as they come. Has she said she wants to flee?" Mr. Rouse asked.

"I don't know. Janie only got here a day ago. We've barely had a moment to say hello, much less share such a dangerous conversation," answered Anne.

"Perhaps we should talk to her, John," Mr. Rouse said.

Even with only the bits and pieces, Juba put together the meaning of their conversation. They wanted to know if she hoped to escape! Her head was very clear now and she knew she must speak up. She swung her feet over the side of the bed and went to the door, leaning on the doorframe to keep steady. She felt her anger, strength, and determination rise up inside her.

She opened the door, and all three turned to witness that she was standing on her own two feet. Taking the cloth from her mouth, Juba announced, strong and clear, "My name is Juba, and I want to be free. Can you help me?"

~7~

Anne

A nne's heart seized in her chest hearing the nursemaid's request for help. She didn't know what to say, but she was scared in a way that she hadn't been since the night she became a widow. The fear was for herself and her family. Was that selfish to focus only on herself and those she was responsible for? What about heeding God's call to help another?

Reverend Fidler and Elias Rouse stood looking at Juba standing in the doorway. Janie wasn't even her real name! Anne looked to the men to see their reaction. The woman had not only declared her true name, but also that she wanted to be free and needed their help.

The Reverend Fidler had stepped into Rouse's barber shop about an hour after Mr. Rouse had pulled Juba's tooth. Rouse and Anne had been explaining who the patient was when she surprised them. The Reverend was well-known and respected in Bedford and a leader in the black church. He was what was called a circuit preacher. He traveled from one town to another, preaching to the African Methodist Episcopal congregations. His home congregation was the Zion Church up the street on Gravel Hill, where many of Bedford's black citizens lived.

Tall and thin, Fidler's hair had started to go white on the sides above his ears. He was gentle and calm in public, but Anne had heard him preach before, and God gave him a solid and booming voice when he spoke God's truth.

"You have found the right people to help you, my dear," the Reverend said as he sat on the barber chair. "Come sit down here on this bench by me so we can talk. I don't want to worry that you may fall over from all that you have been through today."

Anne hurried over to Juba and took her arm. She wasn't hot to the touch anymore like she had been when they brought her in. Her fever had broken. Anne held her steady and helped her onto the wooden bench.

"I overheard what you all were talking about when I woke. You asked Miss Anne if I wanted to run. I need to find my parents in Boston," said Juba.

Mr. Rouse's eyebrows rose. "How is it your parents are in Boston, and you are a slave of a southern widow?" Eli asked.

Anne saw the sadness and anger well up in Juba's eyes as she took a moment before speaking. Anne put her hand on her knee, hoping it would make her feel better, and nodded to encourage her to speak.

"My parents were freed many years ago and moved to Boston before I was born. They worked jobs, and we had a life there." Juba paused, and Anne noticed her hands had clenched into fists. "I was about ten years old when slave catchers took me from a street corner. I was sold a couple of times but ended up with Missus Bass. I don't know anything of my momma and pappa in all these years since. I think of them every day. I have been too scared of being sold further south to tell anyone that I was stolen into slavery. Can you help me get back to them?"

Anne drew a breath. Slave catchers had stolen Juba. She couldn't imagine what that would have been like. Boston was much more progressive than almost anywhere. Quakers like Lucretia Mott, an abolitionist social reformer, and William Lloyd Garrison, the founder of *The Liberator*, the leading abolitionist newspaper, were in Boston. New England was a hub for the abolitionist movement. It was unimaginable that slave catchers took people right off the street and put free people into slavery. But here was this enslaved woman sitting with her who had been born free. She was *stolen*.

Reverend Fidler got off the barber's chair and walked around the room, lost in thought. They all sat silently watching him. He moved to the front of the barber shop and stared out the door. Anne read the look on Juba's face. It looked to Anne as if she was worried that he might walk out but also hopeful about what he might say next.

He turned from the door and walked back to the group. "Juba, I believe God blessed you today with a toothache to bring you to the right people. He surely works in mysterious ways! Mr. Rouse and I are active in this town with what some people call the Underground Railroad. I call it good people who help other good people who need help. Miss Anne's family is part of that work. Her husband was involved too. We can help you," he said.

Anne was quiet but knew she had to say something. She could barely see a way out of her problems. How could she help this woman without risking everything? She flushed with sweat.

"Reverend Fidler," Eli Rouse intervened, "we can't take for granted that Anne can be involved after what happened to Jacob McCoy. We can't place her in any more danger."

"What is he talking about?" Juba asked her.

Anne took a steadying breath and thought about recounting what had occurred last year. She was just starting to put it behind her. She couldn't stop worrying that people in town might discover what had really happened to Jacob. It would put herself, her family, and many others in danger.

"Last August, my husband was asked to bring some escaped fugitives up from a farm in Cumberland Valley. He grew up as a Quaker, and his family had always helped move people who were escaping to freedom. Reverend Fidler and Eli often took people from our farm and got them out of Bedford to the west. Other people would move them to Quaker Valley. There, my family would move them to other Quakers who would take them over the mountain to Johnstown. Everyone worked together to get them as far north as possible to outrun the slave catchers who would send them back to slavery." Telling the story brought Jacob's face back to her.

Anne went on, "Jacob had done this journey many times, first with his father and then by himself. He put the freedom seekers in his wagon, which had a false bottom as a hiding place. Last year, John Morgart, who has a station at his house just over the Mason-Dixon line, brought two men halfway up the valley to his tavern above Centerville. Jacob brought hay for the horses boarded at that tavern. When there was a need, he returned with hidden cargo. He had gone to Morgart's tavern to pick up the two men. He was coming up the valley road when slave catchers stopped him and insisted on searching the wagon." Anne felt her voice crack and she wasn't sure if she could go on. She cleared her throat and continued.

"We don't know for sure what happened, but he must have tried to fight them. Mr. Morgart heard the gunshots ring through the valley. As he rode his horse up the road to see what was going on, he heard the slave catchers' horses galloping toward him. As he hid down in the creek bed next to the road, he saw they had the two black men hogtied, one on the back of each horse." Anne choked with tears and couldn't speak anymore. Looking down, she let the tears run down her face. They splashed onto the wooden floorboards and made dark marks where they fell. Anne broke down weeping at this point and was unable to continue. Juba moved closer to her and took her hand.

Reverend Fidler continued the story. "After the catchers were gone, Morgart found Jacob shot dead further up the road. He brought him back to town and told me what happened. We reported to the constable that he shot him by accident because Morgart thought he was a horse thief. We came up with that story to cover what they were doin' for the Underground Railroad and to protect all the others involved. Many townspeople still think Jacob was a horse thief."

It was as if Anne was living the day she lost Jacob all over again by hearing it out loud. It was hard to keep herself from sobbing. Once she started, she might not be able to stop.

Silence passed for several minutes as each in the room felt the heaviness of the tragedy. The price was high for doing what was right. Reverend Fidler again walked over and looked out the front windows onto the street. Juba held Anne's hand more tightly. Eli Rouse turned away, anger set on his face.

Then he spoke up. "Reverend, there is a lot going on right now. How can we make sure to put Juba on the road safely as soon as possible? There are lots of moving parts with many parties."

"I think you're safe to talk with Anne and Juba, Eli. We still don't know exactly what is going on with Mr. Brown and his plans. I don't know if *he* knows," answered the Reverend.

"Miss Anne ran into us at the Springs a couple of weeks ago when he was here," Elias said.

"You introduced me to a Mr. Smith. I don't understand," Anne said.

"You can imagine the famous—or notorious, depending on the crowd—John Brown must be cautious. I believe he has a price on his head," Elias informed her.

"That tall man with the long grey beard was John Brown, the aboli-tionist?" Anne was astounded.

She was conflicted about what she thought of John Brown. Some said he was a messiah, and others said he was a murderer. The Quakers, being pacifists, put him closer to the latter in that regard. Anne admired his commitment to acting on what he believed was God's law, but she couldn't imagine violating other commandments in the process. He and his sons had recently tried to drive pro-slavery settlers out of their town in Kansas and brutally murdered four of them. The wind was knocked out of her, knowing she had met him on the lawn at Bedford Springs. He'd looked like an ordinary older man, not the larger-than-life anti-slavery evangelist with blood on his hands. Now she understood Eli's reference to her husband "helping the cause."

"He's been making his rounds from here to Maryland and Virginia, trying to drum up support from blacks and whites. He wants to inspire a slave revolt. He needs as many supporters as he can find to create radical change to emancipate those closest to the capital. Then that will further his campaign to rid the country of slavery," Fidler said.

"He was telling me he even played pool with the editor of the Bedford Gazette at the Springs billiard hall, unbeknownst to Benjamin Meyers. He goes by John Smith when he's traveling," Elias added.

Juba was fidgeting while the conversation moved away from her escape and finally cut in. "Does this mean you can't help me?"

"No, not at all, Miss Juba. Apologies for the distraction. We been getting people free one or a few at a time for years. Mr. Brown's big plans are not going to stop that. No, ma'am, no how," the Reverend confirmed.

"Miss Anne, we can't ask more of you than to keep silent. We will be trying to figure out how to start Juba on her way to freedom. We won't ask you to be involved, but we will be gettin' your family out in Fishertown ready for her. You be all right with that?" Elias asked her.

Anne regarded the two men for a long moment, and at last, she looked at Juba. "I certainly would never say anything. Please understand I can't risk losing my job and my farm." However, Anne was sure she was losing something else dear to her all over again.

— 8 —

Harriet

The next day, Harriet played whist in the central downstairs parlor with a group of ladies in the Colonial building. Overstuffed couches and upholstered chairs were scattered throughout the ground floor, along with several polished mahogany card tables. Dark silk wallpaper with scrolls and plumes in jewel-tone colors made the long open space feel cool. Windows faced the front of the hotel, occasionally allowing summer breezes to waft through. The ladies who frequented the cardroom wore elegant but corseted summer dresses with multiple petticoats, making the heat even more oppressive. They enjoyed this spot for socializing.

The ladies Harriet was sitting with that afternoon came from Ohio. Unfortunately, the conversation turned toward politics, which was disappointing, but unsurprising.

The subject had circled the ever-more-common and concerning topic of abolitionism and the growing tension and violence reported in the newspapers. It was a topic Harriet was well acquainted with, so the ladies seemed to want to get her point of view or some tidbits from the Executive Mansion. Both areas were dangerous territory for her.

Mrs. Simms broached the topic. "It seems we are getting closer to the trial about the Oberlin-Wellington rescue. The last Cleveland Plain Dealer I read before leaving home two weeks ago had those involved reduced from thirty-four accused to just a handful of people who will be put on trial. What do you ladies think of that incident? More and more people are banding together in these public shows of anti-slavery support."

Harriet pretended to move her whist cards around in her hand. She hoped Mrs. Gray or Miss Shively might make an opinion first or take the conversation elsewhere so she would not need to share her thoughts on the case.

The Oberlin-Wellington case had been in the papers since the previous fall when it had gotten national attention. Part of the excitement was that federal marshals were acting on the Fugitive Slave Act, even in states where slavery was not legal. The number of people who stood up for the black man and arranged his freedom from capture also made the story sensational.

The U.S. federal marshal in Oberlin, Ohio, had detained a fugitive slave from Kentucky named John Price. Fearing trouble because Oberlin was a staunchly abolitionist town, the marshal quickly got the man out of Oberlin on the train to the nearby town of Wellington. A group of abolitionists from Oberlin followed the party to Wellington, and another cluster of abolitionists joined them there. Thirty-four men forcibly participated in taking Mr. Price from the U.S. marshals and getting him off to Canada for freedom.

Mrs. Gray was the first to answer after putting her jack on the pile of cards and taking the hand, or "trick," as it was called in whist. "I just worry about all this violence and where it may lead. While I think the men who helped Mr. Price get his freedom were brave, I think it amazing no one was hurt or killed."

"I agree with you, Charlotte," replied Miss Shively. "Look what has been going on! That maniac, John Brown, is still on the loose. He is supposedly responsible for the murder of several pro-slavery people at two separate events in Kansas! Women and children as well! I think the U.S. marshals should be out looking for him rather than chasing after black men who have done nothing but try to be free. Mr. Price went to Oberlin because someone told him about the people there who would help him escape north. What do you think of all this, Miss Lane?"

Harriet paused for a few moments. She shuffled the cards for the new hand and could feel the awkward silence and the eyes of her three companions on her. She needed to give a measured response that was also truthful.

"My uncle, the president, has issued a reward of $250 so that John Brown can be brought to justice. I think it's important that radicals like Mr. Brown pay for their crimes against other citizens so that the rest of

America can understand that our officials will not tolerate his kind of tactics," Harriet said carefully.

Mrs. Simms was the first to respond. "Yes, I agree that Brown is a murderous radical, and his brand of abolitionism is dangerous for everyone. But I agree with Miss Shively that the U.S. marshals should be spending their time looking for him and protecting all of us rather than assisting in slave catching!" She turned to Harriet for a response.

Clearly, these northern ladies wanted some tidbit about the president so that they could run around telling others at the Springs and back home. She would not be drawn in or give them any satisfaction. She must support her uncle's position in public.

"Ladies, I would not like to get into this challenging topic today. Rather than try to defend my uncle, who is ultimately the supreme chief of the U.S. Marshal Service, I will conclude by saying the president believes his job is to uphold all the laws of the land. Both enforcing the Fugitive Slave Act through the U.S. marshals and bringing murderers to justice for heinous crimes against citizens fall under his duties as president. While his personal views may be very different, he is duty-bound to United States law."

With that statement, she put down her cards, stood from her chair, and excused herself from the game, leaving the other ladies looking after her. Did she say the right thing? What would they say to their husbands about the conversation? Hopefully that the president had the best in mind and was doing his duty. She suspected, however, that they might make other conclusions. There was a tinge of something else bothering her about the conversation too. Defending her uncle came like a reflex, but she felt conflicted about what she didn't say. Those people were courageous in helping Mr. Price.

Defeated and discouraged, Harriet climbed the stairs to her room. Holding onto the balustrade, she stopped and looked down at the lobby where last summer her uncle received the first transatlantic telegraph from Queen Victoria. Her uncle worked his whole life to serve the public to the best of his ability. He had served in Congress, the Senate, as Secretary of State, and as U.S. Ambassador to both Russia and England. Unfortunately, she understood that, as a president, the tides of national sentiment were pulling him under.

Later that evening, Harriet sat with her uncle at dinner in the grand ballroom. The tables were ablaze with candlelight, though there was still quite a bit of light outside as it was midsummer. At their table was Attorney General Jeremiah Black and his wife Mary, who were from the nearby Somerset County, and Mr. George Hess, a wealthy iron furnace magnate from a town called Nanty Glo, which was a day's travel north of Bedford, with his wife, Lydia.

The fine linen tablecloth was covered with delicious dishes, many of which were favorites and locally grown. Squab in caper sauce and mutton with mint jelly were the main entrees that evening, served with pickled onions and stewed beets, roasted squash, and creamed cucumbers. Her uncle ordered claret for the table, and the ruby liquid seemed to be helping everyone to relax.

Mr. Hess started the conversation with a question for the president. "President Buchanan, tell us about your recent trip down south to North Carolina. With all the current agitation, I'm curious to hear how they received you."

Harriet ate her boiled mutton and listened carefully. How would Uncle Buck respond? Many questions concerning the South from Northerners could have underlying motivations. She was beginning to realize that her uncle didn't always see how loaded even benign questions could be.

"Oh my, George, it was an excellent trip. Everywhere we went, crowds were greeting me and cheering," Buchanan exclaimed. "It was wonderful to see the presidency respected and honored. I haven't had such an enthusiastic reception in quite a while," he added.

The sour expression on Jeremiah Black's face revealed his disapproval. His wife Mary observed the same and opened her mouth to say something to the table. However, she must have thought the better of it and instead stared down at her lamb and vegetable dish.

Mr. Hess responded to the president's account. "I'm glad to hear you had a satisfactory trip, Mr. President. I'm sure the people of the southern states are pleased to have you supporting them and representing their interests."

Uncle Buck's face changed from jovial to serious as he replied, "Why, George, I am surprised at the insinuation coming from you. You and all the American people should know by now that I am a staunch constitutionalist. Therefore, I defend the right of the states to make their own decisions on certain matters not expressly laid out in the Constitution. I do the same for Pennsylvania now that I no longer represent her directly. I act on behalf of the whole nation, and that is my job, first and foremost."

Harriet waited to see if the conversation would continue, but instead, all six at the table sat in awkward silence. A few moments later, the waiter brought out the last course and removed their empty dishes. The conversation shifted to everyone's pastry selections, but Harriet had lost her appetite.

After dinner, she returned to her room and thought perhaps she would feel better after writing a letter to Lily.

Harriet Lane
The Bedford Springs Hotel
Bedford, Pennsylvania
July 11th, 1859

My Dear Lily,

How are things back east with you? In your last letter, you mentioned looking forward to your week in Atlantic City. I waited to write to you, thinking you would only have too much correspondence to catch up on when you returned. How was your trip, and did you make it into the water? I imagine it was refreshing after the midsummer heat and humidity of Philadelphia.

My arrival at Bedford Springs was uneventful. I have settled in and spent some time reading and taking in the mountain air as well as some of the storied waters from the Magnesia Spring each morning since I have been here. I believe my digestive constitution has greatly improved. A young Quaker woman named Anne has been assigned as my lady's maid. I thank goodness every day she has a fine and even temperament and a quiet way about her which has put me at ease. What a difficult first half of the year this has been, my dear friend.

I don't want to belabor you with my troubles, but I need to share an incident that occurred today. I fear I am becoming a bit repetitive in depending on you to voice my fears and concerns about Uncle Buck's current state of affairs. You are the only one I can share my worries with and trust above reproach.

I just returned from dinner with the Blacks and Hesses, which took an unfortunate turn. My uncle was going on about his May trip to the south. The insinuation he received in return from Hess was that he was pandering to Southern interests, and Jeremiah Black neither cut in nor refuted the suggestion. Black is part of his cabinet, for goodness sake!

Lily, I worry that my uncle does not see how he has to be careful of the growing rift between North and South and how being a representative of all needs must be handled quite gingerly. He is not aware of how he comes across and will lose support more and more as his presidency progresses. Unfortunately, bringing it to his attention is not well met.

Please let me know if you have any wisdom for me in these matters. I know you are forever in my court and love Uncle Buck as if he were part of your family. What does your father think of the recent events concerning the president? Has he commented to you, or would he not, since he knows your allegiances?

I must go now, but I look forward to hearing from you before I leave Bedford. Uncle Buck gets a special post every other day here at the Springs. If you send a letter to me at the Executive Mansion, it will get here faster than regular post to Bedford. Your last letter arrived today and was sent before I left Washington.

All my love,
Harriet

— 9 —

Juba

Walking back from the kitchen with a pitcher of fresh milk for the children's porridge, Juba crossed the gravel path between the Colonial building and the Crockford bachelors' quarters. It was still early morning, and the sun had not yet risen over Constitution Hill. The narrow valley stayed shady until almost ten when daylight finally crested the hills.

Mist hung across the hotel's front lawn, held in place by the many trees spreading their arms wide to keep the lawns cool. Closer to Crockford, an old two-story frame structure, she spotted two men to her right. The men were talking under the maple trees in the heavy fog. Getting closer, she saw one was a tall, silver-haired white man wearing a light-colored waistcoat, high collared shirt and silk bowtie. He had a high forehead and slumped shoulders that gave the impression of being burdened. The other man was black, and as she approached, she realized it was Mr. Rouse. Both men turned to look at her, and Juba raised her hand in greeting.

"Juba," Rouse called quietly and waved her toward them.

Juba walked into the grove of trees. She was afraid of getting in trouble if the children woke and she wasn't back with their milk. But, when she left the barbershop with Anne, Reverend Fidler told her someone would find her once they had everything in place. Did Mr. Rouse have plans for her escape?

"*There are many tracks that need to be laid and engines fired to make a safe journey to freedom for you,*" he had said that day before she left him. Juba had believed that the wheels were turning and that she had to wait patiently for more information. Now, here was Mr. Rouse on the lawn at the Springs. What great luck!

"Juba, this is Senator Cameron," Eli Rouse whispered. "He is a friend of the abolitionists and believes people like you should be free." Because of the fearful look she knew must be on her face, he continued to put her at ease. "He was just asking me about some activities here in Bedford that support the new Republican Party and the abolitionist movement. I was telling him about our plans to help you."

She had seen him in the hall in the Evitt building before, and he tipped his hat to her. Now, he did the same.

"Good morning, sir," she replied.

"You are with the president's party. I was told that you are enslaved by the widow. Is that correct?" Cameron inquired. His voice was deep and slow, and he had a deliberate way of speaking.

"Yes, sir."

"Your name is Juba, correct? I think many people here in town can help you to your freedom. I have some connections, and Eli was just asking me to help him with papers for you."

"Thank you, sir. I am so grateful," she replied.

Senator Cameron turned to Eli Rouse. "Send word to Mr. Brown that while I will not condone or support his larger violent schemes, I will be honored to assist in helping this woman of the president's party gain her deserved freedom. It will also serve to undermine the administration and re-election as it becomes public, which is an added benefit."

Juba didn't like hearing about John Brown and his "plans" again. She had a bad feeling about it, but she wasn't sure why. At that moment, though, none of that mattered—she understood the senator would be involved in helping her to escape. She didn't like the sound of his motives either, but all that mattered to her was being free and finding her family.

Eli Rouse looked past her at the buildings to ensure they weren't being watched. "You just sit tight, and we will get word to you here. Many things are going on right now with the cause, but us gettin' you out of town has moved to first place."

"Thank you. I should be going so I'm not missed." Juba nodded to the men and took her leave. She hurried back to the children's rooms, feeling hopeful.

Later that day, she was alone in the Evitt building as the children went off with their mother to play croquet on the lawn. She was carrying laundry down the hall to the washrooms when Senator Cameron stepped out of his doorway just ahead of her. He tipped his hat again and walked past her just as Miss Lane opened the door of her suite further down the hall.

"Janie, do you have a moment that I may talk with you?" Miss Lane asked.

Juba hadn't seen the president's niece much since they had arrived. The last conversation they had was when she was nearly unconscious with pain and fever more than a week ago.

"Yes, ma'am. Let me put this laundry in the washroom down the hall and I will be right back." She nodded and hurried on her way.

Moments later, she knocked on the door of Miss Lane's suite and heard the lady call back to enter. The sitting room was pretty, with soft couches and chairs in fine light-colored cloth. Miss Lane was seated at her desk with some papers and a fountain pen in her hand. She turned away from her writing and toward Juba as she entered the room.

"Janie, how have you been doing since your tooth was pulled? Are you feeling better?"

"Thank you, Miss Lane. I am much better."

"I don't want to interrupt you in your duties, but I did happen to observe Senator Cameron in the hall near you. Perhaps I should warn you about him. He is a political opponent of my uncle's, and I would not put it past him to try to pry information from you or create controversy with our travel party. It would be just like him to embroil you in drama or prey on your position as a servant for details of our stay. I feel it was best for me to be straightforward and talk to you about it so that you wouldn't be caught unawares," cautioned Miss Lane.

"Thank you, Miss Lane, I will be careful. He was just nodding hello to me and didn't say anything," Juba replied.

"Very well then. It just came to my attention, and I thought it would be good to tell you before something unfortunate happened." She smiled kindly at her, then paused and looked thoughtfully at her before she continued. "Are you all right, Janie? Is the widow good to you?"

Juba considered how she should reply. She didn't want to get herself in trouble with Missus Bass. Now that she had hope of an escape plan, she didn't want to draw any attention.

Miss Lane had always been kind to her and talked *with* her instead of *at* her, which was different from most white people. The lady talked to her like a person and not a servant or slave, which was surprising and not unwelcome. Still, things were how they were in the world, and the difference in station and class was a real part of life. It was a big mistake to pretend otherwise.

"Yes, Miss Lane, everything is all right, and the widow treats me good," she replied.

"I've noticed that you do your best to take excellent care of the Bass children every day. You don't have children of your own, do you?" Harriet asked.

"No, ma'am. I haven't had my own yet."

"Every day, you seem to be doing more than what's asked of you. Yesterday, I saw you rocking Eugenia and singing to her after she woke crying from her nap. It's lovely how you mind those children, Janie. Mrs. Bass tells you that she appreciates you, I hope."

"I do what I must, Miss Lane. But it sure is hard not to love little children. They treat everyone with love. We all need to take a lesson from them. Their love makes my days better."

"I understand you have no choice in the matter, but I want you to know I see your love and kindness with the children. Your life as an enslaved person isn't easy. I also see that."

"Thank you, Miss Lane," Juba replied with a bit of disbelief. Where was the lady going with this conversation?

"There's a lot I don't understand about your life, about what you go through daily. I want to hear from you if you're willing to speak," Harriet said.

"What do you want me to tell you about, Miss Lane?" Juba added with hesitation.

"Everything. What your day is like, what you think about, what you wish for . . . I'm not asking to be challenging. I just want to understand."

"I don't know what to say to you, Miss Lane. I feel uncomfortable to share. Forgive me, but it's the truth." How could she get out of this conversation? It was curious though, Miss Lane's questions and that she would raise them. This woman had sat by her side when she was sick and feverish. She'd held her hand and put cool cloths on her head. Could she be honest with her? Could she be honest about what her life was like with a white lady, the president's niece?

"I don't blame you for feeling that way. I've done nothing to earn your trust. I hope that you feel like you *can* trust me, Janie. I want to listen and learn and maybe—if it's possible—help my uncle make better decisions about how to help the enslaved in the South."

Juba looked away. What harm could it do? The lady seemed genuine and had shown herself to be kind and compassionate. But where to start?

After a long silence, Juba began. "I wake up before dawn every morning, and the first thing I think about is surviving. I wonder if today is the day I will make a mistake and be hit or sold off somewhere far worse. I think about my family and how I miss them. I think about freedom, though I don't know if I'll ever be free." Juba was surprised at her own words. They had just tumbled out.

"That's more than I can imagine. I'm sorry," Miss Lane replied softly. She didn't continue to fill the silence. What could be said?

The women regarded each other for a few moments. Juba realized she was looking into Miss Lane's eyes. She wouldn't dare look Missus in the eye or straight at other people of her station. She wasn't afraid, though. She felt seen for a moment.

"It's not in my power to do anything for you, Janie. I'll admit that I am very uncomfortable with your situation, and I am frustrated with myself for not being able to do something about it. I am sure just having this conversation puts you in an awkward position. Please forgive me. I mean no harm or offense to you."

"That's all right, Miss Lane. It's not a talk I have ever had with anyone. But I am grateful that you would think on my behalf and for other people like me. My momma told me a long time ago that there are good people of every shape, size, and color. I understand that you are a fine lady not in a place to oppose your uncle in any way," Juba said.

"I best let you go back to your duties before the children come back with their mother. I thank you for your time and honesty."

"Yes, ma'am." Juba nodded, curtsied, and backed out of the room. She couldn't presume to turn her back on a white person, no matter how honest and kind they seemed to be.

Walking down the hall to the washroom to find fresh linens, she thought about her discussion with Miss Lane. It was very strange and uncomfortable, but not unwelcome. Her morning had started with an exchange with Elias Rouse and the senator, who were both working to help her. Juba smiled to herself. For today—or maybe for many days to come, until she knew more about her escape—she carried a small flame of hope.

— 10 —

Anne

On Sundays, Anne had the afternoon off from work. It was a quiet day at the Springs without planned social activities other than church. She helped Miss Harriet get dressed before a late breakfast and then returned to her farm to spend the day with Joshua. She was looking forward to a day at home. It had been so busy at the Springs that she was glad to spend time with her family.

As she walked into her cozy log house, she removed her cap and set it on the wooden table Jacob had built for her a few years ago. She touched the wood, feeling its coolness beneath her fingers. Even though it wasn't finely polished mahogany like some of the furniture at the Springs, her husband made it with his own hands. Anne treasured it. She spent many hours with him in the woodshop behind the barn, watching him sand it. She'd helped him rub beeswax on it. They kissed when it was done, and she hugged him tightly, thanking him.

She walked past the table to the windows on the other side of the room. She couldn't hear anyone in the house, so she thought perhaps Agnes and Josh were doing chores in the yard.

Looking out the window next to the large stone hearth toward the chicken coop, she could see Agnes and Joshua spreading feed for the chickens. It amazed her how fast her son was growing. As Josh dipped his hand into his grandmother's basket, he quickly jumped away to spread more corn, like a game. Agnes smiled down at him, enjoying his antics. The older woman seemed to have grown younger around his youthful spirit. Anne realized her boy probably reminded Agnes of Jacob as a young lad.

She watched them for a few more minutes, wondering at how much her boy warmed her heart, and then left the house through the back door to join them in the yard. As soon as Josh saw his mother was home, he ran at her. "Mamma! You're here! Grammy said you would be early today," her son exclaimed.

Anne scooped him up and noticed he was getting almost too heavy to lift. "How is my fine boy," she asked, squeezing him tight.

"I am well, Mamma, but I missed you so," he replied, burying his head in her shoulder.

Agnes approached and put her hand on Josh's back. "He sure did miss you, Mamma. He has been talking about Sunday afternoon since last Monday."

"I am glad to have my day here at home. It's hard being gone so much, but I am making real progress toward the taxes," Anne replied.

Pulling her small purse out of her dress pocket, she jingled it to show Agnes that there were coins in it.

"You are a fine girl, Anne, and I am grateful for it. Jacob married a good woman and would be proud of you." Agnes beamed at her and reached up to move a lock of red curls that had fallen out of Anne's cap and over her eye before going on. "I did want to tell you that the constable was here again on Friday and left another notice. He reminded me that we are only two weeks from the first payment being due to avoid the public sale notices in the *Gazette*," she said.

Anne carried Josh over to the bench that sat by the dooryard gate. The gate had a small wooden arbor over it, and she could smell the heavy, sweet scent of the primroses she had planted that were now in full bloom. She had trained those vines three years ago. This was the first summer they looked like she had imagined they would. She had taken pains to plant flowers and herbs that would make their little house look like the little cottages she saw in the block prints she loved in her favorite books. Each little detail on the farm moved her dreams ahead. The thought of losing her home made her stomach clench.

"We are going to make it, Agnes. I will have enough by the end of July to make the first payment," Anne assured her. She looked away to watch Josh, who had jumped off the bench and started stacking wood scraps into the shape of a house.

"That is good news. I also had another visitor I want to speak with you about, Anne." The tone in her mother-in-law's voice made her turn back to her, and she could tell whatever she was about to say was important.

"More bill collectors?" Anne asked. She was trying her best. Why did they keep reminding her of her troubles?

"Not a bill collector. Reverend Fidler came by yesterday. He told me about the young enslaved woman you are working with this summer. I wondered why you hadn't said anything to me about her. He said she is a nursemaid for one of the president's guests."

Anne didn't answer right away. She hadn't mentioned Juba, but now she had to think about why she intentionally didn't talk about Juba or her situation. She thought closely about it as her mother-in-law anticipated a response, and she knew why. She supposed she was not ready to hear what Agnes would say. Now, they would have this conversation for better or worse.

"Did Reverend Fidler tell you they want to help Juba escape, Agnes?" Anne decided it was best to put it all out for discussion and get to the point. She was too tired from work and needed to get through this discussion and return to enjoying her day with her son.

"Yes, he did tell me that. He also told me that you were afraid to get involved," Agnes replied.

"Mother McCoy, you know what happened to Jacob. I can't get involved and risk us losing everything he worked so hard for. We have barely kept the farm going. I will only just make it to the courthouse with the money for the first payment by the deadline. What if I am caught? What if I am fired from Miss Lane's service? The fine for the Fugitive Slave Act is a thousand dollars. There would be jail time as well! I can't go to jail! We could lose this farm!" Anne blurted out, exasperated.

"But we are Quakers, Anne. Our integrity means putting our beliefs into action and above our own needs. Community means that we are to consider everyone, not just ourselves."

Anne looked down at Josh who was sitting at her feet, still stacking sticks into what looked like a small log house, and remarked, "I have been thinking and praying about the right thing to do."

"That is deep and heavy contemplation, indeed. Our Quaker faith teaches us to uphold our integrity and follow our Inner Light. God is telling us the way, even when it might seem at our own cost."

"But Mother McCoy, how do I discern what is truly right? Do I put my family first or help another?"

"Patience and reflection are needed, my dear, for discernment. Listen closely to the whispers of conscience and the guidance of the spirit within you. Sometimes, not acting upon injustice can have consequences. As Quakers, we believe in the power of truth and taking action on what is right. God will help you be certain of the way if you listen."

"But Mother, remember what happened to Jacob? I am so scared." Anne started to cry.

Agnes pulled her close and hugged her, saying, "Oh, Anne, that is where you must have courage. Quakers seek peace, but not at the cost of truth. It is not easy to uphold your integrity and follow the path of righteousness, but it is the foundation of our faith. You won't be alone. The Quaker community of Friends supports and uplifts us no matter what happens. We are never alone in our journey when we are amongst Friends."

Josh ran up to the other end of the yard, where he began hitting a ball with a long switch. "Momma, I want a piggyback ride to see the baby calf in the pasture!" he exclaimed.

Anne walked over and dipped down for her small son to climb on her back and wrap his legs around her waist; his arms tightened around her neck. She nodded with resignation to Agnes to indicate their intention to walk away. She needed time to think. As they headed around the side of the house and down toward the lower field, Anne looked up at the afternoon sun shining over the western ridge.

She closed her eyes and stopped to feel the sun on her face. Then, her skin suddenly felt cool. The sun had slipped behind a large cloud that looked like it might take some time to pass. More dark clouds were coming over the ridge from the north and west. She and Josh would need to enjoy the baby calf quickly so as not to get caught in the rain.

Anne knew that, later that night, she would pray for the whisper of spirit to bring her guidance. She would pray to hear God within herself and listen closely to his counsel. There were always answers, but she could only act on the ones she was ready to understand.

The baby calf was precious, and Josh was excited to pat it. She held him back from running toward the small brown and white creature on wobbly legs.

"Josh, we must be careful. Her momma is right over there near the fence looking at us," Anne cautioned.

"But Momma, I won't hurt it. We feed them every day. Don't they know us?"

"That momma knows we are her friends who bring hay and milk her. But, when a momma has a baby, her first instinct is to do everything to protect that baby. That's her priority, even over food."

"Is that how you feel about protecting me, Momma?"

"Yes, Josh. You are always my first thought and priority." Anne picked him back up again and enveloped him in a warm hug.

As she walked back up toward the house from the pasture with Joshua on her hip, she thought again about the questions swirling in her mind. Sometimes, when she felt lost, she would go to the small plot on the southernmost hill of the farm and talk to Jacob by his gravestone. His spirit was still strong with her when she went there, and she wondered if she should speak with him tonight.

It looked like a storm was heading from the west and about to crest the ridge. Rolling clouds were moving in front of it. The silvery under-sides of the maple leaves on the edge of the forest turned up to greet the rain, and there was the sound of them rustling as the breeze picked up.

Josh was wiggling around, so she put him down on the grass. He ran toward the upper meadow, where his father rested. He was full of life and joy as he ran up the hill, his father's headstone in the distance.

Anne, quite the opposite, felt sad and lost. She wasn't sure if her little one really understood the loss of his father. She tried hard to keep him positive and safe, even when he cried at night that he missed his pappa. The more she thought about her worries as she climbed the rise, the less she wanted to confront them at Jacob's grave.

"Joshua, come back now. The rain is moving in, and we will barely have time to get back to the house," she called up to him.

Josh turned around. With the momentum of his run down the field, he picked up speed, which fueled him with extra joy as he galloped toward Anne. As he hit her legs, she scooped him up. She turned and hurried down the hill with him, using that same downward force to carry herself away from facing a conversation with Jacob about helping Juba escape.

11

Harriet

The first two weeks of their visit went by so quickly for Harriet. Every day was busy with summer activities. There was a dance last night, or a "German," as dances were called at Bedford Springs. Today was a trip to a roadside establishment east of Bedford called the Willow Grove Tavern. There, the party would continue with drinks, dancing, and a dinner the tavern was famous for: chicken and waffles.

Harriet spent the afternoon reading on the porch outside her room and came inside to get ready for the tavern trip. The large party of young people planned to leave at six for the four-mile ride. The Springs made quite a spectacle out of the weekly sojourn.

Multiple coaches and wagons were loaded with revelers, full almost beyond safety. Some riders were crammed in open coaches, while others were hanging on, riding the rails. Harriet intended to sit safely inside her coach. She had seen how some young men would fall off, rush to catch up, and climb back onto the moving carriage. This wagon parade was affectionately known as the "Tally Ho!" and was as much a part of the event as the dinner party at Willow Grove.

Harriet asked Anne to accompany her since the president had declined and it was appropriate to have an escort. Many evenings, she released Anne early so she could go home to her family. Anne seemed agreeable about going along and said having her mother-in-law put her son to bed was not a problem. Harriet planned to have her coach drop Anne off at her farm upon their return. She was interested in seeing a bit more of the town of Bedford and catching a glimpse of Anne's farm anyway.

As she prepared to leave the Springs property for the first time since her arrival, Harriet picked out one of her favorite gowns—a sage green silk damask dress with white lace and a matching travel bonnet that wasn't too ostentatious for the country setting. In Washington, she had become a style-setter with low-cut necklines that had not previously been the fashion, but out here in rural Pennsylvania, perhaps that would be frowned upon. For a trip off the hotel grounds, she might see all manner of people along the way, so a more modest Victorian collar was appropriate. Anne braided and fixed her hair so it wouldn't come loose on the bumpy trip and used extra hairpins in the bonnet.

As the women walked past Hygeia's tinkling water spray toward the carriages lined up by the front gate, coronet blasts called everyone to start loading. Many couples strolled on the grounds before dinner to watch the spectacle of the departure. Harriet turned to see that Uncle Buck was already on the front upstairs porch of the Colonial building. He would give the final wave to set the party off. He saw her looking at him, and they waved at each other. Earlier in the day, when she shared her plans, he was glad she would go and have a good time without him. Now his big grin seemed to her like his blessing for her to have a good time.

There was a commotion once the coaches were loaded, and the cornets blasted again and echoed off the valley walls. The president gave the sign, and they were off. The noisy journey began.

"Goodness, how many do you think are with us, Anne? It looks to me we have a good twenty or more," Harriet shouted over the cacophony of wagon wheels, horses, and cheering revelers.

"Yes, miss, I think at least twenty. I have never seen anything like it," Anne replied, laughing over the din.

They sped down Richard street, and as they reached the more populated part of town, locals lined the road as word had spread that the Tally Ho would be running that evening. People yelled to those on the coaches and cheered as young men on horses trotted alongside the carriages. Harriet waved at the spectators. Some of the parade-like atmosphere was for catching a glimpse of the president's niece.

As they turned east onto Penn Street, the riders of single horses galloped up to the front. Several blocks down, Penn Street ended near the Anderson farm and became Race Street, appropriately named for the straight stretch of road used to race to the foot of the Narrows.

The carriages all stopped, and many riders got out. Four men lined up. Even though they wore dinner breeches and waistcoats, all were poised to take off. One young man with a top hat handed it down to his friend to hold so he wouldn't lose it. A fifth man on horseback galloped ahead to the Narrows tollgate and, taking his hat off his head, waved it to show he was ready.

"Miss Lane, you must be the starter," one of the men on horseback shouted toward her carriage.

Harriet smiled, handed Anne her parasol, and took the cotton stole sitting next to her on the seat before climbing down from the carriage with the help of a well-dressed gentleman. She walked to the line of horses and lifted her stole.

"Ready," she paused, "set," pausing again, "go!" she called out, dropping her arm, and the four horses took off, spurred to action by their riders.

Dust from the dirt track rose, clods of dirt flying, and the thundering of hooves rang through the vale. The sound faded away, drowned out by the cheering of the revelers, many of whom had certainly made wagers. Harriet saw a young man in blue make it across first and raised his fist to the cheers of people watching. The man standing at the finish went to the winner and waved his hat, confirming his victory.

All were having a grand time. As she climbed back into the carriage, Harriet looked over to see if Anne had also enjoyed watching the boys race. Instead, she was looking anxiously out the window in the other direction, toward the north by the river.

"What is the matter, Anne? Are you unwell?" Harriet inquired.

"No, miss, I am all right. I was watching the people standing over there."

Following Anne's gaze, Harriet saw about ten people standing in the field to the left of the carriages. Behind them was a long clapboard dwelling close to the riverside. It had faded red shutters and a porch that needed fixing. She also saw that the people wore homespun, ill-fitting, dirty clothing. Small children stood with a woman holding a hoe near a garden patch. The children were barefoot. All were waving like the earlier crowds, but their appearance was sad and downtrodden.

"That is the poor farm, miss. I feel bad for those people when we are having such a grand time in all our splendor," Anne said quietly. "I don't mean to interrupt your fun. Please don't mind me."

The carriages lurched forward again toward the Narrows toll bridge. Harriet sensed Anne was thinking about something else and not saying it. What was bothering her? She would leave it for now. The din of the carriages and shouting young people swept them on.

Since it was a beautiful summer evening, the dinner party was to be held on the lawn of the Willow Grove Tavern. Harriet had been inside the tavern once but decided that she'd like to take a tour before dinner. The interior was cozy and quaint as she chatted with the proprietor's wife, Sofia Defibaugh.

As Sofia walked her through the downstairs, she pointed out to Harriet how the building had been extended and added on to over the years.

"The main house is a log house underneath the frame exterior. It was first erected right after the War of Independence," Sofia said.

"It's quite beautiful. One could never tell how old it is, as it looks lovely in the frame and plastered walls," Harriet replied.

"We struggle to get by with the railroad taking people off the pike. My husband's family used to do brisk business with drovers coming through, but now our heaviest times are the summer resort season. He is also a blacksmith and gunsmith."

"With six little children, I wonder how you manage such a fine establishment, Sofia."

"We've nearly lost the place to taxes a couple of times, but we make it through. We're grateful the Springs guests like yourself like to come for dinner. It's lovely seeing all the finely dressed ladies and gentlemen dining on our lawn and having a grand time. Certainly, having the First Lady here is an honor, Miss Lane."

Harriet left her shortly after to return to the dining party, crossing the grassy lawn next to the kitchen ell that extended beyond the main house. How were people making do out in the countryside? Sofia suggested that it was difficult for the average person. The recession of 1857 had occurred just as her uncle came into office. Many people were still struggling to get by.

After dinner, several of the Springs party decided to take a walk from Willow Grove, past the blacksmith shop on the property, to the riverside on the other side of the Great Road. Daniel Defibaugh, the proprietor, offered to lead those interested down to the river.

"It will be just about time for sunset through the Narrows," explained Mr. Defibaugh. "It will be worth the walk as sometimes the view this time of the evening is breathtaking."

Harriet and several others were glad to stroll after dinner, which had been delicious and filling. Many of the young men stayed behind to have some locally made whiskey. Ten people made up the walking group. Anne followed closely behind with Harriet's stole and parasol.

The path down to the riverside was steep, and along the way, they passed a shallow quarry filled with clear blue water. Daniel Defibaugh stayed close to Harriet as they approached the footpath, giving her a hand down when it got steep. As they neared the river, the air was full of birdsong, and the evening sun shimmered through a glade of massive sycamore trees. They joined a footpath and walked west, back toward the direction of town.

"I can't get over how beautiful it is out here," she remarked to the tavernkeeper. "It reminds me so much of the area around my home at Wheatland. I surely miss the peace and quiet of the country when I am in Washington."

"Yes, Miss Lane, we are lucky to have the Juniata River winding by the property. It has been a blessing to my family since before the War of Independence. My wife and I enjoy raising our six children here. There are lots of turtles and frogs for them to find. Sometimes, we see eagles fly by. Down that way is a big eagle's nest in a sycamore, and we see them carrying fish in their talons up and down the river. I guess they like raising their young here, too," explained Defibaugh with a chuckle.

As they neared a bend in the river, the view opened, and the pink and gold setting sun could be seen just above the horizon in the west. The mountains on either side were in silhouette, and in the foreground, the river sparkled. The narrow river rolled smoothly by, a continuous silver band, cool and lifegiving. Harriet took a deep breath, and they all stood quietly to take in the scene, which would only last a few minutes more.

Later, as they were returning to the tavern in the dusk, Harriet and Anne were walking together a bit away from the group. Harriet noticed Anne had been quiet all evening and had not eaten much of her dinner.

"Anne, is everything all right? You seem to be more quiet than usual this evening."

"Excuse me, miss, I don't mean to bother you," Anne replied, casting her eyes down.

"Is there something bothering you? I noticed your mood changed after we were at the horse race, but you said you were all right," Harriet said, pushing her for more.

"Well, miss, it's just that I keep thinking of the people we saw there by the road who were dirty and bedraggled. I haven't felt like I could enjoy myself much after that," Anne explained.

"It's very sad that there are souls who live this way. However, it's good there is a place here in Bedford for people who need help. A county-poor home is something that many places don't yet have the benefit of. At least debtors, widows, and orphans get support here in Bedford."

"Yes, miss, I suppose you're right," Anne replied, not looking any less downcast.

How ridiculous of her for not thinking. Anne was a widow. She had mentioned working at Bedford Springs to support her family. The poor farm was more than just an advancement in social services. It was an embodiment of Anne's fears. She flushed, embarrassed that she hadn't thought about how Anne must be feeling.

As she continued to walk and think about Anne's situation, she reflected on her conversation with Sofia Defibaugh as well. And what about Janie? That recent conversation was still on the top of her mind. So many people were struggling, and she had been focused only on her uncle's difficulties and how it affected her. Was this how she wanted to be? What about what Anne had said about integrity needing to be belief put into action?

They were nearing the top of the path back up to the tavern when Harriet stepped up to Anne and put her hand on her shoulder as they continued to walk up the hill toward the tavern.

"Anne, you are a smart, hardworking, and conscientious girl. You will always take good care of your family and do your best. I haven't known you for very long, but I know enough about you to feel sure that you will always do the right thing for everyone."

Anne gave Harriet a worried smile and took her leave to find the driver so that they could head back to town. As she waited for their carriage to be brought from the stable, Harriet looked toward the west where the sky was still deep red over the purple mountains. What did she believe in, and how could she act on those beliefs?

— 12 —

Juba

Juba had the children under the trees on the lawn and was watching them play. They were pretending at croquet, being silly, hitting the balls, and then running after them and laughing.

Sitting on a bench by a large oak tree, Ella, the oldest of the three, directed the two younger ones to fetch the balls for her. Council was following her directions. The boy ran as fast as he could and seemed to be having great fun. Little Eugenia was wandering around between the wickets. She didn't understand what Ella was trying to arrange, but she giggled nonetheless.

While at the Springs, Juba enjoyed being out of Washington and away from the Bass plantation, Riverside, for an extended stay. People here treated her kindly, and since there were no other slaves on the grounds that summer, she felt like most guests and workers saw her as simply another servant.

She thought about the difference as she sat quietly watching the children. Why did she feel there was a difference in treatment? The nearest she came to an explanation was that here she was treated as if some choice was involved. Of course, as a slave, there was no choice. Ever. When to sleep and eat depended on when she was sent to her quarters or what she was given to eat.

A servant, on the other hand, could quit. A servant could ask for higher pay and then, if they didn't receive it, look for another position. A servant usually wouldn't fear being smacked or beaten for doing something wrong—or for no reason at all. Beaten to within an inch of life, in some cases. That changed a person. It changed how Juba looked at the world and how she moved through it.

What she appreciated about being treated like a servant was that she felt like the other servants saw her as a person. Only some of them treated her differently because she was black. The difference was the freedom to be a person, not someone's property.

The Reverend and Mr. Rouse had given her a great deal of hope. There was a supportive group of black and white people in Bedford trying to help slaves flee bondage. That was inspiring and made her flicker of hope grow into a steady flame.

The community amongst those enslaved was different. On the estate and with farms nearby, the slaves in her area depended on each other. They were family, sometimes in reality and sometimes by need. They shared church services and holiday celebrations. They mourned the loss of children sold off or others who passed, old and sick ahead of their time due to hard work and little basic sustenance. At times, those ties were cut off at a moment's notice when a slave was sold away. When the crops were ready for harvest, privileges like Sunday church were suspended or canceled. Before she left Riverside, church meetings were no longer allowed because of rumors of a slave revolt brewing. No one knew where or when, but it was enough to spook all the white folks into not allowing gatherings, even for church. Losing the church services has been a hard blow for many, as they needed the comfort of God's word more than ever to give them consolation in their bondage.

Mr. Rouse and the Reverend were examples to her of another way to think about living. She had lost touch with how it was to live freely since she had lost her life with her parents. Here, over the Mason-Dixon line, black people owned businesses. They moved around town and were part of the community. They had families without fear of being split up by someone else's plans.

Though things had been better at Riverside with the Bass family than the other places she had been, better treatment did not erase the things she had seen and experienced before.

"Janie! Why is Eugenia in front of the ball where she could get hit?!" Missus Bass exclaimed, hurrying up behind her.

"Yes, ma'am, I will surely make her stay here by me." She rushed off her seat to grab the little pigtailed girl to avoid further scolding from Missus Bass. Why could she never do anything right for her? "They are having a good time out here in the sun today. Ella is becoming good at telling her brother and sister what to do."

Eugenia hugged her tight and put her little head on her shoulder. She could tell she was getting close to nap time when she began to cuddle. All the children warmed her heart with their sweet acts of affection. Children didn't care what color the people they cared about were. They took love and gave it back with no questions or judgments. It wouldn't be long before they started following the opinions and behaviors of their mother and other white people around them, though. Ella was already starting to be distant and treat her with less respect. That's just how it was. Losing that innocence and pure love for all was part of life. If only people could hold onto that.

The widow Bass wore a black ruffled skirt with many layers and a hoop underneath. She was trying to sit on the bench next to Juba but was having trouble arranging all her finery. The corners of her mouth pursed, and her brows furrowed. Juba hid a smirk at her mistress's fancy problems. Was she uncomfortable? She hoped so.

"Help me, please!" she ordered, annoyed.

Juba put Eugenia down and stood to give the woman more room. She helped pull the hoops evenly to each side to help her sit, adding, "There you go, ma'am."

"Thank you, dear. It's too hot for all these layers. It puts me in a mood. This travel with the children is a trial, but I am glad they are having a good time on the lawn."

They sat for a few more minutes and watched the children play. Juba made sure to keep little Eugenia close to her. In the distance, near the hotel, they saw Miss Lane and the president walking arm and arm, coming down the path toward them with Anne, Miss Lane's maid, walking behind. As they got closer, the president let go of Miss Lane's arm, said something to her that made her laugh heartily, and tipped his hat in the widow's direction before heading toward the Colonial building. Juba stood to make a place for Miss Lane, who had a dress without hoops but many layers of white lace.

Anne and Juba moved to a bench on the opposite side of the grassy area, bringing young Eugenia to keep a close eye on her. Sitting out of earshot allowed the ladies their privacy, while also giving Juba a chance to speak with Anne without raising questions.

"I understand why you can't be involved, miss, but since your family will be helping with my escape, do you know anything about the plans? When might they come for me?" Juba whispered. It was hard to keep her expression normal. She forced herself not to look around.

Furrows formed on Miss Anne's forehead and her shoulders slumped as she answered, "I'm sorry, Juba. I haven't heard about the plan." She looked like she was about to cry. She sure wasn't good at hiding her feelings.

"Shhhh now. We ain't close to the ladies, but please don't call me by my real name near Missus Bass. She'll have a fit that you even know the name Juba, and it's bound to raise questions."

"I'm sorry, I thought I was being respectful. I understand. I don't want to get you in trouble or arouse suspicion," Anne said, fidgeting in her seat.

"Miss Anne, not to be difficult, but you can't understand half of the trouble I have been through over the last ten years. I had about given up hope. I thought getting out of a bad situation, with cruel overseers and fieldwork, was the best I could hope for."

"Why haven't you told anyone you were born free? Wouldn't they realize they had to release you?" Anne questioned.

"If only it were that simple. When these masters pay a lot of money for a slave, they aren't interested in any news like that. If they found out a slave was free, they'd be more likely to sell them as quickly as possible so they don't lose their money. They would sell the slave as far south and out of the way as they could. I found out early on when the slave catchers first had me. They beat the tar out of me for saying I was free and told me anyone else who heard me say it would too. Even though I was a young girl, they threatened to kill me if I said it again. They told me I'd be better off being quiet and following directions. They said if I acted well enough, I would have a better chance of getting a house job since I was young, pretty, and had lighter skin. They said I had better not cause trouble."

Anne's jaw tightened. The color had risen in her cheeks and her eyes were starting to glisten.

"Now please don't cry. That won't fix what happened to me. Missus Bass and Miss Lane see you looking at me like that, they're going to wonder what we're talking about," Juba gently scolded Anne.

"I'm sorry. I realized long ago slavery was against God's will, and terrible things happened within it. I've read The Liberator and Uncle Tom's Cabin on occasion, but I have never met anyone who spoke of such cruelty from experience. I don't know what to say, Janie. I have so many thoughts and questions."

The children were sitting on the grass a few yards away, busy popping the heads of dandelions and laughing. Missus Bass and Miss Lane stood up and began walking away back toward the hotel, paying no attention to the two women as they left. This gave Juba and Anne more freedom to speak.

"I appreciate you have read some things about what it's like to be a slave, but I don't think you understand what it is to be in someone's power and have none yourself. Having no control over your life or your body is something that can't be described in a book or newspaper," Juba explained. "I know what Uncle Tom's Cabin was trying to say, but a white woman wrote it. She talked to many folks, and what she wrote in the book was similar to things I have seen or heard about from others. A book can't capture the horrible evil and terror millions of people live under every day."

Looking at Anne, she saw no judgment, just intense attention to her words. *Should I go on?* she thought. *I feel like I can trust her, but I've never talked to a white woman about these things.*

Looking off in the direction of the children, she continued. "When I was twelve years old, I started to look more like a woman than a child. The overseer where I was at the time started to eye me up. Every day, I tried to stay out of his line of sight, and he always found a way to leer at me anyway. One of the older women in the quarter warned me he was a wolf waiting to pounce. I lay awake at night, or if I slept, I had nightmares about him. I tried to never be alone with him."

She looked into Anne's brown eyes and there was both horror and sorrow in them. But she was listening intently. She went on.

"Before the Christmas holiday, when the harvest was done, the slaves got their one break of the year and could take several days off. The master wanted a few of us to go over to the neighbor's plantation to help make their barn ready for the slave meal and dance. Each nearby plantation took turns hosting the meal. The overseer chose two men and three women to help the other farm sweep up and hang the pine boughs."

Anne was leaning forward, waiting for the rest.

"When we got to the other plantation, the overseer made up a story that he'd forgotten they wanted me at the main house and would take me back. I watched the looks on the older women's faces. They were afraid for me. On the way back, we came to the turnoff for the overseer's house near the plantation entrance. I knew before we got there he would make that turn to his cabin. Like I said, I was only twelve years old."

Juba and Anne sat in silence for a few moments regarding each other. She saw Anne swallow hard, bow her head, and wipe tears with her sleeve. There was nothing more either could say.

— 13 —

Anne

As Anne made her way home later that evening, her conversation with Juba weighed on her. The things that had happened to Juba were hard to think about. She tried to push the images out of her mind, but they kept overwhelming her. If she felt sick to her stomach just hearing about Juba's experiences, she couldn't imagine living them. She prayed that Juba would find peace and that there would soon be a better future for her. She thought of all the people who might be getting ready to make her escape possible.

It was a summer evening, heavy with the heat of the day, just beginning to ease by the cool air drifting out from deep in the woods. Anne wondered how that cooling breeze would roll down the hills from the trees in the forest. Sometimes, it moved like a roiling swell of air flowing over a person, bringing relief even in the midst of summer. Where did that cool live all day? Did it hide in the shade under the thick green oak leaves? Was the brisk air stored up in the rocky hilltops and then tumbled down after sunset, released from hiding by the setting sun? The crisp wave was at her back as she walked down the slope toward her farm.

Anne couldn't shake the nagging feeling that she should help Juba. She was closer to the situation than all the people in town who, in the past, were involved with Underground Railroad activities. She knew each conductor well; such good people. Reverend Fidler was an outspoken shepherd of the black community and deeply believed in the work God had entrusted to him. Elias Rouse was a caretaker of people's health and the closest thing the black community in Bedford had to a physician. He was hardworking, kind, and freely put himself at risk for the betterment of others.

The next leg of the journey out of Bedford usually led to the Harrises home out near Wolfsburg. The Harrises were gracious people willing to share anything they had with anyone who came to their property. After that, the stops were in Cessna, Fishertown, Spring Hope, and Alum Bank. That was the northwestern route most familiar to Anne. Those places were all part of the Quaker Valley section of the Underground Railroad. Her uncle, Sam Way, was important to that section of that trail. There were other alternate routes out of Bedford too. Some went north through St. Clairsville and on to Altoona. There was also a more westerly route that headed toward Somerset and then northwest to Erie.

As she got closer to the house, she saw there was a horse tied up by the post out in front. Who could be visiting this late in the evening? Agnes had some lady friends who would stop by to quilt, but they would be gone by now to make dinner for their families. She thought about the constable. Given the hour, she figured his duties were long over. He would be home with his family as well. Doctor Watson had a black horse. This fine animal was not black but a large, white, well-groomed stallion. It had an expensive-looking saddle, unusually trimmed out.

Anne opened the rear door to the kitchen. The room was still lit by the dusk light coming through the western windows. There were also candles lit in several places throughout the room, giving a mixed glow of gold and rose to the space. Agnes was sitting at the table, and in front of her, his back to Anne, was a tall white-haired man in a cream-colored suit. The man stood and turned toward her as Anne walked closer. It was Senator Simon Cameron. His white hair was a bit unruly, and his height seemed to make him stoop.

"Good evening, Mrs. McCoy," he began in his deep, quiet voice. "Your mother-in-law has made me a lovely cup of tea. I was explaining to her that I needed to speak with you about the plan to help the enslaved nursemaid of President Buchanan's guest, Mrs. Bass."

Agnes stood up and moved to the stove, saying, "Anne, sit down with the senator. I will make you tea as well."

She was speechless to find Senator Cameron in her home. What about Miss Lane's warning to her about this man and his potential for scandal and conflict with President Buchanan? Her stomach turned.

"Thank you, Agnes, but it is rather late for tea," she said to the older woman. Taking a deep breath, Anne took the basket off her arm and sat down at the table.

"I beg your pardon, sir, but I've told Mr. Rouse and Reverend Fidler that I cannot be involved and risk losing my position serving Miss Lane. I am a widow trying to keep this family farm from tax sale. What about Thomas Miller, the president's valet? He is a Quaker. His people have helped fugitives in the past."

"Mrs. McCoy, it certainly is a beautiful farm. I noticed you have the beginning of an apple orchard along your back field. Many years of cultivating have made this farm what it is today. Your husband had quite a chore clearing all the trees here to make the magnificent view you have now. It would be a shame to lose it," the senator said.

"Yes, sir. My husband was very proud of this farm. I am too," Anne replied warily.

"I understand you are in jeopardy with your financial affairs, but you are in a unique position to help the enslaved woman escape. If we bring another person into the plan, we risk a breach. I did find out the valet is a Quaker like yourself, but Thomas is too close to the president and may have an allegiance that could jeopardize the plan. You have access to the comings and goings of the Buchanan party and when the right time is at hand," he went on.

"Senator, I believe it is the right thing to do for her, but I am in no place to be able to assist," Anne said.

"If we rely on someone else at the Springs to be the first link in the chain, we risk exposing the plan. It would raise suspicions with Miss Lane or the other members of the group. They can't see me anywhere near their rooms without my being suspect."

"Yes, sir, it's very risky," Anne remarked.

"I'm trying to help a soul in bondage. I discovered Juba was born to free parents. Certainly, as a woman of the Quaker faith, you understand the moral implications," Cameron went on.

"Sir, I do understand, and I know more about Juba's situation than I can share, which makes my heart and mind ache for her freedom. The risk to my family's security is a fact I cannot overlook or even take chances with. Miss Lane trusts me, and I cannot break that trust. My livelihood and personal safety, as well as that of my family, would be in danger, Senator." Though her voice was even, Anne could feel the threat of tears behind her eyes.

Cameron regarded her steadily. "I have people who can help, and I want to offer you the funds to cover your debt. Then you won't have to worry about losing your position or coming up against the law if you are found out. I know powerful people all over the state through the courts and the political system who can protect you, Anne," he countered.

Anne's thoughts raced. Was this truly the right thing to do, *and* the answer to her troubles? Miss Lane and the president opposed the senator. How could she trust him? She struggled with herself, unsure whether this was a godsend or her undoing.

"Money is not the point, sir. What of my integrity, my good name? What of the impact on my family if this was all found out? Senator, I am sorry, but I can't help you."

The senator frowned but nodded. "Thank you for hearing my proposal, Mrs. McCoy. I will take my leave and not bother you again."

He stood to leave, and Agnes followed him to the door and opened it for him. Anne rose politely. The senator looked back at her before ducking his head through the low doorframe. Agnes closed the door and walked back to her, standing a moment in silence as if collecting her thoughts.

"Anne, I don't often speak my mind when it comes to your decisions. With Jacob gone, you are left with the heavy burden to carry this family as a man usually would. Senator Cameron's offer would alleviate so many of your concerns. He is answering your prayers and giving you a safety net if you run into trouble helping Juba. I cannot understand how you won't help her safely get to the first leg of her freedom journey."

Anne could not speak. Resting her head on the table, she began to cry. Deep, heaving sobs wracked her, and she felt like she may not be able to stop. She didn't trust Senator Cameron, and she didn't want to disappoint Miss Lane, herself, or Jacob's memory.

Agnes put one gentle hand on her back, patting her as if comforting a child. Anne's crying slowed, but she knew in her heart she would have a long night ahead of praying for discernment and God's light to guide her choices.

✦———━━━———✦

Later, after she'd fallen asleep, Anne woke with a start, her heart racing from a terrible dream. Laying on her back, she stared at the log beams of the ceiling. Finally, she couldn't take it any longer, and she knew what she had to do. She had been avoiding it for days, but it had to be done.

The night was still warm, and the moon shone brightly as Anne stepped off the porch and opened the latch on the gate. As she passed through, the perfume of primroses on the arbor wafted through the air. Walking up the hill toward the southern pasture, she lifted her cotton nightdress so the hem wouldn't get wet with the dew already on the long grass. Moonlight made her way clear, and there was barely a breeze. Jacob's headstone was at the edge of the woods under a huge old oak tree. He had left that tree for shade when he cleared the field many years ago.

Anne had put off having a conversation with him long enough. She prayed each night, waiting for God's answer, but she had only heard her own conflicted thoughts about helping Juba escape, things that could go wrong, and taking care of the family. She needed Jacob's counsel, even if it was just in her head.

Approaching the headstone, her stomach lurched. All the anger, sadness, and fear of being without him rushed in on her. In front of his grave, her knees buckled. Down on her knees, her tears began and wouldn't stop.

"Oh, Jacob, I can't do all this without you. I miss you so," Anne sobbed. "I want to do the right thing. I want to help her, but I'm so scared we could lose everything. What would become of Josh and Agnes? How can I be strong enough to do everything you used to do?"

She bent over sobbing and found herself lying face down in the soft grass in front of the gravestone. He lay six feet below her. His body that she loved so dearly. His body she had made love to, mended too many injuries to count, and washed tenderly in the big metal tub as she poured water over his back while they laughed together.

"What must I do?" Anne spoke into the ground, the tears on her cheeks sticking to the scratchy grass. "Please give me a sign. Show me that we will be okay. I know what you would do. You would help. You would do everything in your power to ensure Juba's freedom."

With those words in her head, Anne stopped crying and swallowed hard. She rolled over and sat up. She looked down the pasture toward the house and at the whole of their land below. She wiped the grass and tears from her cheeks with her hand, then regarded the endless darkness filled with tiny pinpricks of starlight. The conversation was over. Standing to walk back down the hill, Anne saw not one but two stars shoot across the northern heavens.

Her eyes opened wide with awe as she sighed, "Oh my! I hoped for an answer, but I didn't think you'd be so clear about it! You were always the one who liked to answer things directly." She added quietly, "Thank you, my love. I miss you every day."

She made her way toward the house with both peace and a surge of new power in her heart. She knew what she had to do.

— 14 —

Harriet

Harriet awoke to fog sitting in the valley outside her windows and saw dew drops glistening across the resort lawn. Above Constitution Hill, the sunshine was breaking through. Soon, the fog would lift, and it would be a beautiful day to be outdoors. One thing she appreciated on these foggy mornings was that in the narrow valley where the Springs sat, the cool mountain air would stay in the woods for a few extra hours. She planned to enjoy an invigorating walk after breakfast.

It was routine for most guests to eat, then cross over the colonnade bridge to the Magnesia Spring to drink the healing waters. Shortly after the water therapy, strollers would walk in different directions on promenades throughout the trails that crisscrossed Constitution Hill. Covered with hemlock, oak, and maple trees, the shady woods made these paths dappled with sunlight and often full of convivial conversations.

Since it was a Monday morning, Anne wasn't back from her Sunday with family, so Harriet got herself ready to meet Uncle Buck in the dining room for breakfast. As she dressed, she thought about her recent interactions with Anne and Janie. They were both serving her group this summer, but the difference in how each woman carried themselves, interacted with her and others, and moved through the world struck her hard. Though she had considered slavery and its evils before, she hadn't seen it so closely compared to paid servitude as she did in her small travel group at the Springs this summer.

Anne was a free woman, able to own a farm and seek employment where she could find it. Janie was enslaved to Mrs. Bass, who did not own property, have a family, or earn wages to better her life. Anne worried about trying to make ends meet and taking care of her mother-in-law and child on her own. She was able to do so with the satisfaction of leaving at the end of a week's work to go home with money in her pocket. Janie could do nothing but serve Mrs. Bass. She had no way to stand up for herself or make her own choices. Janie's best hope was to be treated with kindness rather than cruelty by her mistress and others.

Harriet walked across the green lawn of the Springs, lost in her feelings. She was ashamed that she had never thought about servitude and its many forms as deeply before. Though in her heart she had always been against slavery, she never put herself in the situation of an enslaved black person. She did not think about it from their point of view. As she climbed the steps to the second level of the Colonial building, she felt a shift in her perspective on the topic inflaming the nation.

Arriving in the dining room, she saw her uncle at their usual table. Seated with him was another familiar Springs guest they often dined with: Major Lawrence Taliaferro and his wife, Eliza. The major had been a faithful public servant and recently retired from service as an agent of Indian affairs in the northwest territories. He had retired to Bedford to suit Eliza, the daughter of a local innkeeper. Major Taliaferro made good on the promise to her that after all their years on the frontier, they could come home. They built a beautiful manse right on the corner of Penn and Richard streets, supposedly constructed from lumber brought from the Taliaferro family's plantation, Whitehall, in Virginia.

Eliza Taliaferro was quite a beauty. Petite with raven hair and dainty features, she was a striking companion to her husband's dark good looks. This morning, as Harriet walked up to the breakfast table, she heard the group was already in a lively discussion. After ordering her tea and a soft-boiled egg with toast, Harriet settled in to catch up on the conversation in progress. Major Taliaferro recounted the recent work that had been done at his home and how the couple were finding life in Bedford after their return from the west.

"I find it very pleasant here, Mr. President. We enjoy being back from the edges of civilization, yet not embroiled in the dirt and crush of the cities. I think after so many years in the broad open plains, I have become accustomed to the freedom the country brings to a man's soul. Bedford is a good in-between for us," the major explained.

"Why, I am glad to hear that, Major. At least you are near Eliza's family and have the goings-on here at the Springs to keep you in the mix with what is happening in Washington. Your time settling some of the Indian unrest won't be forgotten. You never know, an appointment may present itself," Buchanan replied.

"I'm not so sure we want to continue in public service, sir. My wife is relieved to be home. Things have been in such turmoil both in the west and between the states; it seems too much like a viper pit. It was enough for me to try to do right by both the government and the native people in my role. I imagine being the supreme representative of the United States keeps you up many nights, Mr. President," Taliaferro said.

"It is a challenge but an honor, Major. We are currently fraught with struggles as a nation. The slavery question has been ongoing and difficult. Speaking of that topic, have you heard from Harriet Scott, Eliza? I read that Dred Scott passed away in September." He turned toward the major's wife to inquire, and Harriet was surprised her uncle had brought up the subject of the Scotts.

Dred and Harriet Scott were previously close to the Taliaferros. The major moved his slave, Harriet, from his plantation in Virginia to the frontier to serve his wife. There she had met Dred, who was enslaved to another settler. Though both were enslaved, the major had presided over their marriage and had given her over to Dred's owner, Doctor Emerson. The Scotts had tried to buy their freedom several years later but were refused, which began many years of court battles that led to the Supreme Court.

The Supreme Court made its decision that enslaved people of African heritage were not citizens of the United States and, therefore, they did not have citizens' rights. This ruling also gave legs to the property rights of slave owners, binding regardless of which state they resided in, free or slave state. Dred and Harriet had been manumitted after the decision by the family who last claimed ownership. But sadly, Dred died in the fall of tuberculosis, only a year after they gained their freedom.

Eliza looked sad but guarded as she answered the president. "I did get a letter from Harriet after Dred's death. She decided to stay in St. Louise with her daughters."

"Yes, I heard they named one of their daughters after you, Eliza," Harriet piped up, trying to steer the conversation in a more positive direction.

"I was very fond of Harriet. She was a good woman, and I was glad that she was finally free. All the goings-on about the court case and its aftermath have been a trial in itself for them. I am afraid Dred was not in the best health for a long while," Eliza informed them.

Buchanan weighed in, "I was sorry he couldn't live to enjoy his life. I hoped his trial would bring closure to the issues that have burdened the country for so long, and restore constitutional law back to the forefront of people's understanding."

"With all due respect, sir, I beg to differ with the outcome. I think the case has highlighted the foundational injustices of slavery," Major Taliaferro ventured, uncertain of the response his declaration would garner.

"Slavery will take its course. It has already been decided in the north. Coming innovations in farming will make slavery economically untenable without the government intervention that could cause destruction," Buchanan replied.

Harriet looked down at her uneaten food in the awkward silence and felt ill. How had her uncle lost sight of the truth of humanity for the sake of nationalism? Was she powerless to change his mind? For the first time in her life, she felt like there was a distance between them that couldn't be closed. But how could she stand up to him on her own?

After breakfast, Harriet and her uncle walked arm in arm over the colonnade bridge to the Magnesia Spring. There, across Shober's Run, was a pavilion ornamented with charming fretwork and milled spindles painted green and white. The spring gushed and bubbled from the hillside and spilled onto rocks set there to create a small catch basin. A young man was stationed there with a dipper and tin cups to serve guests their morning draft that was part of the resort's medicinal regimens. Harriet still felt uneasy about where the breakfast discussion had gone and hoped the magic waters would settle her stomach.

"To you, my dear, for being the solace in this old man's days," Uncle Buck pronounced and raised his cup in a toast to Harriet.

"Thank you, Nunc." Harriet raised her cup to his and drank the full measure of water. It had a metallic taste and a fizzy quality that wasn't unpleasant. "Let's take a walk in the woods and digest our breakfast."

The president turned, extending his elbow to Harriet for her to take his lead, and they walked from the pavilion toward the Grotto Spring. As they climbed a short set of stone stairs, they came into a grove of tall hemlock trees that towered over them. The hillside was covered with a giant hemlock and a dense cluster of mountain laurels. Above their heads, pouring from the hillside, was another spring. It rushed and tumbled as a small waterfall into a stone pool that disappeared under the path. The water was so loud that they were quiet and stopped to listen for a moment. The clear water sparkled as its wide ribbon splashed. The air was rich with moisture, the smell of hemlock needles, and damp earth.

As they walked on, the pair turned up the hill. Constitution Hill was crisscrossed with many walking trails. Some of the paths switched back and then descended again on the other side and met paths that skirted along Evitts Mountain, which was significantly higher.

"Nunc, I want to talk with you about some of the table conversations I've been part of while we've been here," Harriet began cautiously. "I'm worried by the topics that keep cropping up. I think that you may be losing support with even some of your closest acquaintances." Sometimes it was easiest to talk to her uncle while they were walking. Something about moving forward and not having to face each other made difficult conversations easier.

"My duty is not to please everyone, Hal. The time for thinking solely about my popularity or my convictions is past. Not while I am sitting in my current seat. Are you referring to the topic at breakfast regarding Dred Scott?" He looked down at her, searching her face for a reaction.

"Well, yes, and the conversion at dinner the other night wasn't any less awkward. Jeremiah Black is on your cabinet, and he didn't even defend you when Hess implied that you were catering to Southern interests." She hoped her tone remained steady. He would receive her better if she stayed calm. He didn't like emotional appeals.

"I take exception to the fact that after my whole life in public service representing the best interests of this country, my peers can't trust that my priority is to quell the unrest between the parties and states. By asking the Supreme Court to make a final determination on the slavery issue before my inauguration, I had hoped to put the issue to rest so the country would heal and move on." His voice held a note of resignation.

He looked sad. Perhaps she had offended him. She needed to go on, regardless.

"But Nunc, the decision calls into question humanity itself. Making slaves of African descent ineligible for citizens' rights and relegating their agency as property . . . Can't you see how those with a deep conviction of the sanctity of human life would object? How can there be a compromise when it comes to the truth that we are all human beings?" Harriet pleaded. Had she gone too far? She'd never contradicted him before or presumed even to oppose him.

"Harriet, we have danced around this topic many times, my dear." He paused, perhaps weighing his words like the lawyer he was trained to be. "You know, I find slavery morally repugnant. I have freed slaves myself. We have been friends and neighbors with black people in Pennsylvania all our lives. What I am trying to avert is the bloody collapse of our union over this issue. It could bring economic catastrophe to the South if slavery were abolished before the natural evolution of agriculture. Unrest and violence are what I am holding at bay." He stopped, looking at her as though hoping she'd change her mind and take what he'd said to fortify her unwavering support.

Harriet heard the deep conviction in his summation. This was the justification for the inaction he'd made in public over and over. Couldn't he see this line of reasoning wouldn't satisfy her? Why did he not understand he wasn't making an argument she and other Americans could accept?

They walked for a while in silence. Her uncle had raised her to be kind and to consider all people, as had the Catholic nuns who had instructed her to think and follow God's laws of truth and mercy.

They came to the south end of the trail as they reached a deep ravine. On the opposite side of the cleft was a large rock outcropping covered with thick green moss. At the crest stood several whitetail deer. The doe flicked their tails and stared with big, dark eyes. Harriet and her uncle stood still to watch them. One of the deer stamped and huffed, looking at them—a warning to stay away or stand her ground. Then they all ran as if driven by some invisible sign to make their break.

"Nunc, I know you have the weight of the nation on your shoulders. I cannot question your love of this country and your primary intent to do right by the nation you have served your whole life." She paused, checking his expression to gauge his mood. Would he be receptive to what she had to say? All that she had seen, heard, and thought about the last few days culminated in a flood within her that she had to release. Her fear of disappointing him made her heart race, but she went on.

"However, I simply don't understand how you can believe we live in a nation founded on religious freedom but let laws be set in place that go against God's truth." Harriet looked deeply into his tired eyes. She saw he understood her implication by the sadness in them.

"Hal, patience, and perseverance are also virtues. We can strive for God's will for a nation of freedom. Change will not happen overnight."

Her uncle moved to lead her left with his arm, continuing the path toward Evitts Mountain, but Harriet let go of his elbow and strode in the other direction, back toward the hotel. She walked her own way.

15

Juba

Dawn was just breaking and cool mists rose over Shober's Run and crept across the hotel lawns. Juba enjoyed the early mornings. She could move about without Missus constantly giving her orders or making unnecessary comments about her work. When the children were sleeping, she had permission to leave them for short periods to do errands like getting their breakfast tray or taking their washing to the laundry house.

Given how highly sought after these quiet moments were, before the light moved over the mountains, Juba was up at five in the morning to enjoy the time that felt almost like her own. She planned to drop off some soiled children's clothes at the laundry and then stop by the kitchen. Mrs. Barnes, the early cook, was kind to her, and sometimes they enjoyed a conversation.

"Good morning, Miss Koontz," Juba greeted the laundress as she entered the humid brick laundry building, an extension of the kitchen house. The walls were slick with water rising from the steaming cauldrons.

Lucinda Koontz turned and scowled at Juba, then went back to stirring a kettle of boiling laundry.

"I have some children's clothing with grass stains on the knees that need some extra attention," Juba said as she walked toward the woman, holding the garments to show the problem areas.

"Just leave 'em there," Miss Koontz answered gruffly, pointing to a worktable.

"There's blackberry on this one on the front," Juba said, laying a small dress on the table and showing her the spots. Missus would give her a hard time if the clothes weren't cleaned properly.

"I said leave 'em there and get outta here. I don't like niggers in my laundry room."

Juba stopped dead, looking at the woman. What had she done? The woman was so hostile, all she needed was help with the laundry. Since she had been at the Springs, she hadn't been treated poorly, and she had let her guard down. The pit of her stomach rolled, and bile rose in her throat. Fire came to her cheeks. Her hands balled into fists at her side.

"I was just doing my job. You don't have to be ugly. Today is Thursday, and the children will need those clothes for church before Sunday," Juba said, holding down her tone so the fury wouldn't show through.

"You heard what I said. Get out." The laundress stepped forward. It was clear she needed to leave.

Juba turned and walked out slowly. No good could come from continuing to stand there and be insulted, but she wasn't about to show that she was scared. The heat in her face was cooled by the morning air, and she wiped the moisture and sweat from her brow. As she walked into the main kitchen, Mrs. Barnes looked up from her floured worktable to greet her.

"Janie. Good mornin'," she said with a smile.

"I hope you're having a fine morning, Mrs. Barnes. Mine's not going too well."

"What's going on, my dear?" The cook stopped and dusted off her floury hands over the worktable, then rubbed them on the apron that covered her ample front. She was a big woman with powerful arms that looked like she had been lifting heavy flour sacks and giant cast-iron pots for many years.

"I don't want to make trouble. Your laundress doesn't like me too much."

"Mercy, what did she say to you, Janie?"

"She said she didn't want niggers in her laundry room."

"Oh my! That's not how we are here! Mr. Newman don't tolerate that kind of talk. I'm sorry!"

"Well, it wouldn't be the first time for me, Mrs. Barnes," Juba said.

"That's not the point, Janie. Come sit, and I'll give you a hot roll that just came out of the oven." Mrs. Barnes pointed to an old wooden stool next to the workbench. She walked over to a cooling rack, picked up a roll with a cloth, put it on a plate, slathered some butter on the edge, and set it down for Juba. The steam rose from the bread.

Mrs. Barnes continued, "Let me tell you about Lucinda. She's being hateful to you because she thinks you took her assignment."

"I don't know what you mean, Mrs. Barnes," Juba said, tilting her head. Why was there always something going on she was blamed for and had no idea about?

"She was supposed to be assigned to Mrs. Bass before Blackburn knew she had brought her own nursemaid. Lucinda found out on your arrival that she had to be reassigned to the laundry because it was late enough in the season that the other better jobs were filled."

"Well, that's not my fault," Juba stated, brushing some breadcrumbs off her lap.

"I know, dear. But some people don't think. Some people only know what's close to them and not what is right, fair, or kind."

"But it's not about my color. Not even about me."

"Janie, people haven't realized the world is changing. Hopefully, for the better. Some people have been stuffed away in hollers and never learned anything. People who only see their own people as right. Everything is everyone else's fault. They think black people moved up to the north and took their jobs. They see it as a personal attack. You see what I mean?"

"Yeah, I see it. Down south, we have poor whites. It's about the same. Some don't like the slaves too much. Some treat others poorly at every opportunity," Juba said sadly, shaking her head.

"It ain't right. But it is what it is. The best I can tell you is to steer clear of her and others like her and hope that someday, things might get better. But I guess there will always be those people who don't think," Mrs. Barnes finished.

"Can I take this roll with me, Mrs. Barnes? I'm not too hungry now."

"Sure can, child. And here's the breakfast tray for the children."

Eli Rouse was standing by the far end of the kitchen building, talking to one of the cooks, when she stepped out the door. He caught her eye and signaled for her to wait a moment. When he'd finished speaking with the boy, she walked over, and they both sat down on a bench in the yard by the kitchen garden.

Eli cautioned, "We can sit here and talk, but if someone comes, you open your mouth like I'm checking on your wound."

She nodded and asked, "Do you have some news for me? Is there a plan to help me soon?"

"It's all coming together. You must be wondering what is going on, so I came out here hopin' to find you 'bout the same time as last week when I was talking to Senator Cameron. You get the children's tray each mornin'?"

"I was hoping you would find me. I can barely sleep at night thinking about it all. My mind goes round and round. I'm so scared of getting caught, but so ready to see my parents," Juba whispered, putting the tray and milk pitcher on the bench as her hands were shaking and causing drops of milk to spill on her apron.

"I can only imagine. We will send word up to Boston through the Quaker community. Can you give me your parents' names, Juba? That way, we can link up where we need to get you on your way. Also, I need your last name so we can get you some papers. Senator Cameron will be working on that, but your full name and the name of your parents are needed for those."

"John and Mary Wright are my parents. I am Juba Wright. That is Wright with a 'W.' My pappa always said Wright with a 'W' like Wrong and would chuckle. My folks were always proud that they could read and write and got the joke. People who couldn't read didn't understand."

"All right, Miss Wright," Eli laughed quietly and grinned at Juba. It seemed they both felt a little relief to have a moment to snicker and smile together. "But, back to the plan—we don't have much time." He looked around, making sure they were alone. "Sunday, what time does Missus Bass go to church? Do they go to the services here at the Springs in the evening, or do they go into town to the Presbyterian Church that the president attends sometimes?"

"Last week, they stayed here and went to the evening services, but I have heard they may go to town for the morning services. I am not certain where they will go to church this Sunday," Juba replied.

Eli thought for a moment. Juba could tell this was a problem from his expression.

"I guess we will have to get word to you. We will need two plans and abandon one or the other. Do they take the children with them?"

"Yes, they take the children to church. Missus is very set on them getting used to sitting nicely through the service and learning to be good Christians. She don't take me, though," she confirmed.

"I will meet you Saturday morning at this same time when you come to the kitchen. By then, you should know about their Sunday plans. If they go in the morning, I will come and get you while they're gone. If they go in the evening, I will arrange to come and get you then. Neither time is ideal, as the daylight makes the whole thing more dangerous. Are there other times you're left alone?" he asked.

"No, not really. I am with the children all the time. Missus keeps track of me, especially with the senator close by. I think they suspect that he has his eye on me. Miss Lane already told me to steer clear of him."

"Yeah, that's why he can't be involved. It would be a scandal if he was found out. Some other things are going on with the abolitionist cause, and we don't want to draw too much attention."

Juba didn't understand what he was referring to. The last time she saw Eli and the senator, they made allusions to John Brown, the radical. None of that was her concern, but her escape surely was. How could she sleep at all the next few days, knowing she was so close to being free? Oh Lord, what if she was caught or something happened before they came for her? It was all too much to think about.

Walking back to the Evitt building, she could hear the plates shaking on the tray. She had to stop and take a deep breath before someone saw her or she dropped it. One foot ahead of the other. She could do this.

— 16 —

Anne

As she rounded the curve by Naugle's Mill, Anne heard the far-off music drifting from the ballroom at the other end of Bedford Springs. It echoed through the valley, filling the front lawn with the sound of violin and piano. A blaze of light was shining from the ballroom windows, illuminating the grand portico and entrance. The Saturday "German," or dance, was in full swing. She hoped everyone stayed focused on the fancy ball.

She climbed the exterior stairs of the Swiss House section of the lodging quarters, planning to make her way to the Evitt building without passing patrons or staff. The sound of the music grew louder as she approached her destination, but there was not a soul about, which was a great relief. She needed to make it to the Evitt building and back without having to explain why she was there. Hours earlier, she had gone home for the evening.

Anne tapped lightly on the door, hoping Juba would hear her. "Juba," she whispered. "Juba," she said quietly again.

There was sweat on her forehead. Was there anyone nearby? All was quiet in the rest of the building. The floorboards creaked behind the door, and then it opened a crack. Juba's face appeared in the opening, her eyes wide.

"Miss Anne, what are you doing here so late?" she inquired.

"Grab your things. The plan has changed. I am here to take you away now. It's time!" Anne spoke as quietly as she could in her fear and excitement.

"But Miss Anne, what about the children? I thought Mr. Rouse was coming to get me tomorrow while they were at church services. That's what he said this morning," Juba whispered, looking over Anne's shoulder to the hall.

"We can only worry about you right now. This is a safer plan. This is your freedom! I told Mr. Rouse and the Reverend I would help. We decided that tonight was the best time. Come! Come! The children will be fine," she replied.

Juba shut the door on her. Had the woman lost her nerve or changed her mind? *Please, God, let me help her! Please keep us safe in this escape!* Sweat was beading on Anne's forehead, and she wiped it with her sleeve.

The floor creaked again behind the door, and Anne barely breathed out of fear as she looked both ways down the hallway. Still no one in sight. The music from the ballroom had moved on to a boisterous rondo, louder and livelier with rising and falling waves of sound.

Finally, the door opened again, and Juba slid through, looking left and right down the hall. She was wearing her pinafore and shawl and had what appeared to be her things tied up in a piece of cloth.

"I'm so scared, Miss Anne, but I've waited ten years for this," she whispered, breathless. Anne took her hand and squeezed. They looked each other in the eye, and Anne felt her own strength rise deep in her soul. Could she see the same resolve in Juba's lifted chin and firm grasp of her hand?

"Come, people are working together to help you, but we must leave now while the president, Mrs. Bass, and Miss Lane are at the dance. Miss Lane gave me the night off to be with my boy, so I can't be seen here at the Springs. Let's hurry!" Anne urged.

The women crept as quietly as possible down the hallway. The sweat was slick between their hands as Anne pulled Juba with her, leading the way toward the exit to the stairs on the north side of the building. They were halfway down when they heard footfalls above them. Rather than stop, Anne rushed them down faster. The sound trailed away and, luckily, seemed to be heading upstairs and away from them.

They had to make it down one more flight. Out on the lawn about twenty yards past the Swiss House, they would be covered by laurels lining the path toward Naugle's Mill. Once beyond the sleeping quarters, they would be much safer.

As they made their way out into the night, Anne turned to look back at the Colonial building. The lights were ablaze, but the music had stopped. She hoped the dance wasn't over so soon, as they needed at least an hour's lead before the widow returned and found Juba gone. It started again, and "Listen to the Mockingbird," a popular song that was said to be dedicated to Miss Lane, began playing. She breathed a sigh of relief. No one with the president would leave the ballroom during Miss Lane's favorite melody.

"Miss Anne, I thank you so much for helping me," Juba whispered from behind.

"Mr. Rouse and Reverend Fidler have helped so many people," Anne replied in a hushed voice. "They will know how to keep you safe and move you out of Bedford. They have special hiding places and kind folks that will hide you. My family out in the Quaker Valley will help you, too. Each step is a step further away from Bedford. Each mile will be a mile closer to your parents and your freedom."

Juba nodded as they neared Naugle's Mill, where they would cross to climb the path up Federal Hill. Anne hoped they wouldn't come across someone returning late from dinner in town or a servant on horseback traveling there. The road was quiet as they ducked from a copse of oak trees clustered at the bend.

They were in the narrow gap between where Shober's Run powered the mill and Federal Hill. The mill was dark, and the creaking paddle wheel turned and splashed behind them. The sound faded as they started to climb the path next to the miller's house. They both startled as a bull-frog croaked, sounding almost like a man's voice.

"We can't walk on the road, Juba. It's too risky. We will take this trail up and over the hill to the end of Juliana Street. Jackson's Hotel is up ahead at the top. Hopefully, we can skirt it without seeing anyone. Then we can make it down to the south end of my farm."

"All right, Miss Anne. I'm right behind you," Juba said breathlessly.

"We should be able to get to my farm before anyone realizes you're missing. Reverend Fidler is there waiting for you."

"Miss Anne. What if I get caught? What if we both get caught?!" Juba was breathing heavily. Anne could barely understand her. What she did understand was how imperative it was for them to get to Anne's farm and away from the grounds of the hotel.

"We will be fine, Juba. We are making it away right now. We are on the way." Anne hoped that by continuing to whisper reassurances, she could keep Juba moving.

"There's no snakes out here, is there? Or other animals?"

"Juba, you must quit your worries. Once we make it to my farm, Reverend Fidler will take you to Rouse's barbershop. Then Eli will take you in a farm wagon of feed to the Harris homestead. You will hide there until it's safe for you to go to the next stop," Anne said. The plan made sense and was coming together. The first step was to get safely to the farm. Hopefully, hearing the plan would ease Juba's mind and speed up her climb.

Music from Jackson's Hotel filled the clearing at the top of the hill. It was a shady place. Some people in town said it was a brothel and game hall. Supposedly, men from the Springs or other hotels in town had lost more than a few dollars and some of their morals there. All this was a big secret, and polite people only whispered about the goings-on at Jackson's. Blackjack, whiskey, and women who used their bodies to make money were about the sum of it.

"We must be quiet now. We're nearing a public house where we could be heard."

Juba started to breathe heavily as they made their way to the top of the hill. Perhaps she didn't often walk long distances while watching the children, but this was Anne's regular route home, so she was used to it.

"Are you all right?" Anne stopped to let Juba rest a moment and catch her breath.

"I'm okay, Miss Anne. Keep going. My heart is racing ahead of my feet." Juba sounded hopeful. Making it out of sight of the Springs hotel grounds was making the reality of the escape set in for Anne, and she guessed it would for Juba, too.

In the near distance, piano music grew louder, and a light shone through the woods in front of them.

"We have to go wide around Jackson's. People will be too involved with their entertainment to care about the woods. We need to be careful," Anne warned.

Just then, Anne heard the snap of brush up ahead. It was too difficult to see in the dark, so she stopped abruptly, and Juba bumped into her. Had she really heard something, or was it her imagination? Was some drunk coming down the path ahead, about to find them?

She jumped as a large black house cat rubbed up against her legs. Oh, for goodness sake. Just a cat. What a fright.

South of Jackson's, a small ravine provided cover and the right direction toward the farm. Luckily, there wasn't much underbrush since the trees were tall, and they made a clear pathway up the hillside. At the top of the ravine, they stopped, both women breathing heavily. They caught their breath for a few moments. They were at the beginning of Anne's farmland, which sloped downward toward the house.

As they stood looking north from the crest of the hill, they saw several stars shoot across the sky. Anne was the first to speak with excitement and awe as they watched for more. "Surely those stars are a good sign from heaven urging you north, Juba!"

"God bless, I hope so! Are we almost to your house, miss?" Juba asked, catching her breath.

"Yes, we are getting close. Just down there," she said, pointing.

"You must love having your own home and land."

"My husband cleared the land and built the house. I do love it," Anne replied.

"But ain't you risking your farm and getting arrested by helping me, Anne?"

Anne took a moment to form her reply. "It's hardly worth owning my farm and being free if I'm not helping others and living my beliefs. If I live just for me, it's not really a life, is it? My husband said that, and I do understand what he meant more and more as the days since I lost him increase in number."

"He musta been a wonderful man," Juba whispered with conviction.

"He was, and he was taken too soon. I know he would rather give his life than fail to help people in need."

As they descended the hill to Anne's house, the light in the kitchen spilled across the dooryard stones. Anne took Juba around to the back of the house, carefully rounding the corner to make sure no unknown horses were tied up out front. The only horse she saw tied to the post was Reverend Fidler's. Opening the door, they found Agnes seated at the long wooden table with some sewing. She looked up from her work with joy and relief on her face. Reverend Fidler was in another chair by the fire and gave them a welcoming smile.

"Come in, Juba," Agnes said. "Eli Rouse should be waiting at his shop to take you for the next leg of your journey."

"I know you just got here, but we gotta go. We're gonna cut across to the western ridge and follow it to Gravel Hill and into town to Eli. Are you ready, my dear?" Fidler stood and motioned toward the door.

"Let's go," Juba replied. Anne noticed the trembling and uncertainty had left Juba's voice and was replaced by firm resolve. She would need that for the journey ahead.

Anne hugged her. "Godspeed, Juba. I will be thinking of you and praying for your safe travels. You will be in good hands," she assured her.

Juba's eyes were wide, but then her smile softened, and she took Anne's hands in hers. "Thank you, Anne. I will never forget your kindness and what you've risked helping me find my freedom."

— 17 —

Harriet

The Saturday night German was lively this week. The candles and lamps of the Colonial ballroom were blazing, and the room was full of jovial conversations and laughter. Having been at the resort for two weeks, it felt so good to be relaxed and happy. Luckily, the July afternoon hadn't been hot. All the windows of the ballroom were open, and a light summer breeze came through, carrying the scent of the trees with it, melding with the smell of burning paraffin from the gentle lighting and making even the flames with shades flicker. She had been dancing quite a bit this evening. It was a good thing her green silk dress wasn't uncomfortably warm.

Anne had done her hair up in braids with fresh flowers and ribbons before returning home for the night. Harriet loved flowers and was known for bringing them into the Executive Mansion. Previous first ladies had favored wax flowers, but Harriet thought those were stodgy and certainly didn't bring any fragrance with them. Living in London when her uncle was the British ambassador had awakened her appreciation of horticulture as a lifestyle. Her recent addition to the Executive Mansion of a conservatory greenhouse was a wonderful place to receive guests and provided flowers year-round. The Springs had some lovely flowerbeds, and Anne seemed glad to pick some for her room and her hair to keep up her flower habit.

She was dancing with young Sam Pollock, the son of the former governor of Pennsylvania when the musicians started to play her favorite song. She had a mixed reaction whenever they played "Listen to the Mockingbird." The lyrics were sad, but the tune was lively, and she loved dancing to it. Luckily, no one was singing, so she was able to move to the music.

Sam Pollock nodded to her. "Shall we have another go, Miss Lane? Would you do me the honor?"

Harriet returned his nod and smile. "Yes, thank you, Sam. I do enjoy this song so."

Sam was a handsome young man and was always up for some turns on the dance floor. At twenty-one, he was certainly too young for her, but with his willing attitude, flaming red hair, and knowledge of the waltz and the galop, they made an attractive pair for a few dances. He was staying for the summer as well and often offered his arm for a walk or hand for a dance.

"I understand Hawthorne and Milburn have dedicated their song to you, Miss Lane," he said with a grin.

"So I've been told. I am grateful, as it is a lovely tune. The only part I don't enjoy is that hearing the song means the night is coming to a close. They tend to play it for me at the crescendo of the evening," Harriet said, and they spun around for a few turns and then slowed down to catch their breaths, laughing.

Harriet saw Nunc dancing across the room with Mrs. Bass. He looked happy, and they were laughing as well. It was wonderful that, at his age, he still liked to dance and have a good time. He needed that. It was good for him.

Sam looked over to the president and, following her gaze, commented, "He certainly seems to be having a fine time this evening. I haven't seen him that relaxed since I've been here. He has a lot to worry about lately. Perhaps he's having a reprieve tonight."

"Yes, I am glad of it. He needs to enjoy himself and forget his responsibilities for a moment. They weigh on him heavily, Sam."

The song ended, and Harriet told Sam she would sit the next one out. As she went to stand by the side of the ballroom with a glass of claret, her uncle walked over to her.

"Harriet, Mrs. Bass would like to head back to her rooms. I am going to walk with her. I am tired as well. Without Anne here to escort you, will you make sure to find someone appropriate to accompany you? I think the musicians will play only a couple more songs."

"Yes, I will be fine. Sam Pollock's younger sister is here with her maid, and I will walk back with them as they're also in the Evitt building," Harriet confirmed.

Her uncle nodded and turned to the north end of the ballroom. By the double doors to the grand stairway, Simon Cameron stood engaged in conversation with the widow. Harriet hoped there wouldn't be a scene. As far as she was aware, the senator and the president had avoided each other over the last two weeks. She worried that his evening of merriment had the potential to end poorly.

She watched the two men greet each other and nod politely. Cameron seemed to be drawing him into a conversation already in progress with Mrs. Bass. Relief washed over her as all three appeared to laugh and enjoy their talk, smiles on their faces all through the next song.

Harriet was too curious not to walk over and find out what they were talking about. As she walked up to the trio, Mrs. Bass was fanning herself and laughing. "Oh, Senator, I couldn't possibly have another glass of wine."

"Surely a beautiful lady like you can appreciate a delicious Spanish claret! I have ordered a bottle to be uncorked and brought over so we can all share it. Please, madame!" Cameron implored.

The senator had all his charms on display. Was he making a peace offering? It seemed as if he'd had too much to drink already. He was more animated than usual and also looked flushed.

"Mr. President, won't you and your lovely guest join me so that we can take advantage of the beautiful night and find some common ground here amongst the spectacular mountain air?" chided the senator.

"Well, I certainly appreciate the offer, Simon. That is very cordial of you. But we are rather tired from all the aforesaid mountain air we've had today. Please, let us enjoy a drink together later in the trip, senator," the president replied.

As they were talking, one of the waiters walked up with a silver tray holding four glasses and a decanted bottle of ruby-red liquid. The young waiter started to pour, and the president interjected, "Young man, you will need to find someone else with whom the senator can share that fine elixir. Mrs. Bass and I must be heading for our quarters."

The whole scene was amusing, but as she turned to walk away, there was a clatter and crash. The wine had tipped, the glasses crashing to the ground. The garnet liquid was now on the carpet, dripping off the arm of Mrs. Bass's black gown and on the president's light-colored dress pants.

"Oh my goodness, I am so sorry, Mr. President. I am a buffoon! Waiter, don't just stand there. Find some towels and mineral water! Surely, this place has bottles of mineral water to spare!"

The sour expression on her uncle's face was nothing to trifle with. He was turning red, starting at his tight collar. The evening was taking a bad turn after all, thanks to Senator Cameron.

After the staff helped the president and Mrs. Bass clean up, Harriet went back to Sam and Louisa to recount the ruckus that had just transpired. Perhaps she could have the last dance with Sam and leave the evening on a better note.

◆———————◆

When Harriet and Louisa arrived back at the Evitt building a little while later, they found the place filled with noise and activity. Servants rushed past as they climbed the stairs, and footfalls could be heard in the hallways above. Thomas, the valet, was coming down as they reached the top of the landing. The look of distress on his face alerted her to trouble. What now?

"Thomas, what's going on? Is someone unwell? Is everyone all right? Is the president here?"

"All is confusion, Miss Lane. Mrs. Bass came back to find the children asleep by themselves, and Janie was nowhere to be found. The president is furious. He's sent me to go fetch the constable. Mr. Blackburn is with him and sending others to search the grounds," the valet recounted breathlessly.

"For goodness sake, I am sure she is getting something for the children elsewhere in the hotel. Have they tried the kitchen? Perhaps she went to get the children's milk ahead of her morning schedule since we are going into town for church early tomorrow," Harriet suggested as he continued down the stairs.

"It appears that her belongings are gone, Miss Lane," he shouted as he rushed out of sight, skipping stairs in his haste. There must be a reasonable explanation. How could this have happened? She was both hopeful and afraid for Janie. Then, there was the fallout for Uncle Buck.

This commotion was not what her uncle needed. After a lovely night at the dance, she knew he would be beside himself. After beginning pardon of Louisa, Harriet walked quickly down the hall toward their suites and heard her uncle's voice a hundred feet away from his door. She found his room open, and the widow and Mr. Blackburn stood to the side as he paced the room.

"Harriet," he exclaimed, seeing her in the doorway, "the widow's girl is gone. The way Cameron engaged me like an old friend at the dance—I should have known he was up to no good. We arrived here to find the children asleep without anyone with them. Janie is gone, and so are her things."

Harriet turned to Mr. Blackburn, trying to keep calm and not be swept into her uncle's furor. "Mr. Blackburn, have we searched the kitchen and the walkways out front? Perhaps she's on an errand?"

Mrs. Bass cut in before Blackburn could answer. "She would never leave the children for an errand while the rest of us are not close by. I checked her things, and her kit was gone as well. Nothing else is touched. All my belongings seem to be intact."

Mr. Blackburn looked at the president and then the ladies. "I can't imagine what might have happened. This is a safe place for visitors. I am sure we will find a good answer. I have sent several housemen to the various parts of the resort, kitchen, and stables. Thomas has left to find a horse to ride for Constable Smith."

"Harriet, have you noticed anything odd with Janie? Have you seen her talking to Senator Cameron?" Mrs. Bass inquired.

"I have witnessed nothing out of the ordinary. I saw him tip his hat to her in the hall, and I counseled her to stay away from him and his trouble," she replied. She tried to recall that morning in the hall. Had she missed something?

"I am going to see Cameron in his rooms," the president said as he walked to the door, but Harriet caught his elbow.

"Nunc, do you honestly think if he has anything to do with Janie's disappearance that he would tell you?" she questioned him, hoping to prevent a potential quarrel. The last thing he needed was a political confrontation with Cameron at close quarters on holiday.

Mr. Blackburn was looking out the windows onto the lawn. He turned to the others and suggested, "The girl couldn't just leave on her own. She wouldn't be able to find her way at night. There is little moonlight tonight, and a girl unfamiliar with the area could get lost in these woods. I think she must have had help of some kind."

"You have several negro servants here, Mr. Blackburn. Would any of them help her to escape?" Mrs. Bass asked frankly.

"My staff wouldn't do any such thing. This town and valley are full of people on both sides of the debate, ma'am. While there's word that there are Underground Railroad conductors in and around Bedford, I don't rightly know who they are. Constable Smith may be able to shed some light on that and bring your girl back before daylight."

— 18 —

Juba

Riding in Eli Rouse's wagon, hidden among the empty flour sacks, so many thoughts were racing through Juba's mind as she tried to force herself to sit quietly and still. The first few days were the most dangerous for her escape, and putting miles between herself and Bedford was crucial—even life and death—for her and the people helping her. Was she about two miles from the hotel? By the sounds around her, she was not quite out of the town limits. Mr. Rouse had told her when Reverend Fidler dropped her off at his shop that it would take about an hour to get out of Bedford proper. They would head through an area he called Boydstown and over the north foot of Wills Mountain, then to a homestead of some people named Harris.

"We gonna take you out of town as fast as we can. It's too late to make it all the way out to Quaker Valley tonight, but we got a stop right out of town. You'll be in the woods, tucked in with the good John Harris. His place is farther out but not along the Great Road, so hopefully out of range if they put out a search party. He's got some small caves close to the house on his property that he keeps foodstuff in. He can hide you through the day. Lots of those crevices are small and covered with laurel and not big enough for people in town to know about," Eli had told her as he was getting her buried in the flour sacks.

He added, "These sacks are at least soft and give fair cover. It's not unusual to be headed to the mill at Wolfsburg to pick up grain. At this early hour, we might not pass anyone at all. Hopin' we can turn off the main road before the sun rises."

Juba couldn't stop her heart from racing, and she was breathing fast, too. Her body was shaking. As the wagon moved along, she periodically took a deep breath to calm herself. Heaven forbid someone come along and see the flour sacks shaking or hear her heavy breathing. She tried to allow her mind to drift off to her momma. Would she see her soon? Would she feel her momma's arms around her? She prayed her momma and daddy were well and that soon they would know she was on her way if they didn't already.

Eli was singing to himself over the sound of the wagon wheels grinding on gravel. She imagined he was as nervous as her and trying to soothe himself. Things seemed quiet in the dark of early morning, and she sensed that after what sounded like a bridge was crossed, they had left town and were now in the country. Her heart started to slow a bit, and her breathing came easier.

Then she heard horse's hooves beating the dirt road ahead, moving fairly fast. Every muscle in Juba's body went stiff. As the horse got closer, she could tell it was a single rider without a wagon. Mr. Rouse kept his wagon rolling. She tried to focus on being as quiet and small as possible.

"Good mornin', Mr. Rouse," she heard a deep man's voice say as he stopped his horse. Their wagon came to a slow roll stop.

"Good morning to you, Dr. Watson. You're up awful early," Eli said jovially. Juba was amazed he sounded so calm.

"You know how it is, Elias. These babies come when they come. Some still need attendance if the midwife says so, at any hour," came the answer.

"I'm tryin' to pick up flour from Wolfsburg before the day starts and get back to church."

"It seems you have things to care for, too. Have a wonderful day," the other voice replied. Juba heard him chook to his horse, and then they rode off.

As the sound of the other horse got further away, Elias spoke.

"Well, that wasn't too bad. It's been said Doc Watson has helped the Railroad sometimes. I don't pretend to think he went with my story. I think he knows exactly what the things I got to 'care for' might be. But we don't have to worry about him, at least. I sure hope you didn't fret too badly back there. Downright frightening, I'm sure," Eli said over his shoulder.

After a long time of only horse clopping and the wagon bumping, Eli said loud enough for her to hear, "We goin' turn now and head off the road to Titeytown. We're not far off now. Up and over the hill is all. Be there in jus' a bit."

Juba knew he didn't want a response but was glad for his comforting words. He went back to humming and started to quietly sing:

"De Gospel train's a-comin',
I hear it jus' at han',
I hear de car wheels rumblin',
An' rollin' thro' de lan'."

Mr. Rouse seemed to be trying to comfort them both by singing the spiritual hymn taken to heart by so many enslaved people across the South. It worked to calm her nerves a bit. He went on for several more verses, finishing each with the refrain:

"Git on board, little children,
Git on board, little children,
Git on board, little children,
Dere's room for many a mo'."

A little way farther, the sound of the wagon wheels changed from grinding on gravel to a softer sound, like they were in the woods. Minutes after that, the sound of running water could be heard close by, like a creek.

"We about there, girl. Jus' hol' tight. I can see the Harris homestead up ahead," Eli said to her over his shoulder from the wagon bench. The horse hooves were quieter. She guessed they were on a dirt path. When they finally came to a stop, she heard Eli jump down from the wagon. "Jus' hold on a minute while I let them know we here and make sure all is safe before I bring you out."

Juba heard him walking away and the creek running nearby. A few minutes later, Eli's voice came back, and there was the sound of another man approaching and the two talking together.

"You're safe for now, Juba. You can sit up, and we'll help you out," said Eli.

She could hardly move from being still in one position for so long. She stretched out her legs and sat up straight, taking off the sacks covering her head and shoulders. Morning light was starting to break and mists were rising off the forest floor, which smelled damp and loamy.

"Well, look at that. She is risen!" the other man chuckled.

"Juba, this here is John Harris. He lives here with his growing family and farms his own land. He's going to keep you hid for at least a day or two until we can move you out to Quaker Valley. Laying low a while till after the local law makes its rounds is best. Imagine there's quite a big mess goin' on in town over you disappearing," Eli explained.

"Good evenin' young miss," greeted Harris. "You can call me Uncle John like everybody else. Glad to have you here. We gonna get you a bedroll, candle, and such, then me and my wife Martha gonna take you up the creek a bit where there's a hidden cave in the rocks for your safety during the day. I'm sure you're ready to sleep anyways after all the excitement."

"Thank you, sir. I really appreciate your kindness," she said to Uncle John and then turned to Eli. "I can't thank you enough, Mr. Rouse."

"Aww, you know it's what we do. Jus' the right thing to do, helpin' folks. Now I gotta ride back to town as today is Sunday, and it'll be unusual if I'm missing from church. Should the constable show up there first, he might just figure the Zion Church is the best place to show himself and shake things up a bit, sniffing 'round."

Juba stepped forward and gave Rouse a long hug. Rouse held her warmly. "I almost forgot in all this . . ." He reached into his pants pocket and drew out a cloth purse, shaking it, and said, "This for you. You're gonna need it for your trip. Some 'benefactors,' as they say, done pulled through with coin to get you goin'." He saw by the look on her face that Juba didn't want to take the money, so he added, "You take it now. It's not from anyone who needs extra, and you need it for sure."

"Thank you. Bless you, and please thank everyone in Bedford who has had a hand in helping me."

"Will do, my dear." Eli tipped his cap and climbed onto the wagon.

"Come on, now," Uncle John said with his hand on Juba's shoulder to guide her toward the cabin. "Let's go find Martha inside and we'll take you to the hidin' spot before our children wake up. No need for anyone else to see you that don't need to."

Inside the log cabin, in the warm candlelight, a small woman was moving around the kitchen, making a fire in the wood stove. She turned as John Harris and Juba came in the door.

"Momma, this here is Juba. Eli just brought her out of town. He went west this time instead of north to throw off the route from that last fella's trip who came through and got caught at Cessna. She's gonna stay here a day or two in that cave by the crick. Then we'll get Jim Graham to take her up to the Valley."

"Juba, what a lovely name. Reminds me of Jubilee, which is always a celebration!" Martha smiled.

"Yes, ma'am, thank you. My momma named me Juba 'cause I was born on a Monday, and that's what it means. Also, she said it's the name of her favorite dance. She was dancin' it when she met my daddy," she explained.

"Well, that makes it extra special, a pretty name for a pretty girl. And a girl headed to freedom, no less. Let's take the bedroll and some coverlets, and we'll make sure you are hidden before the sun comes up any further."

The three walked out the back door of the cabin, and the sound of the running creek could be heard close by. The water was about a hundred feet behind the home and down in a small ravine. On the other side was a steep hill thick with bushes with waxy dark green leaves. Following Uncle John, they turned left when they got to the ravine and followed it for a while, coming to a wide log that crossed over the water to the other side. After crossing it and walking up the hill, they came upon a rock outcropping that had more waxy bushes all around its base.

"Come on up here." Uncle John gave Juba his hand to help her up the moss-covered boulders. As Juba got over several, she saw behind the branches of the bushes was a hollow space. At the back was a small crevice between the layers of the rock wall and an overhang of more rock. Uncle John struck a match for a lantern he was carrying and lit up what was a tiny cave with some jars and barrels lined against the walls.

"We use this as sort of a root cellar. Not much here now, but soon we'll be puttin' up more after harvest. Momma's a fine canner. She makes the best dilly beans around. You get hungry, there are a couple more bean jars left," he chuckled, "but I got some bread and cheese in this bag for you too. You be quiet and get some rest. Stay back here now, ya hear?"

"Yes, sir. I'm going to sleep, and I won't cause any trouble or come out until you come for me. Can you leave me the lantern and matches?"

"Sure can, and beside the food in this bag, I put a Bible and a copy of the Bedford Gazette in as well. Can you read?" he asked.

"Yes, sir, I can read. Thank you. This puts you and your family in danger. I don't know how to say thank you enough."

Martha took Juba's hand and patted it between her own, saying, "Don't you worry none. Lots of people will be helping, and your job is just to hide." She unfurled the bedroll and shook out the coverlets on top.

After the Harrises left her, Juba sat down on the bedding and tucked her legs under her. She looked around the small cave and saw some places where people had scraped words and pictures on the rock wall. Some were reddish, some white, she guessed from the different rocks they'd used. How many other people had been hidden here before her, she wondered.

Paul Henry June 1854

Dinah

Elijah Smith 1856

The LORD is my shepherd; I shall not want. He maketh me to lie down in green pastures: he leadeth me beside the still waters. He restoreth my soul.

Juba extinguished the lantern, setting the matches right next to it to find in the dark later. How were the Bass children? Hopefully, they were not upset, waking up without her. All the commotion with her running away must have been alarming for them. God willing, they would remember all the times she had wiped their sticky fingers or sang them to sleep. She hoped they had warm memories of her.

Surely Missus was awful mad at her. As much as she was glad to be away, she didn't want to leave behind bad thoughts about herself. Now she had to leave that all behind. There was no point in these thoughts. She lay down on the bedding and recited to herself, "*The Lord is my shepherd; I shall not want. He maketh me to lie down in green pastures: he leadeth me beside the still waters. He restoreth my soul.*"

— 19 —

Anne

Anne approached the grounds of the Springs and met the road by the miller's house. What would she walk into that morning? Could she arrive to find she'd lost her position or was about to be arrested? Or, would she not be suspected? How would she pretend she knew nothing about how Juba had escaped and where she might be headed? Given how much she knew about the entire escape, that was going to be difficult.

She was raised with a sense of integrity and truth. Keeping in mind the safety of the people involved and Juba's freedom would have to suffice for God's grace and doing what was right. Her heart was beating hard in her chest and her hands were sweaty. Her whole life might change today.

The mill wheel was paddling and splashing behind her, and she rounded the corner in view of the Hotel. Anne breathed in the early morning summer air. How was Juba faring out at John Harris's? God help both her and Juba's strength and spirit over the next few days.

Arriving at what had become her normal Sunday morning start time, seven o'clock, Anne headed down the path at the back of the buildings toward the kitchen. All was quiet as usual at the resort that morning. Usually, she would start her day by getting Miss Lane's tea tray before making her way to her mistress's suite.

As she approached the back door to the kitchen building, she saw several staff members standing outside. She couldn't quite hear them yet, but she saw they were talking with hands and arms flying. Were they talking about the escape? Surely she would be drawn in as part of the presidential serving staff.

Thomas was part of the group and the first to turn to her and ask, "Anne, have you heard yet? Janie is *gone*!"

The two other staff members bid them both good morning and hurried off to their duties, but the valet was eager, wanting to engage in conversation about last evening's events.

Anne weighed her words for a moment while the other staff departed, then replied fast enough not to be perceived as unsurprised. She had thought about this instance and practiced a reply in her head. "Are you sure she's gone?"

She had thought overnight about saying the least possible without seeming to be hiding anything. Unless asked a direct question, others would fill the space if she did not elaborate. This was human nature. Thomas fell right into that expectation.

"The president and Mrs. Bass returned from the dance to find her gone, and the children alone. It was quite a commotion, and they sent me running for the constable," he continued, and she let him ramble on. She would try to learn as many details as possible from him.

"Oh, my goodness. The children were left alone! Perhaps she came to some kind of harm," Anne suggested.

Thomas was excited to give information about his trip to the constable, which was outside his usual houseman duties. "I rode to the constable's house as fast as I could, and he wasn't home. I had to track him down at The Rising Sun Tavern on his wife's advice," he said.

"What did the constable say?" Anne asked.

"He acted a bit in his cups when I arrived and told me to go find his man Sergeant Gladwell, who was on duty. He said he would catch up later after he got home to change. I found Gladwell at his home, and he rode back with me."

"How did that go?" Anne inquired.

"He's pretty green, I guess. He proceeded to ask a bunch of questions and wrote down a bunch of notes in a little notebook. He didn't have a search plan. The president got extremely upset. You've seen how he gets," Thomas added, rolling his eyes.

"Did anyone have any ideas? Did he start looking for her?" Anne really wanted to find out if they were already on Juba's trail or if they had any idea who'd assisted her.

"No one seemed to know anything, but the president suggested perhaps Senator Cameron was behind the girl's disappearance—that perhaps it had been a personal attack on him. Gladwell said he would follow up with the senator. I don't know if that meeting happened or not. They sent me off with a group of housemen to scour the grounds and the woods heading into town. We didn't find her. The only thing going on was a big party up at Jackson's," he said, laughing, before seeming to catch himself and continuing more seriously, "She never said anything to you, Miss Anne?"

"Surely not. She was very committed to the Bass children. I pray she is okay and not hurt somewhere when everyone thinks she's running away."

"Well, I guess they'll find out. Constable Smith finally showed up in the middle of the night when the president had already gone to bed. He told Mr. Blackburn he was going to start searching the town for some of the abolitionists, like at the Zion Church, and sent Gladwell out to send word to the slave catchers south of town, Crissman and Mock. Mrs. Bass said she didn't want any harm to come to the girl and hoped she was okay, but told Gladwell she would give a hundred dollars to anybody who brought her back. I sure am worried for Janie. Those two are bad news."

"Oh dear, the slave catchers," Anne exclaimed. Though she'd suspected they would be brought into the search, an unexpected chill went down her spine at the mention of those greedy men who made money off the bodies of others. They were sickening and violent murderers. It made her think of Jacob again, but she held back her fear to cover herself in front of Thomas.

"I had best get to my work. I am sure Miss Lane is in the middle of the chaos. She always tries to make peace for her uncle," Anne said.

"I don't think it will be such a good day today, Anne. They've already canceled their trip to town for church. I'm glad to be heading upstairs to the garret for a rest, as it's been a long night. Senator Cameron asked me to stop by his room later. I'm a bit nervous about what he might want with me. The president has told me to steer clear, but I can't ignore the request of a guest altogether, especially a senator. I hope you have a good day, Anne." Thomas nodded as he turned to leave.

Anne got the tea tray as planned and hurried to the Evitt building. It was good to have gotten some information before she encountered Miss Lane, the president, or Mrs. Bass.

There seemed to be no outright clues to Juba's whereabouts, and everyone was still getting it together to search for her. Perhaps the delay in organizing the search would give Juba more time to get further away.

As she approached the end of the hall that the presidential party occupied, she saw that the doors of all three suites were open. The President marched across the hall and entered Miss Lane's rooms. Anne slowed down before entering the room to overhear the conversation.

"Harriet, I am vexed and beside myself," declared the President, "this year has been a cauldron of trouble. That this girl has been taken on my summer respite, I supposed I shouldn't be surprised."

"Nunc, please sit. This commotion isn't healthy for you. You look like you've barely slept." Harriet implored her uncle in a calming voice Anne had become familiar with.

Anne set the tray on the service table outside the door and knocked. Harriet spoke the "enter," and Anne carried in the tea tray, glad she had added extra cups and provisions, expecting it would not only be Harriet to serve.

Harriet spoke first, turning to Anne, "Good Morning Anne. We are in a bit of trouble today. Janie disappeared in the night and hasn't yet been located.

"Thomas let me know she is missing in the kitchen, Miss, I hope she is alright." Anne sounded worried, but it was a worrisome situation, so was received as an appropriate response.

President Buchanan was pacing around the room, looking out window to window. He turned on his heel and addressed Anne directly: "Anne, have you seen anyone talking to Janie who might have given her ideas or aided her escape?"

"No sir, I have not seen anyone at the hotel talking to Janie. Could she be hurt or have gotten lost, Sir?" Anne decided to keep steering the conversation toward the possibility Juba was still on the grounds and not escaped after all. The longer the search got tied up close by, the better.

"Getting hurt or lost would be less problematic, but the fact that most of her things are gone makes that particular scenario unlikely. Did you observe Senator Cameron talking to her at any time?"

"No, Mr. President, I have never seen them speaking," Anne answered.

Harriet weighed in on the conversation at this point, asking, "Anne, you are from Bedford. Are there people here who might help the enslaved escape? I don't mean to put you in an awkward position but, if we find her before the slave catchers launch a search, I am sure that would be a much better ending for Janie. I worry for her."

Mrs. Bass walked into the room, diverting Anne's attention from answering a question she didn't want to. The widow interjected, "Well, I have made a full accounting of all of my jewels, cash, and coins. Nothing is missing. I can't believe she could escape without any means unless she was given help. If she has indeed escaped, this makes the rest of my trip very difficult! Not to mention the financial loss to me!"

President Buchanan replied, "If Cameron helped her, he has plenty of money, and she wouldn't need to take anything."

"Nunc, I wish you would stop with your speculations. Just because he is an adversary doesn't mean he would actively undermine you by orchestrating her escape." Miss Harriet reacted.

Anne was putting out the teacups for each of them. Both ladies were seated to receive their tea, but the President continued to pace and look out the window. Anne knew the next few minutes could be crucial to her. Did they have any suspicions?

The president spoke to himself, loud enough for them all to hear, "Abolitionists are behind this, I am sure of it. And the Republicans want nothing more than to embarrass me before the election next year. When I find out who is behind this, there will be hell to pay."

Anne had just picked up a teacup to hand to Miss Lane, but her hands were shaking so badly she had to quickly put it back down on the silver tea service. Miss Lane was watching her. She had seen her hands shaking, and the expression on the lady's face changed. Anne froze with fear.

Harriet looked Anne in the eye, then nodded and gave her a smile. Was it a smile of comfort or conciliation? "Anne, I think we will go down to breakfast and have our tea in the dining room. Nunc, Mrs. Bass, shall we head down for breakfast before it's over? I think we need to leave these rooms and find a change of scenery."

Had Miss Lane guessed she had helped Juba escape, or had she simply assumed Anne was upset by the unsettling conversation?

— 20 —

Harriet

Harriet had only eaten about half of her toast and soft-boiled egg when Thomas, the valet, approached the breakfast table.

"Yes, yes, my good man, go ahead. I thought I sent you for some rest." Her uncle nodded and waved the young man closer.

Thomas spoke quietly so as not to draw attention from nearby guests. "Mr. President, Sergeant Gladwell is out front with the two men who will go find Janie. I was taking my leave when they arrived, and the sergeant asked me to find you. They would like to speak with you for details that might help in their search."

The president, Mrs. Bass, and Harriet had all stood to go downstairs when Thomas cautioned, "Sir, the slave catchers are rather unsavory. I don't know if you want the ladies to go with you."

Mrs. Bass was the first to answer. "Thank you, Thomas. However, she is my nursemaid, and I am offering the reward for her return. I think I can best talk to the men and give them a description. I deal with my hands at the plantation all the time and am not so delicate that I can't handle my own affairs."

"I'd like to go along as well, Nunc. I'd like to understand what the search will entail," Harriet added. Perhaps she could stay close to the situation and learn more about what was going on. She had the sense of wanting to help in some way, but was it to keep her uncle calm, or was there something else tugging at her?

They all walked to the grand portico below the dining room. Harriet recognized the two men as the same rough-looking horsemen that they had encountered in the valley on the way from Cumberland. Still dusty and disheveled, she could smell them as she got closer. They had a musty scent, like their horses, combined with the heavy odor of stale sweat and whiskey. The taller one smiled as they approached, presumably to appear amiable, however his missing teeth made him look menacing. The other, who had red hair hanging long over his collar, took off his hat as they approached.

Uncle Buck began the conversation, and Harriet observed that he didn't offer his hand but nodded in greeting. "Gentlemen, we meet again. I believe we encountered you in the valley on our journey here a couple of weeks ago."

The taller man stepped forward with his hand out to shake. "Peter Mock, President Buchanan. We got word early this morning that you have a slave girl who needs found."

The president ignored his somewhat dirty outstretched hand. Harriet read his disgust and caution.

The man went on, "This is my partner, David Crissman. We need some details about her so we can identify who we're lookin' for."

"Janie was my servant, so I will describe her," Mrs. Bass answered. "I'd like to make sure you understand that I want no harm to come to her. I just want her back where she is safe and well taken care of. She is a good girl, and I don't want anyone to take advantage of her or hurt her in any way. She has a finer life with me than she can have anywhere else out in the world."

Harriet held her tongue. That the widow would refer to Janie as her "servant" was ridiculous. It rankled her, the common Southern justification that slaves were "better off" on the plantations like any human would prefer to be a slave than have choices and the freedom to make their own life. Janie's words about what her life as a slave was like came back to her.

This whole business and her uncle's connection to it was an embarrassment and a shame. Harriet's cheeks started to burn. She pulled the fan out of her dress sleeve to fan herself, hoping no one would take note of her reaction. If only she could walk away, but that would be noticed by her uncle and perhaps others as well.

Uncle Buck and Mrs. Bass continued to speak to the two slave catchers. They didn't notice that Simon Cameron and David Over were approaching the group on foot from the direction of the road. Harriet drew in her breath. This meeting was not going to go well. Mr. Over was the editor of the *Bedford Inquirer*, the local Republican newspaper, which was never kind when reporting on her uncle. The story would be in all the papers across the country before the week's end.

When her uncle finally saw Cameron was near, he spoke under his breath, stepping up to Harriet. "Blast it all! I knew he was going to use this for his own ends!"

"Nunc, stay calm and don't give any information away," she whispered back.

Her uncle greeted Cameron and Over as the two patrollers stepped back by their horses and talked between themselves by their horses. "Good morning, gentlemen. You've decided to join the confusion?"

"Why, Mr. President, it is worthy news that a member of your party has gone missing. This is of great interest to the American people. Your security is of national concern," Cameron commented with a somewhat devious smirk. Harriet noted his smug tone. This was exactly what she had been worried about.

"Yes, sir, it is always news when the president is at the Springs. I hear there has been trouble with one of your so-called 'servants,'" Over said, smiling.

Harriet was sure that the subject of Janie's enslavement was already getting worked into a headline. Cameron would be seeing to it that the whole country knew that the president had a slave with his travel party. Meanwhile, Janie would be hunted like an animal.

Mrs. Bass cut in before being addressed or introduced. "I am quite concerned for my nursemaid's wellbeing, gentlemen. She is a good girl. None of my jewels or money is missing, just her. Without any means, I hope she will be all right and that no one will take advantage of her."

Over was scribbling in a small notebook, and Cameron smiled. Harriet held her tongue, and she wished Mrs. Bass had as well. She was sure that the widow's quote would be in the papers. Her uncle was agitated, and she could tell he was weighing his words so as not to erupt and make a scene in front of the press.

"Simon, we go back many years. There was a time when you were allied with me in Pennsylvania politics. I don't know where we went afoul or why you seek to undermine me at every step since we parted ways. I am going to hold myself back from making further statements in front of the good Mr. Over," he said with resignation.

"Mr. President, I believe you do know exactly why we had a schism in our service to the public. It's the same reason that I have gone to the Republican Party," Cameron returned.

"To get elected? Democrats both in Pennsylvania and nationally decided you had too many shady business dealings and questionable morals when it came to lining your own pockets," her uncle said, his color rising and eyes burning steel blue. At least he got in a good retort, Harriet noted.

"No, Mr. President, I think it was the very parting of the ways that the country is having now. I won't accept other people, no matter what race, being treated as less than human, sir. I will not cross that line to secure votes or favor," Cameron countered. Harriet silently agreed with him. There was the nagging guilt of her betrayal again.

"Is that why you're in the middle of this business, Cameron? Did you spirit my guest's servant away?"

"I beg your pardon, Mr. President, but the woman with Mrs. Bass was enslaved, not a servant. And I can unequivocally assure you I did not spirit her away."

This had to stop. It was going nowhere good. Harriet interjected, "Gentlemen, I think this conversation is ill-timed. Let us get back to the matter at hand."

"More people than you can guess, all over this county, Pennsylvania, and the nation, would help a person to gain their God-given right to freedom. Perhaps you should consider all those constituents, sir," Cameron said, ignoring her.

"Gentlemen, I ask that you take your leave. We are trying to form a search party for the missing woman," her uncle said, dismissing Cameron and the newspaperman.

All eyes went to the two dirty horsemen who were awkwardly out of place in front of the stately Colonial building and its neatly dressed patrons.

Mr. Over addressed the men. "The past few years, the most common direction to find fugitives has been up through Cessna and St. Clairsville. You boys headed that way?"

Mock spoke up. "I rightly think that may be the best way to go. Thank you, sir. We was up that way last time on the chase. No tellin' though where she might be, but there's some safe houses up in St. Clairsville. Constable just told us everyone in town thought to be helpn' escaped niggers was sittin' in church as quiet as church mice when he showed up. None of the usual suspects was missin'."

"We fixin' to catch the wench before nightfall, sir. We be headed north straightaway with your leave," added the second man.

All present avoided each other's gaze and there was an awkward silence. No one spoke objection to the unsavory pair's coarse pronouncements. Surely one of the men would call them out and set them straight? Simon Cameron looked both disgusted but victorious. Was that the most sensible search direction or had Cameron put Over up for a suggested diversion? Better not to express her doubts and ask her uncle why he didn't suspect the obvious potential misdirection.

Back in her room, Harriet paced. This turn of events was a disaster for her uncle but not so much for Janie. What a mess this all was. There was nothing she could do. On the one hand, she worried for Nunc. This situation was everything she had been concerned about before they had even left Washington. But there was a more important issue that had made itself clear. Janie was a person. And there were thousands of people like her, either trapped or on the run. Her mind was spinning. She would write Lily and sort through it a bit.

Harriet Lane
The Bedford Springs Hotel
Bedford, Pennsylvania
July 15th, 1859

My Dear Lily,

I hope that you are well and enjoying Saratoga. I trust the Barcrofts are good company. Have you seen Armand Fitzpatrick this year? If you see him, please give him my best.

I am sorry that I constantly seem to need you to prop me back up lately. The political climate in Washington was stifling, and although the mountain air here in beautiful Bedford is clean and clear, the atmosphere here this summer has been unusually oppressive. A few weeks ago, I shared my concerns with you. My uncle brought not only Mrs. Bass to the Springs but also her nursemaid, who is an enslaved black woman. I knew there would be trouble and have had a bit of unpleasant back-and-forth with my uncle on the subject. In the end, he sticks with his "landowners' rights and states' rights" position, et cetera, et cetera.

Lily, the woman has disappeared. Nunc is certain that Simon Cameron has something to do with it and is behind her presumed escape. Cameron's Republican affiliation with abolitionists and Free Soilers has made Uncle sure that he has arranged her flight to embarrass him in the run-up to his potential re-election campaign. While his bringing an enslaved woman with our party was probably not well known up to this point, now the incident will hit the newspapers this week.

I am mortified, in the first place, to condone Janie's enslavement by association, and I am vexed that the widow has offered one hundred dollars for her safe return. Can you imagine!? Between you and me, I am hopeful that Janie is safe and am glad for her freedom. There, I said it.

I would also like to confide that I am not so sure that the senator is the instrument of her freedom. The constable told us he would be following up with the abolitionists in town. I will only tell you that I am worried for my maid, Anne. I have come to enjoy her quiet and steady company and earnest spirit. I have seen a goodness in her I can't fully describe but admire wholeheartedly. She is a Quaker, which I think I have mentioned previously. Her nervousness after Janie's disappearance has me wondering. You are quite aware as a Philadelphian that the Quakers are fervent supporters and often agents of the Underground Railroad. What can come of all this?

Please keep me and those around me in your thoughts and prayers. Say a prayer for Janie and her safety, too. I will be praying for us all at tonight's evening church services for God's grace in these matters.

All the best,
Harriet

— 21 —

Juba

It was a good thing it was the height of summer, as when Juba awoke, the damp coolness of her hiding spot was seeping through the coverlet. Had it been later in the year, she would have been too chilly to sleep. It was quiet, so it took her a moment to remember where she was.

What time of day was it? She had woken from her sleep a couple of times while it was still light out. Now she was sure it was night again, as it was very dark with no light creeping into the cave. There was the lantern where she had put it with the matches right next to it. Lighting the wick, the orange and yellow flame made her a little less chilly.

Juba stayed wrapped up in bedding and propped herself against the rock wall, putting the newspapers and Bible on her lap for a little reading. Perhaps it might distract her until someone came to check on her. Hopefully, that would be soon as the anxiety of capture pressed on her, though she had just opened her eyes.

She skimmed the front page of the *Bedford Gazette*. On the right, there were notices and listings of Bedford Attorney Services. There was a verse that looked like a song or poetry toward the middle. Down on the lower right-hand side, she saw a headline that caught her eye. *Old Osawatomie Brown Secret Guest at the Bedford Springs.*

The story went on to say that the violent abolitionist John Brown came through Bedford on June 25th. The editor of the *Gazette*, Benjamin Meyers, had inadvertently played billiards with him in the game room at the Springs. He had been introduced as "John Smith," and Meyers put together the encounter after reading that Brown was last seen in nearby Mercersburg. John Brown at the Springs. Where she had just escaped from!

Meyers recalled the "taciturn" and unpleasant demeanor of the tall, thin, older gentleman. He went on to proclaim the visit was a reckless and wanton affront to the soon-to-be arriving president, who had a July vacation to the resort planned. There was a price on Brown's head for the murders of five pro-slavery citizens in Kansas.

She couldn't believe it. Juba set the paper down—John Brown at the Springs. She was aware that he was a white abolitionist who thought slaves and everyone wishing to help them should revolt and use violence, if need be, to ensure freedom. She also knew that, like her, many were petrified of the cost of failure that such a revolt could bring.

Goodness, that was news—John Brown in Bedford. She had gotten used to hearing a lot of national news and inside goings-on while in Washington with Mrs. Bass. Thank goodness she was getting away from all of that. She put the paper away and decided the Bible might be more comforting.

She read some more, had some of the bread Uncle John left for her, and then there were sounds of someone approaching the entrance to her hiding spot. John Harris stuck his head into the opening and smiled, saying, "Good! I see you're up."

"Yes, I have been awake and reading. I had that tasty rye you gave me and some cheese. Thank you."

"Well, I've come for you. During the day while you was sleepin', the constable came through looking for you. He searched the house and then went on to the neighbors. He didn't find what he wanted and left. I came to get you to come out and sit by the fire with our neighbors, the Grahams, and us for a bit since it's late now and no one's comin' out this way. We got some left over from dinner if you're hungry."

They crossed the little creek and walked back toward the house. Fireflies rose out of the grass and Juba saw the glow of a fire and a few figures gathered around it as they got closer.

"James and Mary Graham, this be Juba," Harris introduced them, and the couple stood, the man tipping his hat to her.

"Welcome to Little Africa, Juba," James Graham greeted her warmly. He was a tall, thin man wearing overalls and a coarse cotton work shirt.

"Why do you call it Little Africa, Mr. Graham?" she asked.

"Well, the white folks in town started calling it that. We liked that name better than Nigger Hollow. There's one of those not too far off from here. Then, some of us were talking about how there was a movement to send black people back to Africa after freeing the slaves. We decided that we love our homesteads and we don't want to go nowhere. So, this is our Africa," he chuckled as he explained.

Juba couldn't help but smile in return as these people seemed kind and happy. They were a comfort after the events of the last couple of days. The group was all quiet for a bit, and Martha Harris brought her out a bowl of savory chicken stew.

The bubbling sound of the creek was not far off. The stars were out, and the wooded area that the Harris log home sat in was so pretty, even in the dark. What it must be like to have your own homestead and neighbor friends close by, Juba thought. A community of people you knew and who all worked together must make a happy heart. They were all so generous, helping others find their freedom and peace.

After she had eaten, she decided to ask about the news article she had read earlier. "I read in the Bedford newspaper that John Brown may have been in the area a few weeks ago. What do you think that was about?" she asked.

The two men looked at each other, and Harris nodded to Graham as if to confirm it was okay to talk. "Heard through some folks in town that Mr. Brown has all kinds of plans going on. He was here trying to round up support from the people at the Zion Church who want to help our brothers and sisters in chains, so to speak," said Graham.

Uncle John spoke next. His expression didn't look as happy as it had up to that point. "Crazy talk that could get a lotta people hurt or killed, as far as I can tell. I want freedom for all those poor souls in slave states as much as anyone, but I don't think violence is going to do anything but create more pain and suffering for everyone."

Mr. Graham added, "Buchanan needs to stop playing both sides and make changes. What about 'All men were created equal?' Every person has a right to the pursuit of happiness. Black folks keep gettin' further and further from being treated like people."

"I agree," said Uncle John. "That gotta be fixed first before the black people can be accepted as citizens. Acting like violent animals gonna make the white people afraid, and that just makes things worse."

Graham was quiet for a minute, and Juba felt like she wasn't sure what to say. She understood better than they did what hung over all those enslaved people all over the South. She couldn't explain the constant fear of beatings. The everyday worry about family being hurt, split up or sold. Sold as property. How could she explain what it was like to be sold? That was the anger that simmered in her heart and in the hearts of so many. Somewhere on the edge of total loss and sadness was a seething anger that wanted *everything*. Everything that every person wants, no matter what color.

"I told our group that I thought some of John Brown's plans would get him and all involved killed. He came here looking for support to take the president from the Springs and hold him at a secret location to bargain for emancipation. They goin' to find out that the South ain't going to give up nothin.' They'd let that president from Pennsylvania die. Crazy talk. He got other plans too, just not for Bedford." Harris kept shaking his head in disapproval after he'd finished.

"Eli gonna put himself in harm's way, and Reverend Fidler too. Just knowing the man's plans and being associated with John Brown is trouble," added Graham.

Juba couldn't believe what she was hearing. Kidnapping the president was craziness. Mrs. Bass and the children could be hurt. Miss Harriet, too. John Brown did not seem to have any worry about people getting hurt or killed in his fight.

"You mean there is a plan to take President Buchanan right from the Springs? He's only staying for another two weeks. When is this supposed to happen?" Juba was barely able to speak through her fear and racing thoughts.

"Don't rightly know. We both said no way. There might not even be any local support anyway 'cause so many like us thought it was crazy talk. You'll find a lot of folks willing to help fugitives get free, but most want none of the trouble John Brown talks 'bout," Harris said.

James Graham stood up and added, "That's right. Getting people on their way is about all I got the heart for. Tomorrow I'm hoping to hear from Spring Hope that it's clear to bring you over there for your next stop. We gonna wait to take you until the catchers move through. Might hear word at the Wolfsburg mill tomorrow. If that's the case, I'll come take you tomorrow night, Juba."

After saying their goodbyes, Mr. and Mrs. Graham walked off into the night, leaving Juba sitting with Martha and John Harris. They talked about their children and their work. They shared a bit about how they got to Bedford and decided to stay and build a home and a life.

While Juba was listening, she couldn't help worrying about what she had heard about John Brown planning to harm the president. Her worry for Mrs. Bass and the children wouldn't stop. She was glad to be on her way to freedom, but the thought that they might be hurt or killed was more than she was able to sit still with.

———

The next day, Juba was told Mr. Graham would be up for her after midnight. She had tried to sleep most of the day but had too many thoughts racing around her head. What about the harm that might befall Mrs. Bass and the children, not to mention what kind of chaos could come from harm to the president or Miss Lane? It was impossible to push those thoughts out of her head.

She recalled that early morning coming upon Eli Rouse and Senator Cameron by the bachelors' quarters. What had they been talking about before she arrived? There was part of the conversation she heard between them that, at the time, she didn't understand, and she couldn't recall their words now. She lay on the bedroll, bundled against the damp in her rocky hiding place. She just couldn't remember, but it might be important.

Hours later, she woke from a fitful sleep. The daylight was still slanting into the small cave, so she knew it wasn't nighttime yet.

"Send word to Mr. Brown that while I will not condone or support his larger and violent schemes . . ."

That's what she now remembered the senator had said to Eli Rouse. Senator Cameron had said he would help her escape but didn't support John Brown's plans. That must have been about the kidnapping, she thought.

She read some more of the newspaper and then picked up the Bible, hoping that flipping through it would lead her to a comforting verse. Finally, she found the apostle Paul's letter to the Philippians.

"Let each of you look not only to his own interests but also to the interests of others."

At this point in her journey, Juba wasn't sure she had any way to help herself, much less consider the interests of others. How could she help the Bass children, Mrs. Bass, Miss Lane, and the president if she couldn't go back to warn them? She would have to let that go. There was too much else to worry about, like her safe escape out of Bedford County.

By the time James Graham came for her, the kidnapping information had settled, and she decided she had better focus her mind on her escape. Graham and Harris loaded her up in his cart with crates of peaches and cherries to move her to the next hiding place on the Bedford Underground Railroad. The Grahams told her that Spring Hope was the next stop and that the next few hiding places would be with Quakers.

— 22 —

Anne

The ritual of Anne fixing Miss Lane's hair had become somewhat of a habit for them over the past weeks. Anne enjoyed methodically brushing Harriet's hair. She would frame her mistress's face with ringlets and braid the side and back into a low chignon. In turn, Harriet seemed to relax into the soothing experience and relished having her long hair handled gently. Anne would hear Harriet's breathing grow slow and then, occasionally, a sigh of pleasure. Gathering the flowers in the Spring's gardens was another lovely part of this ritual. Harriet would lift the blooms from the basket and smell them before handing them to Anne in silence.

This morning, their routine was a welcome respite from the stress of the last two days since Juba disappeared. What was Miss Lane thinking about? There wasn't the casual ease she usually felt between them, but she was glad for the quiet, nonetheless. As Anne bound the second side of Harriet's parted locks and started to work the silky rose-gold strands into sections, there was a knock on the door to the porch outside.

"Anne, please check who it is and see if it can wait until after breakfast."

"Yes, miss," Anne answered, dropping the bundle of hair and turning to the door. When she opened it, Anne saw it was Amos Gladwell, the police sergeant. She had seen him in town, sometimes with the constable.

"Good morning. You would be Mrs. Anne McCoy, Miss Lane's maid?" Gladwell greeted her, tipping his wide-brimmed felt hat.

"Yes, sir, I am Anne McCoy. Miss Harriet has asked that callers find her after breakfast, please," Anne informed him politely.

"As a matter of fact, I would like to speak with you, ma'am. I'm taking statements on Saturday night's incident with the missing slave woman. Will you be available in the next hour?" Gladwell inquired.

Miss Harriet heard the exchange from inside the suite and interjected on Anne's behalf. "Mr. Gladwell, Anne will be available after she helps me dress for breakfast. I'd like to be present, as it wouldn't be proper for you to meet with her alone. Will that work for you, Sergeant?"

"Yes, Miss Lane. I will be back shortly. Thank you," he answered from the porch.

"Thank *you*, Sergeant," Harriet concluded.

Anne tipped her head and shut the door as Gladwell stepped away. Moving back to Miss Lane, she picked up where she left off with her lady's hair. The awkward silence was heavy, and Anne's face flushed. It was a hot July morning, and she suddenly felt on fire. She was sure Harriet's questions were coming even before her mistress spoke.

"Tell me, Anne." Miss Harriet's voice wasn't harsh, but it was firm.

Anne's heart raced as she tried to gather her thoughts. For the past two days, she had struggled to decide what she would say in the case of this conversation. She knew it would change the course of her life one way or the other. If she lied her way out of this situation, she will lose Miss Lane's trust and probably her employment. If she tells the truth, she is sure to lose her employment, but at least she would be honest with Miss Harriet and retain her integrity. Honesty could get her arrested and fined, which could lead to losing the farm. Maybe she should have accepted Senator Cameron's help after all and not stood apart on principle. Danger lurked for everyone else involved, not just herself. So far, following what she knew deep inside to be right had been her guide. *Do what is right.* Anne found a sudden strength and knew what she needed to say.

She took a deep breath and looked at Harriet's reflection in the mirror. Their eyes met. The expression on Harriet's face was gentle, concerned, and questioning.

"You know I am a Quaker, miss, as we have talked about that fact and a little about what being a Quaker means for me and other Friends," Anne began. "God's way and God's light live in every person. You and me, and everyone. People of all colors and religions. I am here serving you because I am a widow, and I need to take care of my family by earning money. My husband was a good man. He was the most kind-hearted and diligent young Quaker man I knew. Jacob cared deeply for what was right in God's eyes. His inner voice told him to help black fugitives."

"Go on, Anne," encouraged Harriet. Her hands were clasped and Anne could see her nails were digging into her palms.

"About a year ago, he was killed in the valley below here helping fugitives. The slave catchers shot him when he tried to stop them from taking two men he was helping escape. They left him by the side of the road. He bled to death in that ditch. The man who had handed off the freedom seekers found Jacob, but he was already gone. They brought his body home to me. We had to make up a story about his being mistaken for a horse thief so other conductors in the Underground Railroad wouldn't be discovered. The very men who are now hunting for Juba may be the same terrible men who shot my Jacob." Anne's voice trembled and then broke off. She had trouble speaking through the tears streaming down her face. Her chest heaved, and she knew she would sob in front of Miss Lane if she said anything more.

Harriet looked horrified; she had covered her open mouth with her hand halfway through Anne's account. She was silent as Anne paused, then took her hand, which rested on her shoulder. Anne glanced away, collecting her thoughts as she wiped her tears with her free hand.

"Did you help Janie?" Harriet whispered, staring at her in the mirror. Though Anne was looking away, she could feel her steady gaze.

Anne took another deep breath, and the clarity of truth rose in her chest, welling up into words. She turned back to look at Harriet in the mirror.

"I wasn't going to. I've been so blessed to be working for you, Miss Lane. My family—We have already been through so much. But, despite telling multiple people that I would not help, I kept hearing in my heart that I must. So, I did help her. She's supposed to be a free woman, Miss Lane. Her parents are freemen in Boston. She was stolen off the street up there and sold for a profit by slave catchers! Her name is not Janie. Her name is Juba Wright. Mrs. Bass renamed her." Anne was out of breath by the time she had it all out. Her heart was pounding so hard she felt dizzy.

"Anne!" Harriet gasped.

Anne was silent. She had said enough.

"Anne, don't tell me anything more. I cannot know more. Finish my hair and get me ready for breakfast. I need time to think before the sergeant comes back."

Anne's hands were shaking, but she did as her lady asked.

A knock at the door came just as Anne finished putting flowers in Miss Lane's hair. Time moved too fast, and the knock gave both women a start. Anne went to the door and found it was Thomas delivering the morning post. He handed Anne a letter for Harriet, and Anne thanked him and shut the door.

They had been mostly silent while they went about the morning dressing routine, both lost in thought. Harriet opened and read the letter, then put it down on her dressing table, frowning, and stared off toward the windows. Anne wondered if perhaps it was bad news from Washington.

Moments later, there was a second knock at the door. Anne looked at Harriet, who nodded, consenting to her answering the door. Sergeant Gladwell greeted Anne, and she brought him into the suite. Harriet remained seated in an upholstered wing chair, looking uncomfortable but calm.

"Please, Sergeant, have a seat. Perhaps you would like to use my desk to write your notes more easily," Harriet graciously offered.

Anne was trying to control herself, but she was shaking. Her whole life could change in the next few minutes. Could she lie? Surely, she couldn't lie in front of Miss Lane, if at all. This was the very moment she had dreaded for days. And now, here it was. She remained standing as the sergeant sat down and opened his notebook.

"Sergeant, why is Anne being questioned in this investigation?" inquired Miss Lane.

"Well, ma'am, I am questioning everyone who has had contact with Mrs. Bass's slave woman," Gladwell said.

"Am I to be questioned as well? I have had contact with her throughout our stay here."

"No, ma'am."

"Well, why not, Sergeant?"

"You are not considered a suspect, Miss Lane. You are part of the president's travel party."

"A suspect in what, Sergeant Gladwell? Are you sure a crime has been committed?" Harriet asked.

"Well, no, ma'am. I am not sure a crime has been committed. Helping slaves to escape is a violation of the Fugitive Slave Act, so I must investigate if anyone assisted in the woman's flight," the sergeant explained. He looked uncomfortable; his brows furrowed, and he fidgeted in his seat.

"So, you would interrogate Anne but not me? Would you question the widow?" Harriet stood from her seat, walking to the window to look out.

"Yes, ma'am, I have already questioned Mrs. Bass," Gladwell confirmed politely.

"I insist you question me as well. Who knows what relevant information I may have that we don't realize could be useful? Question me now, and then you may move on to my maid." Miss Harriet was firm, and the sergeant looked less sure than he had been when he walked into the room. Anne guessed he knew he had lost control of his interrogation.

Miss Lane had made it possible for her to know and prepare for potential questions. Harriet was trying to help her, even in this small way. She could do this. She would pay close attention to the questions, then answer to the very best of her ability and try to not uncover her involvement without lying.

Her lady remained standing, seeming lost in thought for a moment while Anne waited for Gladwell to speak. He would not contradict the president's niece.

"All right, Miss Lane. I will respect your wishes. Do you mind if I begin? Are you ready?" Gladwell said, deferring to her, though his frown revealed that he was not happy with the new direction of his interrogation.

"Yes, Sergeant, I am ready for your questions," stated Harriet, walking back to him.

"How do you know the missing woman?"

"My uncle, the president, invited a guest with us this summer to join us in our visit to the Springs. Mrs. Bass brought Janie, an enslaved woman, as the nursemaid for her children."

"In your conversations with Janie, did she say anything about her treatment by Mrs. Bass or indicate she had thoughts of escape?"

"No, sir. She told me Mrs. Bass treats her well."

"Did you see anyone Saturday evening, or at any other time during your visit, talking to her who might have assisted her in escaping?" the sergeant inquired.

Harriet took a long pause to think, looking out the window at the bright green lawns and dappled sunlight. Birds were darting and swooping from tree to tree. Anne waited, hardly able to breathe. How would Harriet answer, given what Anne disclosed to her before Gladwell arrived?

"No, I've only seen her talking to our party. I'm sure she had opportunities to speak to other people, but I never observed her talking to anyone outside our group."

"Have you had anything go missing, like money or jewelry, since your arrival, Miss Lane?"

"No, sir, nothing of mine is missing," Harriet answered.

"Thank you, Miss Lane. That will be all for the moment," Gladwell finished. "I'd like to move on to questioning Mrs. McCoy now. Is that all right with you?"

"You may proceed," Harriet answered curtly.

Anne was seated at the back of the room. Gladwell turned the page in his book, wrote a bit, then turned to her and asked, "How do you know the missing woman?"

"I met her when the president's party arrived. We are both in service to the president's guests this summer."

"In your conversations with Janie, did she ever say anything about her treatment by Mrs. Bass or indicate her wish to flee?"

Anne reflected for a moment, trying to think of the correct answer. She looked to Harriet, who nodded and gave her a resolute expression that lent her courage and support.

"She said she was well treated by Mrs. Bass, although she did tell me of terrible mistreatments at former plantations. She said she was glad to be a nursemaid and that she cared deeply for the children. She told me of her wish to be free." Anne paused and saw the expression change on Gladwell's face.

"Go on, tell me more about that conversation, Mrs. McCoy. Did she ask you for help?" Gladwell stood, leaving his notebook and walking toward her.

She decided to go on the best she knew how. Calling on her Inner Light, Anne searched for what was true and right deep inside her heart and she continued, "She also told me she had been kidnapped from free parents by slave catchers. She said she was a free child stolen from her parents many years ago." Anne looked earnestly at the sergeant.

The sergeant's eyebrows rose, and he squared his shoulders. "Are you telling me Mrs. Bass's nursemaid is illegally enslaved, Mrs. McCoy?" His tone held a note of challenge.

"That is what she told me, Sergeant Gladwell," Anne confirmed. She looked at Miss Lane, who must have seen her silent bid for help.

"Sergeant Gladwell," Harriet interjected.

Anne trembled, her heartbeat racing. Either her lady was going to help her, or this could be the moment she was exposed for what she had just told her. She would be in violation of the Fugitive Slave Act for assisting an enslaved person to escape. She held her breath.

"I believe this drastically changes the trajectory of your investigation. I think perhaps your work is cut out for you. You'd best get going on the new information and direction of your investigation."

It seemed the sergeant was satisfied to follow Miss Lane's suggestion, as he picked up his notebook and prepared to leave. "Do you have any other information, Mrs. McCoy?"

"Her real name is Juba Wright, sir. Her parents are both free and living in Boston," Anne replied.

"Thank you, ladies. This is certainly remarkable information that I must investigate further. Please excuse me." He nodded politely to both as Anne let him out the door. Anne was relieved but still trembling inside as she turned back to the room to face Miss Lane. What would Miss Lane say to her?

— 28 —

Harriet

Harriet and Anne walked back from breakfast in silence. Harriet hadn't said more than a few words to her lady's maid since they had closed the interrogation at her suite with Sergent Gladwell. Luckily, Uncle Buck had been wrapped up in his consternation about his political woes and the coming news articles about Janie's escape. Or rather, Juba, which she was now aware was her given name. What a remarkable turn of events!

Nunc spent the meal dominating the conversation. Mrs. Bass had said little, for which Harriet was relieved. No one had asked her about Anne or the questioning with Sergeant Gladwell. She knew soon enough that Gladwell would catch up with Mrs. Bass and the president and tell them about the latest developments.

When she returned to her rooms, she pulled out the letter she had received just before the sergeant arrived from her sleeve and read it again.

Lily Macalaster
The Grand Union Hotel
Saratoga Springs, New York
July 18th, 1859

Dearest Harriet,

The Bancrofts and Armand Fitzpatrick send their fond tidings.
Saratoga has been rainy this year, and I am playing a lot of whist.
I am missing your gaming savvy and partnership. Last evening,
the skies cleared up, and I saw several shooting stars. George

Phillip Bond from the Harvard Observatory is also here with some lovely telescopes set up for guests to view the stars. He says that now into early next year, we will be seeing frequent meteor showers. Isn't that exciting?

As for your troubles, or rather your uncle's troubles, I hate to say he brought this on himself. Much as I love him as my own family, you tried to warn him of the potential problems before you left for Bedford.

In your letter, you asked me one question: "What can come of all this?" I would like to propose that you not only use your influence to ensure that your good woman, Anne, is not implicated in the matters but also, knowing your kind heart, consider what you can do for the betterment of the situation. You are strong enough to make your own choices and have a beautiful heart that I know will make this situation better for all. I believe you understand what I am saying.

For now, I will leave my desk and end this letter. Please enjoy the time you have left out at Bedford. I look forward to seeing you after your return to Washington City. I will take a train ride down from Philadelphia, and you and I can share some much-needed time together. I leave Saratoga on August 15th.

All my love,

Lily

Harriet reflected on Lily's words: *Consider what you can do for the betterment of the situation.* Could she help Juba and Anne without being seen as betraying her uncle? The more she learned, the more complicit she would become. She could not stand by and not help. She was involved now and she needed more information.

Anne tidied the room while Harriet sat on an overstuffed chair, lost in these questions.

"Anne, do you know where Juba is now?" she asked plainly.

"Well, miss, I am not sure how long it will take to travel undetected. I believe before she leaves the county, she will be up in the Quaker Valley at some point and perhaps at my uncle's farmstead. There are Quakers up through that valley who transfer people as safely as they can. Each stop moves a fugitive farther and farther north. Sometimes they are in haymows. Sometimes they can rest in secret hiding spaces under houses."

"It is quite brave when you all are risking so much, Anne," Harriet remarked. She could sense that Anne seemed more like herself and more willing to share.

"Yes. Given the risk to the enslaved person and whoever is helping them, it does take courage and conviction from all involved. I try to think of the great risk of violence that the enslaved persons endure if they are caught. While the free conductors face fines and imprisonment, which is certainly a disaster, the enslaved person may face death by brutal beating for running away. Worse than that is the possibility of being sold far south, which can mean a long, slow death in the cotton or sugarcane fields."

Just then, there was a knock at the door. Harriet nodded, and Anne went to answer. Out in the hall stood young Thomas Miller.

"May I come in, please? Anne, your uncle is unwell, and your family is asking for you. I must get horses ready to take you as soon as you can go," Thomas whispered with insistence.

"Please let him in, Anne." Harriet had heard the valet's appeal. Was what he said true, or was this another part of the plan? Was someone so close to her uncle's service involved in the escape as well?

"Miss Lane, I am sorry to disturb you, but I have come to ask for Anne's leave for the rest of the day. Word has come to the front desk that her uncle is quite sick, and her family is asking for her."

Was this all a ruse? Hopefully, Anne's uncle was well. She decided to go along with it, as Anne was obviously needed either way.

"Anne, you may take the time to visit your family. Thomas, please wait outside for a moment while I have a word with Anne."

Later that morning, Harriet made her way across the gravel path in front of the Swiss House and toward the fountain of Hygeia. What a remarkable week it had been. Her thoughts were full of doubt and questions about right and wrong. She had spent most of her life in support of her uncle. She had depended on him as a parent and cared for his health and well-being. What if he found out all she had discovered and kept from him? It felt like a betrayal. Could it ruin their lifelong relationship? He had said that she was his only comfort. Oh, Nunc!

Never had she outwardly opposed him or done anything that might be construed as counter to his beliefs or wishes. By hiding what she knew about Anne and Juba's escape, she was acting against her uncle. But there was no other way about it. She could not look at herself in the mirror if she turned in Anne and shared what she had learned of the escape. It would have to be as it was. Harm would not come to her uncle from the loss of the woman. Mrs. Bass would find another nursemaid, probably another enslaved woman, unfortunately.

Juba was legally a free woman, as she had been born free and taken into slavery. But that wasn't the point. The point was living according to her convictions; she was now aware that she hadn't been acting on what was right. Her uncle rested his conscience on the greater good of keeping the nation intact. Harriet knew now that slavery contradicted everything the nation was supposed to stand for.

Approaching the stairs to the colonnade, she met Mrs. Bass, who had her children in tow.

"Good morning, Harriet. Would you care to help me take the children over to the Magnesia Spring? I could use your assistance since I am without a nursemaid."

"I would be glad to come along. Will Mr. Blackburn find you another nursemaid for the rest of your stay?"

"He has sent me Miss Koontz from the laundry, but I am not sure I want just anyone caring for my children. Janie was a good girl," the widow remarked, leading little Eugenia along by the land. She seemed to struggle with the little girl's wriggles, and she let her hand go to skip by her side. Ella marched ahead, not much interested in her younger siblings.

The two women followed the children and walked across the colonnade bridge that spanned the lawn, the road, and then Shober's Run. The walkway led to the shady gazebo where they would take a draft of the waters and enjoy the gushing sound of the spring coming from the hillside. Harriet hoped it would settle her stomach, which was in knots.

After they took their cups and seated themselves in the shade, they continued their conversation.

"How are you faring with Miss Koontz?" Harriet inquired.

"Well, I can't say I like her very much. She is a bit impertinent in her attitude and doesn't take direction very well. The children don't seem to care for her either." Mrs. Bass brushed what seemed to be invisible crumbs off her black satin skirt, her always downturned lips finding their normal resting spot that appeared to make a permanent scowl.

"Perhaps give her some time to adjust. I think that Janie was an excellent nursemaid, Mrs. Bass. She cared very much for your children, and they for her. She will be very hard to replace," Harriet replied, trying to be upbeat.

"I just can't understand how she could leave us like this. I took fine care of her, and she had an easy life with us," the widow said.

"As much as she cared for your children, why would she forget about her own life?" Harriet said carefully. This was dangerous territory. She had a feeling the widow wouldn't grasp what she was getting at.

"Her own life? What do you mean, Harriet?"

"I mean her desire to have a life of her own and the freedom to make her own choices. Perhaps she wanted her own children and family." Harriet knew she was going too far, but it was too late.

"Why do you imagine she would think like we do, Harriet? I don't believe the slaves consider those things."

Harriet took that in. Why had she even started this conversation? She knew very well of the Southern sensibilities about slaves. She had not seen anything to indicate that Mrs. Bass would think with any empathy toward hers. Perhaps this was just sport for her own confirmation.

"Why do you think they wouldn't? They are human. They love and care and dream, like any of us."

"I really don't think so. I've heard that they don't think in the same way whites do."

Harriet sighed, frustrated and disgusted. What could she say now without being rude? She was aware of evil hypotheses about racial differences. She realized now that she had ignored or excused them. Those wrongs were now glaring and evil to her after what had transpired since her arrival at the Springs. Her sentiments on the matter had changed and she couldn't see it any other way. Her questions and vague postulations had hardened into an anger at injustice and there was no place for tolerance.

"Why would thousands of enslaved persons risk their lives to escape? Do you think those who try are just a deranged handful? I am sure every single slave in the Southern states hopes, dreams, and plans for how they can find their way to freedom. There is no human nature that is different by color. Like you and I, everyone is born with a desire to live their best life on their own terms." Harriet's voice was strong and clear. She stood, unable to sit still any longer. Her fear of being disagreeable had left her. Standing by her principles felt right.

"I think you are overthinking this, Harriet. I am shocked at your tone and implied insolence." The widow looked embarrassed and started fanning herself, looking around to see if anyone nearby had overheard.

"I am shocked at your lack of understanding of the desires of the human soul." Harriet left her and marched back across the bridge. Surely, she would have to answer to her uncle if the widow told him of their conversation. But perhaps the woman would be too embarrassed to admit to it after all.

— 24 —

Juba

Mr. Graham had gotten Juba as far as the Miller farm. He introduced her in the middle of the night to a kindly Quaker farmer who showed her to a hiding spot in the hayloft of his barn. The night had been cool, but as she tried to sleep through the day, the barn got hotter and hotter.

Just as she thought she would roast in the hayloft, the daylight started to fade. What a relief it was as the cool started to seep back into the space. Mr. Miller had told her he would return at dark with provisions. He said he couldn't give her a candle to read by, for safety reasons and to avoid making her hiding spot known with the glow.

The light around the edges of the door had started to recede. Hopefully, she will receive food and water soon. The hay was not an unpleasant bed, but the smell from the animal stalls made it hard to breathe. Besides her physical discomfort, she had been lost in her thoughts and worries and had been thinking a lot about her parents since she woke up.

What if she couldn't find them? What if something had happened to them, and they weren't still in Boston? What if they were dead? The thought of trying to figure out a free life without her momma and pappa was a bleak one, so she pushed it away. Instead, she tried to imagine her momma's arms around her or the way her pappa would pat her on the head and smile down at her when she asked him a question. Her thoughts and worries raced through her mind.

She heard the creaking of the heavy barn door down below and the rustling of the animals at the arrival of a human. *Oh, Lord! Please let it be Mr. Miller.* She hunkered down under the hay, just in case it was not.

There was the sound of heavy boots on the ladder, and a gentle voice said, "Juba, are you awake? Are thee all right?"

It was the Quaker man. She poked her head up out of the hay.

"Yes, sir. I'm awake. Just thirsty and hungry. I'm sorry to cause you trouble."

"Now don't thee worry about anything. I brought thee a pail with some supper and a skin with some more water in it. Give me the other one back and I'll refill it for the next time I'm up," explained Miller. Juba saw his bearded face in the light from the lamp he carried. As he was setting her provisions down on the floor for her, they both froze at the sound of approaching horses off in the distance.

"I best climb down the ladder to look at who's coming. Hide deep in the hay in the back corner. There is a false wall there. Keep thee quiet until thee hear me come back and tell thee it's safe," the man said as he backed down, his voice quiet but urgent. Juba went to crawl toward the back of the hayloft and remembered to go back and grab the provisions. She found the extra boards that created a space to hide and concealed herself behind them.

There were muffled voices down below. They sounded not too far off, and she could make out two distinct voices along with Mr. Miller's. Fear made her blood run cold, and she held her breath, trying to hear what they were saying. The voices grew nearer and louder, sounding gruff and angry, but she couldn't make out the words. What was happening? Every nerve in her body was tingling. Could she run? How would she get out of this loft without using the ladder? She buried herself further back into the hay behind the small hip wall the Quaker had told her about. It was now harder to hear what was going on. Minutes passed as the voices grew more distant, then came closer again. Then the groaning sound of the barn door was followed by clearer conversation.

"Must not be hiding in the spring house or the chicken coop. How about in here? No tellin' where you sympathizers will hide these niggers," came the voice of a man from below.

Another man added, "You best get her out of this barn. We'll find her if she's here, and if you give her over, we won't speak against you at the hearing. It could save you jail and a lot of coins!"

"Brothers, I told thee already. I haven't seen any fugitives. I beg thee to leave my property and let my family be," Miller implored, but it came across more like an order.

The sound of overturning milk cans and slamming stall gates came next, and Juba held her breath. Boots were climbing the ladder and then hitting the planks of the loft. There was the scratching, raspy sound of hay being tossed toward the front of the pile where she was hidden. Her heart pounded in her chest, each beat so hard she feared it might burst. She pressed her hand over her heart to still it, but it only made the thumping louder, louder—like it might give her away at any moment.

"Let's try the house. Perhaps she's inside," the first man shouted up the ladder. Then she heard boots on the ladder again.

"I beg your pardon! Please do not bother my wife and children," replied Miller as the voices trailed off toward the house.

Juba heard pounding on wood, which she decided was the door to the house.

Miller called out, "Gentlemen, I pray thee, I am a God-fearing man and a pacifist. At this moment, I have my gun aimed at my front door and will momentarily fire. It would be in your best interest to leave my property before it is fired and may hit thee!"

Muffled voices moved farther away, and Juba heard horses' hooves pounding the road, presumably away from the Miller house.

Minutes passed and she stayed hidden until finally Mr. Miller's voice came from the direction of the ladder. "Thee should be safe for the time being. Those men have gone away."

"How will I make it through this journey with the slave catchers on my trail, Mr. Miller?" Juba asked him as his face crested the top of the ladder. She wiped the sweat and tears from her face with the hanky he handed to her.

"Peter, please, my dear. Mr. Miller is too formal. You will put one day and night in front of the other, and with friends to help thee and God watching over, you will make your way home."

Terror and bad dreams racked her sleep that night. Nightmares about being captured, being lost in the woods alone, and about the Bass children being taken by slave catchers filled her mind. The last nightmare about the Bass children was particularly horrible, and she woke from it calling out and reaching for them. Juba sat awake and waited for the morning light to show through the cracks in the barn so she wouldn't have to dream anymore.

———◆——— ——— ◆———

The next day, Juba was introduced to Samual Way. Mr. Miller had said the slave catchers had moved out of the area, so he hid Juba in a wagon of milk cans by day to take her to the next station of the Underground Railroad. Mr. Way was a giant of a man with kind blue eyes. He was as big as any man she had ever seen and had a thick long white beard but not a hair on top of his head. He explained that Anne was his niece and that her father was his brother, who lived on a farm a mile or so down the road.

"I know it was difficult for Anne, with all her troubles, to help me break free. I am forever grateful, sir. Your family are good people."

"The world is full of good people, Juba, but some who have lost their way have made life these days hellish, particularly for those who are held in bondage. Each soul we can help to freedom can spread the word of God's light and help the light grow," Mr. Way explained.

"I am grateful, sir."

"Give thy gratitude to God, Juba. We are all given a life to do our best by his guidance. I am heartened Anne was able to help thee. She is a fine girl, and I know that last year, she went through a horrible loss. Jacob McCoy was a good man who helped many people. The ugliness of our current state of politics in this country is shameful. Most people in this country came here to find religious freedom. It is a corruption of God's will that the freedom of others is not a foregone conclusion because they are of a different color."

He took her to some rocks at the back of his fields. This hiding spot wasn't exactly a cave but a collection of boulders that made a shelter. The rocks were more in the open than the other areas she had been hidden, but at the back of a series of corn fields. Mr. Way read the concern on her face when they arrived.

"Please don't worry about this spot. I call it a matter of hiding in plain sight. We've had many people come through here, and all were kept safe. The beauty of this spot is the catchers don't search out in the fields, as we've seen. They usually hunt through the barns, houses, and outbuildings. No one has ever found anyone we have put out here. We're careful when we come out to bring food and water so as not to draw attention. Might be I need to fix a fence out here or plow a new row over the next few days," he explained with a wink.

Even though she was scared, Juba couldn't help but smile. She wondered if he'd had Anne's red hair before he went white and lost it on top. With his size and jovial personality, he must have been quite an interesting character in his youth.

"Do thee read? I brought thee newspapers to help pass the time," he said as he helped her carry a quilt and a cloth bag of other provisions to the rock shelter.

"Yes, sir. I like to read and will be glad to have something to help me keep my mind off my worries." Juba thanked him, and he rode off back to his homestead. She saw the smoke from the chimney of the two-story log house off in the distance, closer to the road. She couldn't quite see the house as the corn was high that time of year and close to her hiding spot.

The sun had set, and it was time to settle down on the quilt and rest. The newspaper she opened first included a story about her escape. How odd to read about herself. The story quoted Mrs. Bass as saying she was a good girl and that nothing had been stolen. The article reported Mrs. Bass wished her well and hoped no one would take advantage of "Janie."

"My name is JUBA!" she exclaimed out loud.

But what about the kidnapping of the president? What would happen to those three small children if Missus was hurt or worse? She didn't want harm to come to the president or Miss Lane either. They had always been kind to her.

Juba looked out of the rocky area toward the north. Where was the North Star? Yes, there it was. No clouds to obscure it. The North Star had become the beacon for so many enslaved black people like her, looking for freedom in the north. Here she was, already in the north and on her way to freedom. How many countless souls searched for this star and got courage and comfort when they found its bright light?

She stared at the beautiful sight for several minutes and caught a glimpse of a shooting star heading east. North and east were the directions where she hoped to find her parents. Perhaps the shooting star was a good sign.

It felt good to settle into the soft quilt. She was so tired. Every muscle in her body ached for rest. But then, just as she began to drift off, she was startled awake. What was that far-off sound?

There was the sound of horses coming from the direction of the road below the field. Maybe it was just a passing neighbor. *Oh my God, it's getting closer.* Maybe Sam Way was bringing her some supper? As she waited, she heard clearly there was more than one horse. She backed into the small rock enclosure as far as she could. It was too late to run. Her heart thundered so hard she could hardly think.

As the horses slowed to a stop, she heard two men speak to each other. She recognized the men's voices from the Millers' barn. Hugging her legs tightly to her, she made herself as tiny and hidden as possible. Bile rose in her throat, and she thought she may be sick. There was the sound of a match strike. Oh, dear God, a light was coming closer to the rock opening. Was there anything to fight with? She picked up a stone slightly bigger than her hand. Could she fight off two grown men?

A man's face appeared at the opening in the rocks, illuminated by flickering torchlight. "Well, look what we have here," he said, sneering.

Another face appeared over the man's shoulder, his scowl menacing. "Looks like the boy down the road was worth payin' some coin to after all."

She should have sprung at them, but she was frozen, backed into the cold, hard crevice with nowhere to go.

Juba recognized the faces of the slave catchers she had seen by the side of the road in the valley below the Springs the day she had arrived in Bedford. They wore the same sickening smirks and dirty clothes now as they did that day.

"Come 'ere." The taller man reached in and yanked her arm so hard pain seared through her shoulder. She dropped the stone in her other hand with a jolt. Hitting her forehead on the rocky overhang, she dropped to her knees, and he wrenched her arm hard again. This time, a muscle in her arm tore and burned.

"Get up off your knees, girl. You been too much work already. I can't bring you in looking like you're hurt. You ain't hardly gonna be worth a dollar." He looked down at her on the ground.

A drip of sweat ran from her temple, and she wiped it with her hand before pushing herself up with her good arm. There was blood on her hand. She realized she was bleeding from where she hit her head on the rocks. Her head throbbed.

"Stand up and don't smear your nigger blood on me," the shorter man ordered. He had a chain in his hands.

"Stand the hell up, or we'll make this worse for you," ordered the other.

The pain in her body didn't even matter. Her hope of freedom and seeing her parents again was crushed, and she felt the life bleeding out of her dreams. She wasn't sure she could stand. Her head spun, and it was hard to focus her eyes.

"She's a pretty darkie, ain't she, Pete?"

"We gotta keep her in one piece. The widow won't want her messed up if we gonna get our reward money," the shorter one said.

The taller man let go of her hurt arm and stepped toward his horse, sneering, "Nobody will believe her if we do things they can't see. It's her word against ours. Get'er secured with those chains."

— 25 —

Anne

"What's going on, Thomas?" Anne whispered as they approached the stables at the south end of the Springs property. They were finally out of earshot of anyone and at liberty to speak.

"Don't fret now, Anne. Your uncle is only worried sick about Juba's safety." He was walking fast as he talked, giving Anne a smile and a wink as they hurried into the stable.

"Thank goodness." Anne took a deep breath of relief. "I suppose that is honest in its own way. Have you been in on this the whole time?" she questioned, in shock. No one had told her Thomas was involved! "Are we going to Quaker Valley?"

He continued to saddle his horse, talking and working at the same time. "I had no idea any of this was going on, but the senator pulled me aside Sunday afternoon as he didn't want to contact you for your safety. He said he had found out from Elias Rouse that I came from a Quaker family out in the Valley. He asked me if he could trust me and my integrity. I told him that I always do what is right in my heart, so it depended on what kind of information he would entrust me with."

"So now you're involved too and we're going out there?" Anne was trying to catch up to the change in plans. This was all so unexpected.

"We must make haste. Senator Cameron gave me the freedom papers he acquired for Juba Wright, showing that she was born to free parents."

"How did he get papers so quickly?" Anne was incredulous.

"He knows people who know people, if you know what I mean. The paperwork will keep her safe for the rest of her journey. We've got to catch up to her before those grimy scoundrels do."

"How are we going to find her? Where is she?" Anne felt her heart starting to race.

"She must be somewhere out in the Valley. We'll follow the route they had planned for her." He continued to check the fit of the reins and saddle on his ride.

"Oh, Thomas. Now you are tangled in all this, too. Why do you need me?"

"I was a child when I lived out in Quaker Valley when we were in school together. I can't say I know where I'm going when I'm out in the Valley, so I need your help tracking Juba down. Also, she trusts you and may not trust me since I work with the president. She may be at your uncle Sam's, Penrose's, or as far north as Walker's."

Thomas had finished getting the first horse ready and went to lift another saddle. "You ride, don't you? Will you be all right on the horse yourself, or do you want to ride with me?"

"Yes, I have ridden all my life. I want my own horse, thank you." She frowned as it wouldn't be proper for a widow to ride with a man. She hadn't done that since Jacob was alive. He lifted her onto the saddle gently, making sure her feet were planted in the stirrups before handing her the reins and letting go. How kind of him to give her a hand mounting. It was all right to accept help from a gentleman. He could saddle the horse for her and take the lead. He was an old friend, after all. She gave him a warm smile as thanks.

They rode out of Bedford north and west toward Quaker Valley. Anne knew it wasn't good to push the horses, but they had to catch up to Juba as soon as possible to avert disaster. Saying prayers as she rode was the only way Anne could tamp down her fear and keep moving forward.

About an hour outside of Bedford, past the town of Cessna, another rider came into view around the next bend. As they got closer, there was the sound of hooves beating hard and fast on the road and heading their way. The man was bent low over his horse's neck and using his reigns to urge the horse faster. They had no weapons; hopefully, it was not danger closing in on them.

Thomas was in the lead but reined his horse so Anne could draw even with him.

"We best find out what this is about," Thomas said as the rider charged closer.

As the gap between them closed, Anne saw the horseman sit back, slowing his horse to meet them. It was William Penrod, a man from Quaker Valley she knew.

"Good day! I am in a rush to find more men. There are slave catchers harassing the Miller's house about a half mile up the road. They are pulling apart the floor, trying to access the crawlspace below. They're sure a woman is hiding in the house that they're after."

"The Miller's! That's my uncle's house!" Thomas exclaimed. He gave Anne a quick look of alarm and urged his horse forward up the road.

"Have they found a runaway, William?" Anne asked.

"I don't know what's going on. I only heard the commotion up the road and got close enough for Margret Miller to tell me they were in the house. She asked me to go find help."

"We best hurry! Thank you, and God bless!" Anne prodded her horse to catch up to Thomas, who was now a cloud of dust ahead of her. Were they going to find Juba just as she and Thomas caught up? What would they do? Surely they wouldn't accept the freedom papers and let her go without a challenge?

As Anne turned up the lane to Miller Farm, she saw a small log house with a covered porch. Several people were standing in the yard, and she caught sight of Thomas dismounting near the dooryard gate.

"Pray thee, get out of my home!" Peter Miller was dragging a man by the arm forcibly out the door, shoving him off the porch and going back inside. Soon, another man came stumbling out the door and down the stairs.

Anne watched from the garden gate. Two lathered horses were tied nearby on the post with threadbare pack saddles. The angry trespassers strode from the house toward their horses, hastily untied, mounted, and rode off up the lane.

"What in the world happened?" Anne asked as Margret Miller, Thomas' aunt, approached the gate.

"About an hour ago, they rode in here like they owned the place and began to turn our barns, outbuildings, and home inside out, looking for Juba."

Thomas was still on the porch. He was trying to calm his uncle, who was furiously gesticulating and pacing, presumably recounting what had happened to Thomas. As Anne and Margret got closer, she heard his rant.

"They would not leave and were sure that she was here! They've torn apart the feed bins and half our parlor floor!"

Thomas peered in the door, reviewing the damage. "Those were not the slave catchers that I saw at the Springs."

"Many groups of men have searched through the area. The bounty on her has many seeking her for the reward."

Aunt Margret stepped closer, "Thomas, I am worried for thee and Anne. These are dangerous men."

"Thank you, Aunt Margret. We must go. We'll be careful. We have her freedom papers. Was she here? Where is she now?

"I took her out to Sam Way's this morning," Uncle Peter reported. Anne released her breath. What a relief. God willing, she was still safe, and they would find her soon.

＊━━━━＊

After a half hour-ride, they approached her uncle Sam's homeplace. Trying to calm herself, she tried to think about how she missed living out in the valley. Summer was always beautiful outside town, with the deep green hills rising all around and the neatly laid-out fields full of corn and buckwheat lush in midseason. Following Dunning's Creek, they passed the Quaker meeting house in Spring Meadow. It was a small log cabin. It looked so much smaller to her now than when she was a girl—all those years sitting at a desk and all those meetings sitting silently, waiting for God's answers. *God help us to find Juba before the slave catchers cause any harm.*

Uncle Sam's log house was quiet when they arrived. There was no one answering at the house and no one in the yard. They finally found her aunt Alice out in the spring house. "Anne, I am so glad thee have come." Her aunt exclaimed, rushing out of the small stone building. "Your uncle went out to bring Juba some food this morning, but she was gone. We are worried sick." Anne hugged her tightly. It was the worst news. Juba had been captured before leaving Bedford County! Where was she? Which of those awful men had her? How long had they had her?

Aunt Alice continued, "Your uncle and some other men just headed to the Fishertown meeting house to figure out what to do next. I'm surprised thee didn't pass them. They think that the catchers have taken her to town. We're scared to death for her and for those who have helped her."

"How long has she been missing from the shelter?" This was what she had been afraid of—that they would not catch up to Juba in time with the papers. And where was she now, at the hands of those awful men?

"Perhaps she was taken as early as last night? Perhaps they have brought her to the magistrate in Bedford to invoke the Fugitive Slave Act," Alice said.

Now, they must turn around and hurry back to Bedford before Juba is returned to the Springs. After the ride from Bedford, both horses drank deeply from the burbling spring. Anne washed her hands in the cooling water to try to ease the blisters and soreness from the reins. Thomas fidgeted and paced, ready to go.

"Aunt Alice, we must go. Take care. I hope to visit you and Uncle Sam again soon." Anne spoke her goodbye as Thomas helped her back onto her saddle. Another ten-mile ride back to town would be difficult on the horses. They needed to go right away if those men were hours ahead of them. *God be with Juba in their custody.* She pushed thoughts of what may be happening to Juba away and tried to focus on the trail. Those thoughts were too unthinkably horrible.

— 26 —

Harriet

It was hard to go to sleep that night after everything that had happened. Harriet's mind was racing with so many different thoughts. How to reconcile them all? Finally, she did settle into a fitful sleep.

Hours later, she woke with her heart racing. The cotton sheets were damp with perspiration as her head swam, dizzy with sleep. A terrible tingling and tightness ran through her. Was it from her thumping heart or turning stomach? She was awake, but the images of her dream were vivid and wouldn't leave her.

She was a small girl hiding in a dark room. Looking out a window, she saw another window visible across a courtyard with a light on, illuminating the people inside. Harriet didn't recognize them as anyone she knew. She watched as a man and woman moved, not fully dressed. She should look away! Who were they? Harriet didn't know them. The man was white, and the woman was black. He struck the woman hard across the face, and the woman fell out of Harriet's sight. No! Why did he hit her?

She shouldn't be watching, but she couldn't move away. She should cry out for the man to stop, but she couldn't make herself known, or she would get in trouble. Shame filled her, but Harriet couldn't turn away. Trembling, she hid behind the heavy drapery.

Steps were coming down the hall in her direction. Someone would find her watching! Making herself as small as possible, she held her breath as the doorknob rattled and the door creaked open. Perspiration beaded on her forehead. Heavy footsteps entered the room while a match struck. Through the drape, candlelight brightened the room. Shaking, she held her breath and tried to keep still. Who would find her? Surely, she would be punished.

"Harriet, are you in here?" demanded her uncle's voice. He sounded angry. Her heart was beating so hard it felt like it would burst. Could he hear it?

Slippered footsteps padded down the hall, and a woman's familiar voice came into the room. "She's in here hiding. Search behind the furniture and drapes. Harriet, come out here!" That voice was angry, too. That was the end of the dream.

Now lying awake, shame prickled Harriet's face, and her stomach turned. Thank goodness it was only an awful dream. As she sat up and relived the images, she recognized that the woman's voice calling her out in the dream was her own.

The sun had started to crest Constitution Hill, and a pale purple glow lit the walls of her suite. She couldn't stay in her bed any longer. Perhaps she could shake off the leftover dread that clung to her if she got up. She needed to splash her face with cool water and change her damp shift.

As Harriet dressed in silence, her thoughts continued to race. There seemed to be a momentum within her, but to what end? Fear and shame were not emotions she had dealt with in many years. She'd met her circumstances head-on, through moving to foreign countries and traveling throughout the United States to campaign for her uncle. She held her head high and took on the role of First Lady like she was born for it. Now the thought of having to look her uncle in the eye knowing she had been complicit in covering for Anne, made her tremble. How would she face him?

After making herself presentable, Harriet left her rooms. Perhaps some tea would soothe her, and she could take a walk in the misty morning air. She needed to shake off the awful feelings that hung over her from the dream.

As she moved down the hall, she hoped not to meet her uncle. It felt like her shame was an ugly frock that he would notice on her right away and point out for what it was. She hurried her steps to pass his suite, but her uncle's door was open. He was seated at this desk and hailed her to come in. How would she hide all her worries and feelings? Should she?

"Good morning, Hal. You're up early today."

"Yes, I couldn't lay in bed any longer, so I decided to get up and walk down for tea." Her mouth went dry, and her palms were moist.

Her uncle's desk was a mess of papers. His glasses were perched on his nose, and the desk lamp was lit. He must have been at his desk since before sunrise.

"Did the courier come already, Nunc?" she asked.

"Unfortunately, yes. It never seems to be good news these days when I receive my delivery from Washington." He removed his glasses and rubbed his reddened eyes.

"Any news of Janie?" Harriet asked carefully. Would Juba be found and Anne implicated? What would happen then?

"No word," he answered, distracted, as he picked up papers from his desk and continued, "News from Kansas. The convention in Wyandotte successfully accepted that Kansas would not be a slave state. It will go to Congress this fall."

"But that is good news." Harriet stepped closer even though she wanted to back out of the room. Maybe he would understand which way the tide was turning.

"You have heard all my thoughts on this, Harriet. But let me elaborate again. I am glad that the mess in Kansas may be nearing an end. Let's hope the bloodshed will end. I fear that the news will have the southern states in an uproar."

"But, Nunc," Harriet started and was curtly cut off.

"Let me finish. This was elected by the citizens of Kansas. At least I hope so. The other three constitutions for the state were fraught with fighting in the streets and illegal voting by border state infiltrators. I will stick to my position that popular sovereignty is the essence of the constitution, and in this case, it has prevailed for the better. It is the consequences which could be disastrous."

"I see." Harriet was unsure what he expected her to say and didn't trust herself to make any spoken opinion. She exhaled and released her clenched fists.

"I spent the morning writing this," he stood and handed her a piece of his correspondence.

She read through the draft of an official statement. She had previously seen his drafts of such presidential missives and recognized the format.

He would pass it on to his secretary to be cleaned up and then sign and seal it before having it sent with the next day's courier to Washington. The heading was "Findings of Independent Investigation into Violation of the *Act Prohibiting the Importation of Slaves of 1808.*"

Late last year, Harriet had been outraged to hear that a ship called *The USS Wanderer* was discovered to have come into the port at Jekyll Island, Georgia, with five hundred humans on board that had been illegally taken and transported from Africa. Shocking facts had been uncovered. Eight hundred captives had started the journey in chains, and through sickness and maltreatment in subhuman conditions, only five hundred arrived on U.S. soil. Slave importation had been made illegal more than 50 years before.

The unfortunate people on *The Wanderer* were sold in Georgia at a public auction without concern for violating federal law or injustice. Northern newspapers repudiated the transgressors as treasonous, and the President had publicly condemned all involved and called for their arrest and federal prosecution. Her uncle had also dispatched his investigator, a Mr. Slocum, to quietly find out if the importation of slaves was an ongoing and wider practice.

"Mr. Slocum has found no further evidence," her uncle said as she read through his missile, "so now we will proceed in the fall with the trial of all those involved with *The Wanderer.*"

Harriet didn't know what to say. There was more to say than she could articulate.

"Are you all right, Harriet? You are not yourself this morning." It was as she feared; her feelings were obvious. *I must find a way to get away and recover myself.* Her mind raced for words.

"Is this what you thought your presidency would be like, Nunc? Is this how you thought your life of service would reach its pinnacle?" She regretted the words as soon as they came out of her mouth. Where did they come from?

Her uncle stood quietly. He looked at her for a long moment. He was seldom speechless, but as his mouth opened to respond and closed again, his face sagged. There was a glimmer in his eyes, lit by the lamplight. Were they tears? Turning from her, he walked to the window.

In awkward silence, Harriet felt her own tears rise, and she swallowed to hold them back. The heaviness in the room hung like morning mist over Shober's Run. Was his silence anger at her or resentment of her question? Or perhaps at himself?

He took a deep breath and then let it out, staring out the window. "No, my dear. My time in this land's highest office is not at all what I expected."

— 27 —
Juba

There seemed to be no one else around out in the fields who would hear her if she screamed. As the taller man turned his back to search his pack for something, the short one lurched toward Juba with the chains. In a few moments, she would be chained. Then, who knew what could happen? Right now, she was still free. Her body exploded with a surge of energy and fury at that moment that she had never felt before. She would not willingly give up herself or her freedom again.

As he leaned down to grab her wrists with the chains, Juba sprang to her feet. Forcing her wrists upward under the thick chain, she knocked him square in the chin. He fell backward with the force of the heavy lock. His lip split, and there was a loud *crack* as the lock connected. Stumbling for balance, he dropped the chain and spit out a tooth and a gob of blood. She didn't wait to see if he fell. Juba ran into the corn.

"Goddamit, Pete!" the other man swore.

She had to run away fast. It was dark out, and she hoped to gain distance while they recovered from the surprise of her sudden bolt. But where would she go? Green stalks and leaves streamed past her in the dark as she cut through several rows. It was hard to see anything, and she stumbled several times over the uneven clods of dirt and the brace roots of the corn. Juba's mind raced and terror choked her making it hard to breathe as she ran, but her body was weightless as she tore through the corn toward the farmhouse. *God help me!*

Behind her, the men were cursing, and there was the sound of them tearing through the corn after her. "You go left toward the house and I'll cut across!" one man shouted, "You're a worthless piece of shit, Pete!!" he swore.

Juba couldn't tell if one man was behind her or both, but she kept running. Perhaps she could escape to the corn crib, which she noticed when she arrived. Or better yet, to the barn for a horse. Could she escape with a horse?

Suddenly, her world turned upside down. She tripped over the stiff corn stalks and grabbed desperately at other stalks on the way down, but they were no help. As she landed on her hands in the dirt, the pain in her left shoulder took her breath away. She gathered herself up and paused to listen. The men weren't close. Hopefully, they had lost track of her. She got back up and ran.

As she got close to the edge of the field, she saw the barn through the corn. Did she dare break into the open? Listening closely, the sound of breaking stalks and their shouts to one another were distant enough to embolden her to make a dash for the barn, about twenty yards away. With all her strength, she ran toward the barn door that stood ajar.

Inside the barn, stalls lined the far wall. Two horses were in the closest stalls. They lifted their heads as she ran toward them. As she quickly lifted the hasp to enter, the horse whickered and shifted. She didn't know horses very well. How was she going to ride this giant animal?

"Hey boy, you gonna help me and be nice?" Her quavering voice broke as she whispered and patted his neck with shaking hands. Was this the way to make him settle? She couldn't tell exactly what color he was in the dark, but he had painted light spots down his nose and back, and his dark eyes shifted around, looking at her. He tossed his head, snorting.

Muffled curses came from outside. She had to go! Juba negotiated around the horse to the back of the stall. How would she climb on? She would have to use the stall itself and then hope to hang on without a saddle or reins and with a hurt arm. That would have to do.

"I'm gonna climb on now, boy. Please be good." She whispered and patted the horse one more time before jumping off the sideboard of the stall and swinging her leg over the horse as she lay across his back. He danced and shimmied.

"I know you's in here," the catcher's voice was unmistakable as he entered the barn. "I don't hear the corn russlin' no mo. I comin' for you, nigger!"

Juba put her head down on the horse's neck and held her breath. The animal danced a bit but didn't snort or buck. Her heart raced. It can't all come to this, can it? After all that she had come through and all the people who helped her, she had to keep fighting!

The man's footsteps were quiet on the packed earth of the barn floor. She held her breath and sensed him coming closer. Was he close to the stall? She held on tight and kicked her feet into the horse's ribs. The horse grunted, bucked, and then whined and took off, forcing the stall open and knocking over her pursuer as she bolted toward the wide-open door.

"Goddammit!" he yelled behind her as she clung for her life, holding onto the mane with her hands, her legs clasped tight. Her injured shoulder hurt as she held on, but she had to keep hold. Juba crashed out into the night. Where was the other catcher? She couldn't sit up to look behind her, or she would fall off. The horse seemed to have a direction of his own. She hoped it was away from danger.

They galloped down the lane. Juba's thoughts raced. Where would she go? She had no sense of direction, but she had to put distance between herself and the catchers. As she rounded a bend, she heard hooves beating behind her. Up ahead was a gate. Oh, God, help me. What will the horse do at the gate?

As they closed in on the gate to the road, the horse slowed and stopped. Juba slid off and ran to find the gate latch. Looking back, it was too late. The taller man was almost right on her, and the other was behind him.

"Good try. But you ain't gettin' away, you bitch." He swung a rope over her head, lassoing her like stock.

"Careful Dave, she's a mean one." The other man arrived, his lip noticeably swollen as he spit blood into the dirt.

"No more messin' around. Let's jus' get'er to town."

Crushing disappointment hit her like a horse kicking her in the stomach. She had been so close to freedom, fought so hard to keep it, and lost.

28

Anne

Evening was falling when they made it to the courthouse in Bedford. Tying up their horses, Anne and Thomas caught sight of the two slave catchers skulking across the street from the jail toward the courthouse.

"There are those two good-for-nothings," declared Thomas, brow set in a scowl.

"They may have taken her to the jail for holding, unless they took her out to the Springs already," Anne replied. What had they done with Juba? Had they come in time?

"Let's hurry to the jail and see if the constable has her. Perhaps we can catch them before they take her back to the widow." Thomas was already striding across the street to the small two-story brick building that served as Bedford's jail. This was a whole new side to her childhood friend that she had never seen. His resolve gave her renewed energy to press on through her exhaustion and fear. Anne scrambled to catch up. Built in the late seventeenth century, the building had been the site of Indian raids and patriot jailbreaks where their kinsmen were freed from the British. Its patina of age and history made it imposing, even for its small size.

The process set out by the 1850 revision of the 1793 Fugitive Slave Act gave financial incentives to slave catchers or anyone who might help capture and return enslaved people. Bringing the alleged escapee in front of the court paid ten dollars if the captive was confirmed enslaved, in addition to the bounty paid by the owner. If the captive was a freeman, the captors would still receive five dollars. This created a brisk business for slave catchers, leading to horrific consequences for black people across the North. Judges also were enriched for handling these cases: five dollars for a case and ten more if the hearing resulted in the return of the enslaved to the claimant. Hunting fugitives on the Underground Railroad was a lucrative business for the morally bankrupt.

As they entered, Sergeant Gladwell rose from his desk. "Well, it seems we meet again, Mrs. McCoy. What can I help you with today?"

"Sergeant, I understand that perhaps Mrs. Bass's nursemaid has been brought in?" Anne inquired. Thomas stood behind her, waiting to be addressed but close enough that Anne felt safer and like she had an ally.

"Why yes, she arrived here this morning. She was just taken to the courthouse to go before Judge Kimmel," Sergeant Gladwell replied and then turned to Thomas. "Seems I just talked to you as well. Quite a week for you two. Has the president sent you both to retrieve the slave woman? She should be ready to go soon. The judge will be making orders and speaking with the men who found her now."

"Thank you, Sergeant. Yes, we are here for her!" Anne confirmed as she and Thomas hurried out the door.

Across the town square stood the stately Bedford Courthouse. Built in the federal style, the red brick structure had white trim, window casements, and two-story white columns. It was designed by the architect Solomon Filler, who also designed the Bedford Springs Colonial building. The similarities between the two elegant buildings struck Anne for the first time as she crossed the street and climbed the stone double staircase to the entry doors. The double door had two over three panes and a Palladian window that brought light into the broad entryway.

Once inside, Thomas and Anne raced up the staircase two steps at a time. The courthouse had another double interior staircase, bowed like grasping arms. The courtroom doors at the top of the stairs were open, and as they entered, they saw Judge Kimmel facing both Juba and the two slave catchers. The judge peered over his spectacles with challenging brown eyes. His gaze darted to the rear of the courtroom when he heard the commotion of Anne and Thomas reaching the top of the stairs and practically running inside.

"Can I help you? The court is in session," the judge demanded. The dozen or so other people in the courtroom all turned to gawk at them. The widow wasn't among them. Perhaps she wasn't coming. Perhaps it was a preliminary hearing, so she hadn't been summoned.

Anne stepped up to the aisle and raised her hand, holding the freedom papers. "I beg your pardon, Your Honor. I come with urgent information. This woman before you is Juba Wright, and she is a free woman with documents proving she was born in Boston to free parents."

"Come forward, young woman. This is highly irregular, and I can hold you in contempt for interrupting court," the judge scolded.

Anne was waved forward, and Thomas sat down in the back pew of the courtroom. Anne walked to the bench and nodded at Juba. There was a bandage on Juba's forehead, and blood seeped through it. She also held her left arm as if it was hurt. There was a deep burning in the pit of Anne's stomach. The physical damage to Juba was sickening. She must push thoughts of what those horrible men might have done to her out of her mind for the moment and tend to her as soon as she could.

She handed the judge the documents, and he took his time reading through them. Anne peered over at the slave catchers who she sensed were glaring at her. The shorter man had a grotesquely swollen split lip caked with dried blood. Did Juba inflict that? She hoped so.

"Miss Juba Wright, is that your name?" The judge turned to Juba.

"Yes, sir," Juba answered quietly, her eyes averted from him.

"You are the daughter of Thomas and Mary Wright of Boston?" he questioned. He sounded increasingly annoyed.

"Yes, sir. Those are my parents." This time Juba's answer was stronger.

"As I said, this is most irregular," the judge said, continuing to look through the papers. "I notice that these are certified by federal commissioner Johnson Hall in Philadelphia." He looked up and over his spectacles at Anne. "Where did you get these?" he demanded.

Anne didn't know what to say. Thomas had gotten them from Senator Cameron, but who knew where he had obtained them? She was scared to mention the senator. He had been clear that he didn't want to be identified.

Thomas stood in the back of the courtroom and interjected, "Your Honor, I received the papers."

The judge looked cross. He dropped the papers on his desk and looked back at Thomas. "And who might you be, young man? I could hold you in contempt for interrupting my session! Come forward!" he ordered. Anne was getting increasingly worried that they would all end up arrested. They had come so far to get Juba free. Would Thomas keep the senator out of it too?

Arriving at the bar, Thomas stood respectfully quiet.

"What is your name, and where did you get these papers?" the judge demanded.

"Your Honor, my name is Thomas Miller. The papers came from Philadelphia to the Bedford Springs, where I am a valet." Was that enough of an explanation? The judge looked at Thomas incredulously and said nothing. Anne's heart raced and she could see Juba looked unsteady. Surely the judge knew the president was in town, as well as many other dignitaries. Would he press further?

The judge scowled and continued, "I have no way of knowing if these are legitimate. The Fugitive Slave Act requires certification by a federal commissioner before I can free this woman and invalidate the owner's property rights. Take her back to her cell!" He hammered his gavel and turned to the bailiff.

Juba's knees began to give out, and Anne and Thomas moved to steady her. How could all be lost after all Juba had gone through? How would she get the care she needed so badly? It was not supposed to end like this.

"Excuse me, Your Honor." A deep and steady voice spoke from the back of the courtroom. All eyes turned that way to see who dared to interrupt this time.

Senator Cameron stood at the back of the courtroom, his hands resting on the last row of seats. He leaned forward and continued as Judge Kimmel's look of recognition seemed an unspoken invitation. "I procured those papers from Philadelphia and gave them to that young man for Miss Wright." He walked up the aisle in his light summer suit as calmly as if he were taking a walk across the lawn at the Springs. Anne was shocked and could see all the other bystanders were as well. All eyes watched him saunter forward.

He continued, arriving at the bar. "As a U.S. senator, and a representative of the Federal Government, I can vouch for the validity of these documents and their veracity in invalidating the Fugitive Slave Act as it applies to this fine woman, who was born free."

The judge cleared his throat and answered, "Senator Cameron, thank you for clarifying this issue and saving time and taxpayer dollars by avoiding the need for an extended trial." He turned to Juba. "You are a free woman. Now, please take leave of my courtroom so that I can move on to other matters." The judge handed Juba the papers.

Anne squeezed Juba's good arm. Was Juba standing a bit taller? She thought she could hear her exhale. What a miraculous day!

Turning to the two slave catchers, who had been watching the whole time with mouths agape, Judge Kimmel continued, "Mr. Crissman and Mr. Mock, I think perhaps that you are out of order here, presenting a free black woman to me. I hereby hold *you* in contempt. I am also appalled at the condition of this woman, who appears to have sustained recent injuries. I have several other warrants back in my office for your arrest on other matters. Allegations that you may be responsible for the shooting of Jacob McCoy, a Bedford man, were posted to me earlier this week for inquest. I must investigate these charges as well. Thank you for coming in for custody." All eyes went to the disheveled pair.

Could it be? Who had filed charges?

Chaos ensued. Crissman turned to flee, but the large and imposing bailiff standing to the side stepped out into the aisle and blocked his way, grabbing his arm.

Anne hugged Juba carefully. The women held each other, and she felt Juba's body shake as she broke down crying. As she held her close, sobs wracked Juba's thin frame and Anne felt burning tears running down her own cheeks. Thomas laid a gentle hand on both as if to silently steady them. The senator nodded to the three with a polite smile and Anne heard him quietly ask the judge to see him in his chambers.

Juba Wright was free and the men who should be in chains might finally have justice served to them. Yes, it was a miraculous day.

Juba, Anne, and Thomas walked outside to the town square in silence. The sun sank low toward Wills Mountain in the west. Thank goodness they had gotten to court on time. Juba looked exhausted, but she held herself straight, and there was a gleam of hope in her eyes.

Anne took the sash from her dress and helped fashion a temporary sling for her arm. Everything was so overwhelming that she wasn't sure what to say. What could one say after everything that had happened?

Thomas spoke up first. "With it getting late in the day, I think you should stay with Elias Rouse for the night before you head north. He can tend to your wounds as well, Juba. I think he has some information about your parents."

"Yes. I need some rest before I get on my way. I didn't sleep at all last night. They had me tied up on the back of one of their horses. My head and arm hurt so bad. I was scared to death of what would happen next," Juba said quietly.

Anne walked with her arm in arm to the horses.

Thomas, untying the reins, added, "The Pennsylvania Railroad is just north of here in Altoona, and then from there you can get to Philadelphia. From there they can send you on a train to Boston."

Juba took Anne's hand. "I need to tell you something, and you must act on it right away."

"What is it, Juba?" Anne asked. She heard the alarm in Juba's voice. What now?

"In my travels, I heard some talk about John Brown, the abolitionist, being in town recently. He is working on some kind of plans, and I think they might include trying to create national attention to ending slavery by kidnapping the president. People here do not want to be involved, but there may still be a plot. I am so worried for the Bass children, and I don't think putting the president's life in jeopardy is right," Juba blurted out rapidly, looking around her to ensure no one close to the public square overheard.

Thomas cut in. "We have to get this information to the president and his footmen right away so that they can put extra protection in place," he declared.

"Thank you, Juba. After all you've been through, thank you for thinking of everyone's safety," Anne said. "Thomas, you will take Juba to Elias, and I will ride back to the Springs to tell Miss Lane." Anne's heart was racing as she wondered how she was going to explain all that had happened to Miss Lane. She hoped she would believe her, as it was so incredible that she hardly believed herself what had occurred the last few days.

Anne hugged Juba, holding her close and whispering, "You are strong. You are free. Be well, friend, and help others be free in person and spirit. It is what we do." Stepping back, the two women looked deeply at each other. Soon, Juba's injuries would heal, and hopefully, her hope for her future would heal as well.

Anne quickly remembered she had something else for Juba. She pulled a small bundle out of her pocket and pressed it into Juba's hands. "Take this for your safe travels. It is help from another friend."

— 29 —

Harriet

Harriet had returned from dinner and was resting in her suite. She thought about writing to Lily but decided she was too upset and disquieted to put together a letter that made sense, even to her best friend. How could she set down her thoughts in a way that summed up all the different things she was thinking and feeling if she did not understand them herself? Sitting at her desk, she stared out the window at the greenery of the trees outside, which were rustling in the mountain breeze.

She owed her life to her uncle, who had taken her in and raised her as his own. What would have become of her had she not been taken care of by him? Her life would have been much smaller and contained almost assuredly within a hundred square miles around Lancaster and Mercersburg. Not to disparage anyone of a simpler life, but she was glad for all she had seen and experienced with her uncle. She had lived and learned so much, from the Midwest to across the Atlantic in Europe. Through all those travels, her uncle had been her protector and her biggest emotional support. He knew all her foibles and particularities, and she knew his.

What had come to Harriet in the last weeks at the Springs was that she was still learning. All that growth and seeing so many people and places had made her a woman who understood there were infinite ways to experience the world. People came from many stations, cultures, and races. Every person has a different life and perspective. Each was as valuable and noble as the next.

The mounting issues the question of slavery had raised for America were ripe for hard decisions. Harriet knew it but feared what that meant for the country and, personally, for her uncle. A small tap at the interior hallway door roused Harriet from her reverie.

"Yes, who is it?" she called out.

"It's Anne, Miss Lane. I am back from my uncle's farm, and I must speak with you right away."

"Anne! Come in."

Anne opened the door and came in, closing it behind her. She looked to Harriet every bit as if she had ridden all day. Her hair was coming loose from under her bonnet. It looked as if she had tried to push it up underneath, but tendrils of red hair were escaping haphazardly in all directions. Her pinstriped pinafore was dirty, and Harriet smelled sweat and horses as Anne came closer.

Anne dipped her knees in a curtsy. "Miss Lane, please excuse my unkempt appearance, but I have come with some important information that I must speak with you about right away for your safety."

"Goodness, Anne, what is it?"

"While I was out in Quaker Valley, I got the news there may be a plan to kidnap your uncle. The radical abolitionist John Brown has been in Bedford looking for accomplices before you arrived."

"Kidnapping the president is treason!" Harriet exclaimed. "Is there more information, Anne?"

"All I know is many local abolitionists who were approached refused. I don't know if the plot has any supporters."

"We must tell the authorities and immediately put my uncle under extra protection. Please ask Mr. Blackburn to call for local law support, and I will gather the auxiliary guards to put them on alert. Thank goodness nothing has occurred on our visit up to this point."

"Yes, miss. I came as soon as I could."

"Is your uncle all right, Anne?"

"I believe he is improving. I best hurry." Anne dipped her knees and hurried out the door.

It struck Harriet that Janie's escape, or Juba's, she corrected herself, may have created enough law presence and chaos to delay the kidnapping plans. They needed to get extra security in place before anything further developed. She owed a debt of gratitude to Anne for her message. The threat of violence would alter their stay at Bedford Springs immediately.

That night, Harriet could not stop thinking about the events of the past week. The news of John Brown and his plot to kidnap her uncle staggered her. She was glad for the extra lawmen with guns stationed about their rooms and on the hotel grounds but was still unable to sleep. She was also worried for Anne. Anne's part in the escape of Mrs. Bass's nursemaid was still on her mind as she lay, unable to sleep, in her bed, hours after Mr. Blackburn had sent another lady's maid who had helped her out of her corset and into her dressing down. The crickets outside her window were louder than usual. She got out of bed to look out the porch door, hoping that watching the fireflies rise off the lawn would be a comfort. Their tranquil beauty, sparkling on and off like tiny twinkling stars in the night, had been a favorite of hers since she was a small child.

Troubled and unable to go back to bed, she opened the porch door to step outside for the cool breeze coming over Constitution Hill. Further down the porch, she saw the lamps in her uncle's rooms were still lit. Retrieving her wrap, she padded down the painted porch boards, which were cool on the bottom of her bare feet. She tapped on the door and heard her uncle's chair slide back from his desk.

"What are you doing awake, my girl? You should sleep better than an old codger like me." Uncle Buck sighed as he opened the screen door for her to enter.

"I couldn't quiet my mind, but I saw your light was on. Isn't it late, Nunc?"

The president was still wearing his trousers and dress shirt, though his collar was undone, and he wore slippers. He lifted his pocket watch from its nesting place in his pants pocket. "It is past midnight. I've been working on a draft and have sent for Ben Meyers from the Bedford Gazette with an editorial I want him to publish as soon as possible."

Harriet raised her eyebrows in question. She was afraid of what her uncle might need to say at such a late hour, especially after the disquieting news about John Brown's plans. She sat down on the settee and looked up at him, giving him the cue to tell her what was on his mind that demanded immediate publication.

"Hal, I've decided I need to make it clear I am not going to run again. In my inaugural address, I promised to only sit for one term. The Pittsburgh Post-Gazette keeps speculating week after week that I will announce a second run and make myself a liar. I have nothing left to offer this nation. I have done my best. It has not been enough to quell the madness surrounding the question of slavery. It is not enough to implore the abolitionists to accept they are going to bring bloodshed and anarchy."

"Nunc, you have given this nation your whole life."

"Not all of it. Just all I have to give, and I am done. I will step aside and hope better men can make amends and keep this federal union from imploding."

It was hard to reconcile both her huge sense of relief and the heavy feeling in her heart for her uncle's loss. She sat for a few moments and watched him read over the draft he had been working on. She held off saying anything as silence seemed, for the moment, to be the best support she could offer.

Running his hands through his tousled hair and furrowing his brow, he finally turned to Harriet and read aloud. *"I am issuing my final and irrevocable determination to retire,"* he read from the paper in his hand.

Harriet nodded and looked deeply into her uncle's eyes. "If that is what's best for you and this country, Uncle, then I will always support you. I do hope you won't disclose what we've learned about John Brown's intentions."

"Certainly not. That would only serve to further his causes and make people more aware of his activism. My resolve not to seek a second term has nothing to do with that madman. I will not be bullied."

A knock at the door broke their moment of quiet counsel. Uncle Buck got up and opened the door to the interior hallway. One of the armed guards stood outside.

"Yes, what is it?" the president queried.

"Mr. President, Benjamin Meyers is here to see you. He says you sent a carriage for him," answered the guard.

"I did. Please send him up."

Several minutes later, after another knock, Benjamin Meyers was presented at the door.

"Come in, come in, Ben. Thank you for coming at such a late hour," said Buchanan.

"Yes, sir, of course. I thought the driver was joking, but he made it very clear you wanted me to come, no matter the hour. I am grateful to be called by the president. How can I be of service?" Mr. Meyers replied as he stepped into the room. He was a middle-aged man with dark hair and a rumpled shirt that looked like he had grabbed it off a chair and thrown it on after being awakened.

Seeing Harriet on the settee, he nodded. "Good, ah, morning to you, Miss Lane."

"Good morning to you, Mr. Meyers. Thank you for coming at such short notice," Harriet returned.

The president stood from his seat at his desk. "Ben, the Gazette has always been a friend to me. I am sure you know George Bowman, the editor before you, has gone on to greater things in Washington as the printer for the House, Senate, and my Cabinet. I appreciate that the Democratic voice is strong here in Bedford. I don't know if you read yesterday's Post-Gazette, but they want to paint me as a liar, saying I have plans to run again next year. I need to make it clear I plan to retire to Wheatland when my duty to this nation as president is done." With that, he handed the paper in his hand to Mr. Meyers.

Meyers read through the draft and, when he finished, looked at Harriet and then back to the president. "Is this what you wish me to print, sir?"

"Yes, I want you to print it as I have written it. I want it in tomorrow's paper, and I want you to send it out to Pittsburgh, Harrisburg, and Philadelphia. It will spread from here at home in Pennsylvania and make my intentions clear."

"I'm sorry about your retirement, sir, but I appreciate your confidence in allowing me to be the first to publish your words on this matter," Meyers said quietly.

Harriet spoke up. "Mr. Meyers, Bedford has been our summer home for many years. Her pristine beauty and verdant tranquility have given my uncle an indispensable haven to rest and recover from his duties in the nation's highest office. The Bedford Gazette, as the Democratic paper, has been of great support and we thank you. Unfortunately, the past fortnight has proven even the healing waters and this remote location away from the capital cannot keep the president's difficulties at bay. The floodwaters of national unrest are poisoning even Shober's Run. We will be leaving Bedford sooner than usual and heading back to Washington."

— 30 —

Juba

Juba sat in the backyard of Mr. William Nesbit's house in Altoona, Pennsylvania. It had been an exhausting week. Though she was helping William's wife, Sarah, boil the laundry, she was able to sit down briefly under the shade of a maple tree and catch a few moments to reflect on the recent events. She wiped her brow with her sleeve and took a deep breath of fresh, cool air away from the boiling wash kettle. She was relieved her arm was feeling better, and she could take off the sling she had been wearing. The wound on her forehead still ached. Would she always have a scar there to remind her of those awful men? She would put all those dreadful thoughts, along with the memories of the disgusting overseer, into a box out of reach of her thoughts and feelings.

Thomas Miller had taken her from the courthouse to Elias Rouse's care. Mr. Rouse had worked out a route for Juba to get north to the Altoona station of the Pennsylvania Railroad for travel to her parents in Boston. When she got there, he had a letter from her mother waiting for her.

Her head spun with the excitement of seeing her parents. In her heart, she had already mourned their loss and accepted that she would never see them again. Now, she was on her way to her momma and pappa. It did not seem real yet. Juba had read the letter from her mother dozens of times in the last week.

Her first stop outside Bedford was north to a place called Sproul with Mr. Madera, an ironmaster's foreman who was also an outspoken abolitionist. Mr. Madera was a stoic and quiet man who didn't smile much or have any humor, but he and his wife Jane had kept her overnight in their home, making her comfortable and welcome. She had not gone to sleep in a real bed with a coverlet since leaving the Springs. She slept so deeply in her new safety that she woke with a start, dizzy from sleep. Juba had looked out the window to remind herself where she was. Rolling hills and cows grazing showed her she was safe on the Madera farm.

After the night at Sproul, Mr. Madera took her to Sidney Carr's barbershop in Hollidaysburg. This was another step north, closer to Altoona. Mr. Carr was quite a character and recounted for her many stories of the fugitives he had helped over the years.

He was especially animated when he told the story of Jacob Green. Five years earlier, Green, a fugitive of Virginia, was pursued by a man named Parsons. Green boarded a train near Hollidaysburg, but Parsons was closing in, boarding the same train. Green jumped off, recognizing his pursuer, who got off as well. A General Potts of Altoona witnessed the chase and intervened, telling Parsons he must take Green to the magistrate and adjudicate the matter as per Pennsylvania law. The altercation gathered momentum, and more locals joined. Many black citizens arrived, including Sidney Carr.

Sidney laughed with glee and excitement as he told Juba how, in the confusion and growing crowd, he was able to grab Green by the arm and spirit him away to Chimney Ridge. Up on the ridge was a group of black free people's homes, where Green could hide for several days. He was then conducted north to Canada. Sidney took great joy in finishing the story.

In the end, Parsons filed a suit against General Potts for resisting the Fugitive Slave Act. The general, in return, issued a warrant for Parsons for kidnapping. In court, Parsons' lawyers asked for all charges to be dropped on both sides due to the violent and unseemly behavior of his client, as reported by the witnesses.

Juba reflected on the stories she heard along her trip as she sat by the boiling wash. It was a relief not to be on the run. And there were things she was still sorting out in her mind. For many years, she had understood the northern states were a destination for freedom. Now, it was plain to her that the Mason-Dixon line was not a clear boundary on the map that changed everything upon stepping over it. It seemed, at least in Southern Pennsylvania, there were hateful as well as loving people. There was fear as well as freedom for black people.

Her newfound habit, when she thought too much about the things that gave her terrible nightmares, was to pull her mother's letter from her pocket. Though it was starting to be a bit dog-eared and worn at the edges, the letter brought her comfort. As she unfolded the letter to read it again, Sarah Nesbit came out from the back of the house with her small son on her hip. She sat down next to Juba in a second chair, resting the boy on her knee and bouncing him to keep him content.

"I saw you take that paper out your pocket a bunch o' times. What you got there, Juba?"

Juba liked Sarah very much. They were the same age, and Sarah's open and friendly manner made her comfortable sharing her thoughts.

"It's a letter from my momma. Elias Rouse and abolitionists in Bedford were able to track down my parents in Boston, thank God," Juba explained.

"How is your momma doing? She must be over the moon you are headed home. How long since you have seen your parents?"

"Ten years. Seems a whole lifetime."

"What did your momma say in the letter, if you don't mind my asking?" Sarah asked.

Juba read the letter to Sarah.

Mary Wright
156 Belknap Street
North Slope/Beacon Hill
Boston, Massachusetts
July 20th, 1859

Dear Juba,

God is surely wondrous and delivers miracles to us every day. When I got word from Mr. Hayden, one of our black community leaders, that the office of Senator Cameron of Pennsylvania had contacted him and you had been found, I knew a miracle had occurred.

Your pappa and I live in North Slope, near Beacon Hill, in Boston. We are told you are headed this way and may arrive by train as early as August 5th. Lord be praised.

*We are both as well as can be expected. We pray with all our
hearts you are as well after all you must have been through. I will
await the day when I can put my arms around my precious baby
girl again. We have so much lost time to make up for. Your loving
family is waiting for you.*
    I love you dearly,
    Momma

She looked up from the letter at Sarah, who, midway through the
reading, had placed her hand on Juba's knee. Sarah had stopped bouncing her little boy, holding him tightly with one arm as if imagining the
loss of *her* child as she listened to the letter.

"Juba, we're going to take you to the train station tomorrow, and
you're going to be putting your arms around your momma in no time,"
Sarah said quietly, squeezing Juba's knee. Juba hardly believed it herself,
but after hearing her mother's words and Sarah's, she was starting to
believe it was true.

———◆——◆——◆———

The last time she was on a train, Juba had watched the gently rolling
hills and broad open fields of Maryland pass her by. She had seen black
people bent over tending to crops in those fields and had known they
were slaves laboring in bondage. After taking the Pennsylvania Railroad
out of Altoona, she changed trains in Philadelphia and then New York.
Juba had left New York on the New Haven Harford Railroad, heading north to Boston. On this trip, she noted small towns with white
clapboard churches and farmsteads interspersed between rocky, green
wooded ridges. She saw black and white people working with mules and
horse-driven plows in the fields. She sat in a railcar with other black
people and some poor whites.

As she sat on the last leg of her rail journey on the Albany Railroad,
she noted the seats were old and worn but much better than the benches
of southern railcars for similar passengers. She rooted through the travel
bag Elias Rouse had gifted her, which held some personal items and a
nightgown collected from other ladies from the Zion Church in Bedford.

Her thoughts drifted to Anne. Had she gotten in trouble for helping
her? Lord help her good heart. Did Miss Lane know what Anne had

done? Hopefully, Anne had reached Miss Lane in time to give the president's party a chance to avoid the kidnapping plot.

As she searched in the bag for her new comb, she came across the small bundle Anne had given her. She had been getting by with some coins, a few paper bills, and her free papers wrapped and tied in a hand towel from Bedford Springs but had forgotten about the tiny parcel.

She struggled to untie the ribbon that bound the yellowed linen handkerchief but finally was able to untie the knot after picking at it for a bit. She heard some coins jingle. Coins were a good thing! Opening the bundle, she was astonished to find several gold coins inside. There were five one-dollar Indian heads and three larger twenty-dollar gold coins, with the head of Lady Liberty on one side and the eagle seal of the United States on the other. She quickly put the coins into her bag so people around her wouldn't see how much she carried.

Anne couldn't possibly have that much coinage to give. She pressed the hanky out on her lap to look at it, smoothing it with her shaking hands. She noticed on the back there was some embroidery in one corner. Turning the linen over, she could see the letters "HRL" were carefully stitched in gold thread. The hanky was from Miss Lane. "Help from another friend," Anne had said. Juba smiled in wonder and tucked the hanky into her bag like a precious treasure.

It was hard to sit still for the next few hours as the rural views gave way to more densely populated areas as they approached Boston. Mr. Nesbit said he would send a message from the telegraph office the day she left, letting her parents know of her arrival date in Boston on the Albany Railroad afternoon train. Would her parents be able to greet her at the station? They probably had to work and would not have the freedom to be there. She had so many questions about their lives and how they had fared over the last ten years. Did they have other children now?

As the train pulled into Boston, Juba and the other passengers began to move around and ready themselves for the end of the journey. Children cried as they were awakened from naps, and the woman in the next seat started talking to everyone around her about her excitement at seeing her son in Boston after years apart. Juba clutched her bag to her chest, her heart racing with expectation, and felt a flush of panic. How would she find her way to her parents' address if they weren't at the station?

She had come through so much worse; she would figure it out.

The station was chaos. When she traveled with Mrs. Bass to Washington, luxury afforded easier travel, and everything was taken care of by servants or other slaves. She stepped off the train and headed down the iron stairs, clutching her bag. The last thing she needed was to have her things stolen in the crush of the city, especially now she had her freedom papers and the gold coins.

As she walked along the platform, she spotted a sign for the main terminal and followed the line of passengers moving in that direction. She would need to climb a covered staircase over the tracks. Whistles for other trains were blowing, and a haze of sooty smoke was in the air.

So many faces were streaming by. People of every size and color were crushed together, and the acrid smell and clouds of coal smoke hung in the air, making everything look a bit murky. Heart beating hard and fast in her chest, she looked around frantically for her parents. Her memory of their faces was as if another mist hung in her mind. Ten years had passed. What if she didn't recognize them? She was a woman now. What if they didn't recognize her?

As she exited the tunnel that crossed the tracks and found the iron gates marking the entrance to the train station, she felt like she was seeing a ghost. Or an angel. Maybe her mind was making things up. A small, plump black woman with her mother's face stood behind the gates. The woman's hair had a streak of gray, and she had circles under her eyes, but it was the face of her momma.

Their eyes met, and Juba tried to press through all the travelers but couldn't run like she wanted to because everyone was crowded together. *There she is! I must get to her.* Momma was waving and staying in place rather than fighting against the pressing crowd. The smile on her face was like sunlight beaming through the gray dusty air.

Juba finally reached her. "Momma!" she exclaimed as she threw her arms around her.

"Baby girl!" her mother whispered so quietly only Juba heard her awe and relief as her strong arms wrapped around her.

Juba breathed in her mother's warm scent. Could you smell love and safety? She had dreamed of that perfume in her worst moments for the past ten years.

"Baby girl," her mother repeated as they held each other tight, and the world streamed by.

— 31 —

Anne

Anne had to weave her way through the interior hallway of the second floor of the Evitt building as it was littered with steamer trunks, baskets, and crates. She was trying to hurry along as she had arrived later than usual. Miss Lane had told her to catch up on her rest and not bother to come before breakfast. Anne was grateful as she felt stiff and sore from her day on horseback. The walk over Federal Hill hadn't been easy, but she was the better for it.

As she was passing the president's suite, she caught sight of Thomas carrying a trunk out into the hall.

He tipped his head to her, smiling broadly. "Hello, Anne. I hoped I would see you. How are you faring today after all the chaos of the past few days?"

"I'm all right, Thomas. I was relieved to go home for the evening and get some rest," Anne answered.

Thomas, quite tall, leaned lower to whisper to Anne. "I presume you were able to share what Juba told you about the kidnapping plot with Miss Lane? I noticed there are extra guards stationed everywhere, and their departure is sudden and almost a week early."

"Yes, Miss Lane was grateful for the alert. The information must have changed their plans. God only knows what John Brown will do, Thomas," Anne replied.

He smiled shyly at Anne and picked up an empty crate. "I've got my work cut out for me today. Anyway, I'm so glad you're safe."

"Thank you, Thomas. I must be on my way to help Miss Lane in her packing." She tipped her head, smiled back, and hurried down the hall.

She found Harriet surrounded by dresses laid over couches and chairs. Her personal kit of brushes and perfume bottles was gathered in a cluster on her dresser. In her absence, Anne saw that Miss Lane had started packing for herself.

"Anne! I am so glad you're here! I do hope that you got some rest. I fear I am making a mess of gathering my things for the trunks. Please help me put my clothing in order and pack everything. We leave at noon by stage to make it to Cumberland to catch the evening train for Washington."

"Yes, Miss Harriet. I'll be sorry to watch you go, but I'm anxious for your safety," Anne replied, picking up dresses on her arm to fold into trunks.

They were quiet for a few minutes, both busy gathering, folding, and loading the trunks. Miss Lane broke the silence. "Anne, I've given you the highest recommendation to Mr. Blackburn, and he returned the compliment by letting me know that he will be assigning you to another woman who is due to arrive next week."

"Thank you, Miss Harriet. Your praise means so much to me. I am grateful your good report has earned me more work, which I need to support my family."

"Anne, I will miss your quiet company and able service. I know you have responsibilities here in Bedford, but after you put things in order over the next weeks, I would love for you to come work for me down in the capital. Is that something you would consider? I would pay you handsomely. Wages down in the city are higher than up here in Bedford, and there is an opportunity for your family to make a new life with more stability. It could be exciting to serve at the Executive Mansion."

Anne paused. What an honor for Miss Lane to desire her continued service. It was tempting, but she loved her home and quiet life in Bedford. Leaving would be like starting a new life. She didn't want a new life, but she didn't want to disappoint Miss Lane, either.

Continuing to fold dresses to keep her hands busy, she replied, "The offer is so kind of you, miss. Respectfully, my place is here in Bedford. My family needs me, and there is a lot of work to be done here." Miss Lane was gazing steadily at her. Their eyes met, and her lady regarded her deeply. They both nodded. It seemed Miss Harriet understood Anne's work could be more than work at the Springs or on her farm. Somehow, they had found common respect for each other even with their very different stations in life.

A few hours later, the housemen had carted away all the trunks and boxes to load into the carriages. Anne had helped her lady get dressed for travel and did her hair for the last time. Anne answered a knock at the door and found Thomas smiling down at her.

"The stagecoaches are ready, Miss Lane. The president asked me to come and let you know it's time to leave," he alerted the women from the threshold.

"Thank you, Thomas. I will be along momentarily," Harriet answered.

Thomas left, and Anne shut the door. Miss Harriet gathered a small bag and her shawl. She peered into the mirror of her dressing table, and Anne brought her travel bonnet, which the lady took and tied under her chin over her golden hair. Anne had put it in braids and pinned it, much the way she had seen her lady wear it on the day she arrived weeks before. Harriet looked at Anne in the mirror for a moment and then turned to embrace her.

Anne breathed in her fine perfume and felt her warmth. It made Anne's heart warm as well. Harriet stepped back and regarded her for a moment.

"I hope you won't find it strange of me to say, Anne, but I care for you very much. I feel somehow we are kindred spirits. I want you to understand that I have grown from your spirit and respect your integrity and honesty. Please write to me if you change your mind about Washington. I expect, if you are available, we can have next summer and other summers here in Bedford together. I will insist on it to Mr. Blackburn."

"Yes, miss. You will find me here, and I will look forward to the opportunity." Anne smiled freely back at Miss Lane and felt her face flush, thinking, *This fine lady with a fine heart will be in my life and future in some way.*

At noontime, Anne, Thomas, and the rest of the Springs staff saw the presidential travel party off from the grand portico with Mr. Blackburn at the head orchestrating the send-off. Anne returned to finish cleaning up Miss Harriet's suite, stripping the linens, sweeping the floors, and giving the wood furniture a new sheen of linseed oil polish. With the windows of the room open and the mountain breeze coming through, she thought about the early spring when all was new and fresh at the Springs and everything that had occurred since then. It seemed like a year ago rather than several weeks. She felt like another person altogether. Her daily sadness over Jacob's loss was starting to soften into something akin to the need to honor him with how she lived each day. She had a strong feeling that he was with her still and always would be. She was proud of herself for being strong and was sure he would be proud of her, too.

As she walked home that evening, the coins Mr. Blackburn had paid her jingled in her apron. The first payment for the taxes would be made tomorrow, and hopefully, she would begin her next assignment and be on track to have the rest by the September deadline. She may need to sell one of her goats, but the farm would be safe for now. School would start by the time she finished at the Springs, and this year, she would inquire about finding work as a teacher or tutor at the new normal school on Juliana Street.

As she descended Federal Hill toward her farm, so many thoughts swirled through her mind. What about Harriet's offer to go to Washington? She loved the beautiful green forest around her, and as Anne reached the border of her land she could see Agnes and Joshua below near the house in the dooryard feeding the hens. The field below the house was turning gold from the summer sun, and a few cows grazed at the neighbor's field on the other side of the creek. The summer heat had dried up most of the flow, but there was enough to create a glint of evening sunlight over the bubbling water and smooth rocks that lay on the bottom. There was no way she would ever leave Bedford. She loved her family and her farm and would find a way to make it all work.

Joshua saw her approaching and ran to meet her. She gathered him up in her arms.

"How is my boy?" she asked him as he wiggled against her.

"Mamma, you're back!" He buried his head between her neck and shoulder.

"I am! Have you been good today for your grandmother?"

"Most of the time," he replied as she laughed and set him down.

Agnes opened the gate for them, and they met her in the yard. "He is wearing me thin with all his questions, Anne. It's your turn to take over answering." She sounded cross but gave a smile. Anne knew she was all right. "Did the president leave today? We heard coronets through the valley about noontime from over Federal Hill."

"Yes, they are headed to Cumberland and back to Washington. Hopefully, with all the auxiliary guards, they will be safe and have spoiled John Brown's dangerous plans."

Walking back into the house, Anne took off her bonnet and tousled her hair to shake it out. It felt good to relax and be home. As she entered the room, she saw a large pitcher full of bright yellow black-eyed Susans, blue chicory, and white Queen Anne's lace sitting in the center of the table.

Agnes entered the room, and Anne asked, "Were you and Joshua out picking flowers today? That is quite a bouquet; it must have taken you both a while to gather them."

"No, it wasn't our doing. I was going to mention it to you. Thomas Miller was here not too long before you came home. He brought the flowers." Agnes smiled.

Anne didn't know what to say. It was awkward to show pleasure in the gesture in front of her mother-in-law.

Agnes added, "He has grown up so much since I last saw him out in Quaker Valley at Meeting with his uncle. I remember you two were friends at school. He has a warm smile that makes his eyes shine."

"Yes, and like I mentioned yesterday evening, he helped me find Juba," Anne answered, still feeling embarrassed.

"He left a note for you." Agnes picked up an envelope off the table and handed it to her.

Anne noticed it was the Bedford Springs stationery. She opened it and read the brief note. Agnes walked away and Anne was grateful for the privacy. She should say something of the letter to her mother-in-law, but it felt a bit strange.

"He asks if we might ride out to a First Day Meeting in the valley sometime when we both have a Sunday off."

"That sounds like a grand idea," Agnes said, stepping up to Anne with a smile, she patted her hand that rested on the table.

"Yes, I think so too." Anne smiled as she tucked the note back into the envelope and her pocket.

— 82 —

Harriet

Waiting for Lily to arrive was difficult. Harriet bustled around her rooms at the Executive Mansion, waiting for word that the coach had arrived from the train station carrying her best friend. It seemed like ages since she had been in Lily's calming presence, and Harriet had so much on her mind that she could only discuss with Lily. She knew from experience that she would say things in their conversation that she could not fully verbalize to herself. Their kind of friendship, full of sharing and truth-telling, was what made her love and value Lily so dearly.

Finally, Harriet could not stand her own company from anxious impatience and decided to go down to her new greenhouse off the west terrace. Constructed of wood and glass, the greenhouse was quite warm in late August, but the bright sunlight on the greenery and the heady scent of flowers gave her some diversion and peace. After reviewing the last few weeks, she still had many questions and worrisome thoughts. Slipping on some cotton gardening gloves, she hoped the rich smell of dirt and making a small arrangement of begonias for her sitting room would focus her racing mind.

As she filled around the lovely lacelike pink flowers with soil, the clay pot slipped off the potting bench and crashed to the wooden floor. How was she so clumsy? Nothing was right with her. Even her time with flowers couldn't go smoothly. She bent down in frustration, struggling with her tight girdle as she tried to pick up the broken shards. Dipping her knees instead, she cleaned up the mess, but felt anger and sadness welling up inside her. Harriet's pent-up frustration poured out. Hot tears streamed down her face, already damp with the heat of the greenhouse.

She was below the level of the potting table, and the gardener was out on the grounds; at least there was privacy to cry. Frustration from the pressure of the growing turmoil of her uncle's presidency and her inability to change that for him or protect him from scathing press and political attacks took its toll.

The housemen's bell rang toward the front of the house, and she quickly stood, wiping her tears from her cheeks with her sleeve. She placed the pot shards on the bench and took off her garden gloves. It would most certainly be the bell announcing Lily's coach. She shook her skirts of any loose dirt and ran her hands over her hair to smooth any errant strands, then headed for the main house to greet her best friend.

Lily directed the men unloading her trunks and bags as Harriet arrived on the front steps. The circular gravel driveway of the mansion was used only for official guests. Still, Harriet asked the footmen to give Lily the respect of arrival as her most important visitor. The bronze statue of Thomas Jefferson in the grass circle out front looked on in stately approval as Harriet gave Lily a warm, welcoming hug.

"Thank God you're finally here," exclaimed Harriet as they embraced.

"Yes, thank goodness indeed, my dear! I thought I would melt from the insufferable heat on the train, and the carriage ride wasn't much better!" Lily replied.

"Come, let's leave the porters to carry your things up to your room. You're in the west wing in your usual room near mine. They know where to take your things," Harriet said, motioning toward the men carrying Lily's trunks and then grabbing Lily's hand to pull her up the entrance stairs.

"My dear, you are awfully anxious. May I change out of my travel clothes and take off my hat before we catch up? Surely you can wait a few more minutes so I won't be distracted by the perspiration which has soaked my person through and through," Lily said.

"Oh yes, Lily, I'm sorry. I have so much I need to talk with you about. Forgive me for being rude and not considering your comfort. I am a poor hostess."

"You can make it up to me by telling me how glorious I look in my new hat and travel dress," Lily quipped.

"Gorgeous as always," Harriet responded with a chuckle at her friend's humor.

Harriet walked Lily to her room, leaving her to freshen herself, and asked her to rejoin her in the sitting room down the hall when she was ready. In the meantime, Harriet called for one of the housekeepers to bring them some lemonade and tea cakes. Lily found Harriet perched on a lounge chair, reading through some letters as she entered, but Harriet dropped them on a side table immediately upon catching sight of her friend.

"I have read this letter twice and have nothing to show for it except the knowledge that it's from Mary Black, thanking me for the time we shared in Bedford last month. I can barely think, Lily, for all that is burdening my mind," Harriet stated, exasperated.

"Do tell, Hattie. What is bothering you so? It's been pressing down on me from hundreds of miles away for weeks, and as I traveled closer, it's been heavier than the oppressive Washington air." Lily sat down on the lounge closest to Harriet.

She was heartened to hear her friend's term of endearment for her: *Hattie*. She collected her thoughts. Where to start?

"This summer has been a cesspool in Washington, and the fetid pollution of politics followed us to Bedford. I got some rest and fresh air, but by the end of the trip, I was exhausted from the intrigues that found us in Bedford." Harriet stood from the bench and began to pace around the gilt furniture.

"Well, I guessed as much from your letters. And you left early, but I didn't get a chance to learn why. You didn't say in your last letter anything about coming back sooner."

"I couldn't put it in writing in case my letter got into the wrong hands. We learned that John Brown may have been forming a kidnapping plot, taking advantage of our vulnerability in Bedford. We left as soon as we caught wind of the potential plot. My lady, Anne, the Quaker woman I told you about, brought the danger to my attention. We are so grateful!"

"Kidnapping! Oh, Harriet, I have always feared for you and Buck in your notoriety. That is horrifying. John Brown is a madman!"

"Lily, the issue of slavery is bringing disaster to this country."

"What of Mrs. Bass's nursemaid? I am glad for the woman. I have to say the abolitionists in Philadelphia would be proud of their Bedford brethren. I trust you did your best to support Anne?"

"Juba is her name, actually, it was changed when she was enslaved! I don't know for sure where she is, but I believe she is safe and free. I did what I was able without drawing any attention. The woman was stolen as a child from her free parents! I had no idea that happened to people! Why don't we know that these things are happening?" Harriet paced the room and pulled at a hanky between her hands before she went on, "Can you imagine? Can you imagine all these years of her life taken from her and her family? It breaks my heart." Harriet paused, and both women sat quietly for a moment.

"I can't believe it either. I also had no idea that free black people were being stolen off the street. I had no idea that kind of horror was happening up in the North. I am so glad that you are listening to your heart. I am proud of you, dear friend." Lily smiled at her and they both sat in thought for a moment.

Lily broke the silence in a whisper. "I know you, though. You felt disloyal, didn't you?"

"It is right for her to be free. Even if she wasn't born to freedom, all should be free. I can't stop thinking about these laws and institutions my uncle keeps beating his fist about. They are wrong. How can one man do these things to another? The enslaved are people. They cry for their lost parents, and they cry for their mistreatment. They howl for the freedom that lives in their hearts, just like it does ours. We fought for freedom from British oppression only to oppress others?" Harriet began to cry and was unable to talk.

"What changed for you, Harriet?" Lily asked. They both sat quietly again until Harriet collected her thoughts.

"I held her hand while she cried. Anne risked her future and her family to help the other woman. That made me wonder what was wrong with me. Why didn't I see it more clearly before? These are people no different than us. Juba opened my eyes to this. I am so grateful that I met her. I didn't become her friend, per se, but she made me realize that I must no longer be complicit in accepting slavery as a political problem." Tears flowed freely down Harriet's cheeks again. "These tears are coming now because I see everything so clearly. I should have understood all this before. It took this experience to make me see and really understand."

"Did you tell your uncle?" Lily reached her hand over to Harriet's. Harriet read the worry on her friend's face. Lily loved Uncle Buck like her own and understood he was like a father to Harriet. He was everything to Harriet. She still didn't know how she could be honest with him. She was too afraid he would see her assistance to Anne and Juba as a violation of his trust.

"No. I couldn't. I tried to have a conversation with him on several occasions about slavery, but he couldn't separate the politics from the people. I guess the Union and Constitution come first at the cost of humanity." She heard her own words and felt a huge loss. She had looked up to him her whole life, and now she could see he was far from perfect. The larger-than-life man who had been the central figure in her young life was flawed.

"What's next?" Lily asked quietly.

"He's already decided not to run again. You read it in the Inquirer, surely?"

"Yes, I did. It made Father and me quite sad. We hoped he would change his mind."

"Don't be sad! Oh, Lily. He can't work through this." She paused to collect herself and then continued, "He thinks there will be bloodshed with secession, but there is blood on all of our hands while people are enslaved. Perhaps the next Democrat or these new Republicans can get the nation sorted out. My uncle has tried his best. I love him, but I can't agree with him. I can't ignore any longer what I feel is right in my soul. We must have hope. Slavery must end."

Lily got up and walked to the west-facing windows overlooking the top of the greenhouse. Harriet watched silently, the sticky tears on her cheeks drying and tightening her face.

"I am sure many good works will come from your heart, Harriet Lane." Lily turned and smiled at her friend from across the room.

"I haven't really done anything but been a loyal niece and able host-ess. There is so much more I need to do."

— 33 —

Juba

It was a long day for Juba. She had started the day by lighting the laundry cauldrons at four in the morning and ended it after dinner was served and cleaned up at Mrs. Hayden's boarding house on Southac Street. The days were getting shorter at the end of November. It was good working for Mrs. Harriet Bell Hayden because of her employer's work as a waystation and safe house for black people fleeing north. Some were heading on to Canada, and some would filter into Boston life and take their chances staying on in the American north. Mrs. Hayden had been a slave herself and took a leadership role in the black community in the North Slope neighborhood, advocating for black people and working with abolitionists, both black and white. Juba remembered Anne's words when they parted: "*Help others. It's what we do.*"

Three months into living in Boston, it was a relief to have found work, and the long, hard days doing housework in the boarding house kept her busy and with some money coming in. She was full-hearted, helping the people who stayed there, hearing their hope and gratitude. She had felt the same since she had met good people like Anne, Reverend Fidler, and Elias Rouse in Bedford.

She planned to stay with Mrs. Hayden for a few months while looking for a position where she could use her reading and writing skills. Her mother sometimes was able to take on tutoring to supplement her regular pay as a cook, and perhaps she would be able to find something similar. Still, most black people could usually only obtain manual labor jobs, even in Boston.

She was relearning the community after being gone for so many years. The North Slope of Beacon Hill was a congenial, predominantly black neighborhood with older brick homes. She figured about half to be boarding houses, which made the big mansions that had once been inhabited by whites more affordable for the black families who managed to buy them. It also created a way for black women to make a living, as they were the managers, making sure the laundry was done, providing three meals a day, and keeping a firm hand on the order in the house. In the meantime, their husbands would go out and find day labor around town or at the docks or work as servants in the white neighborhoods.

Mrs. Hayden's husband had prospered and owned a clothing store. Lewis Hayden was active in the abolitionist movement and was a leader advocating for black people's rights.

It was shocking when Mrs. Hayden reported that John Brown had stayed at the boarding house earlier in the year. The neighborhood was gripped by news of John Brown's disastrous raid on Harpers Ferry, Virginia. In mid-October, John Brown and twenty-two others had seized the federal arsenal. They had hoped to take the weapons and incite a massive slave revolt to force emancipation. It was not well plotted, and ten of the men were killed, two of Brown's sons among them. Five, including Brown, had been captured and were standing trial for treason.

Newspapers ran daily stories of the proceedings, and Mrs. Hayden was proud to tell Juba she had lodged such a strong supporter of black people. She declared she was devastated that he was in the middle of a fight for his life. Mrs. Hayden told Juba she had never met a white man so passionate about helping black people and ending slavery. His staying in the black-owned boarding house made it clear to Mrs. Hayden that he wasn't just another white abolitionist who talked but didn't act. In her opinion, Brown believed in and acted as if blacks and whites were equals.

Juba had thought about telling Mrs. Hayden about John Brown coming to Bedford, where she had escaped from, and plotting to kidnap the president. She thought long and hard about Harpers Ferry and how many of the men with Mr. Brown were now dead. What if the Bass children were listed among John Brown's casualties? She admired his passion for helping black people, but the gentle Quakers who had helped her did so without violence. Their commitment to peace, service, and integrity seemed a better way. She decided it was all right to keep quiet about what she might know about John Brown.

Walking toward her family's room on Belknap Street in the near dark, she was tired to the bone, but on her walk home each night, she made a point to end her day by remembering to be grateful for her freedom. She had little money in her pocket but enough to pick up something at the market if she needed it, and she had the liberty to go home in peace. Hopefully her mother would be there when she arrived.

The boarding house was three stories tall, and their rooms were at the top. As she climbed the wooden stairs, there was the sound of low voices between the families in the other parts of the house and the leftover comforting aroma of what had been for dinner. Ham and beans, perhaps? Whatever it was, it smelled like home and love. Though she had already eaten at Mrs. Hayden's dinner after serving, she was filled again and gave a sigh of relief.

"You're later than usual today, Juba," her mother said as she stepped into their main room.

"We had more guests tonight than usual for dinner. That took a while to clean up." Juba sighed.

"I got the mail from the post office. You have a letter. Looks like it's from Mr. Rouse." Her mother nodded toward the table.

Juba picked up the post. Indeed, the sender's name was listed as E. Rouse, but oddly, the return address was Canadian. Carefully, she opened the envelope so that she wouldn't smear or rip the return address.

Elias Rouse
Post Office
London, ON Canada
November 15, 1859

Miss Juba,

I hope this letter finds you well in Boston with your parents. Are you settling in, and have you found work? After you left Bedford, the president departed quickly with Miss Lane. I have not seen Miss Anne since Thomas Miller brought you to my shop with your free papers. I am glad to know her and Thomas. They are fine people.

These are crazy times for folks, both black and white. Surely, in Boston, you have read the news stories about John Brown's

misfortunes in Harpers Ferry. This year has been a difficult one. I
was so relieved we moved you out of Bedford and north before the
whole Mason and Dixon area exploded like a rifle blast.

During the ongoing trial for John Brown's crimes, the federal
authorities seized his letters from his wife. In that correspondence,
he mentioned many men throughout New York, Pennsylvania,
and Maryland whom she could turn to for help if he went
missing or was arrested. I was one of those men, along with Rev
John Fidler and Joseph Crawley.

John Brown came to Bedford and visited the Springs as
"John Smith" early in June. Though the others and I felt his plans
were too risky, we have been associated with him. That was too
close for comfort for me, so I closed my barbershop and took my
wife, Mary, and my young son, John, up to Canada to stay with
relatives. Hopefully, we can return when things settle down.

I am writing to check on you and ask you a favor. Would
you please keep my whereabouts a secret from all except Frederick
Douglass? I have enclosed a second envelope addressed to him,
as he is also in hiding in Canada following John Brown's raid.
I would be grateful if you could mail it to him with your return
address. I would not like to have mine known. Your help would
keep both of our locations safe.

God willing, there will be a positive change with the upcom-
ing election since Buchanan is stepping out of the way. Perhaps
the Republican senator from Illinois, Abraham Lincoln, who I
am hearing so much about, can take a firm stand against slavery,
and we can all move on from the tragedies black people live with
every day.

Please write to me about your new life with your parents. I
think of you often and hope the best for you, Juba.

Best regards,
Elias Rouse

Juba folded the letter and put it back in the envelope. She would
write to Elias later and confirm that she mailed the post to Mr. Douglass.
Douglass was a great man. She had read some of his writings and had also

seen his abolitionist newspaper, *The North Star*, at Mrs. Hayden's in the sitting rooms. What an honor to do this "favor" for Mr. Rouse. She owed him and several other people her freedom.

While she was reading, she heard her mother in the background doing chores. Mother's work was never done.

"Can I help you, Momma?" Juba asked.

"Baby girl, how about we just take a minute to sit? The night is warm for the middle of November, and I could use some fresh air. Let's go up on the roof," her momma suggested.

The two women climbed up the ladder in the back bedroom, where there was a hatch for fixing the roof and for the chimney man to access for cleaning. They had found a bench up there, and with the colder weather closing in, they enjoyed going out with their wool shawls and looking at the stars.

Settling close to each other for warmth, they both took a deep breath of crisp evening air. The salty sea air from Boston Harbor filled Juba's lungs. That smell wasn't wholly pleasant, but it was a welcome change from the thick brackish air of Mississippi or the more recent forest mountain air of Pennsylvania. The scent of Boston was the smell of home.

The days were getting short, and though it wasn't late, the moon and stars were clear in the cloudless nighttime sky. The women sat quietly for a few minutes until her mother finally remarked, "You doin' all right working at Mrs. Hayden's, Juba? That work is a bit heavier than being a nursemaid for little children."

"Yes, Momma. I'm fine. It's a place to start, and I meet so many nice guests who need hope. I'm helping others, just like those who helped me find my way home and be free. Most I've met left their families behind or are trying to find their people who have already gone north. I am so grateful my family is close by," Juba explained, putting her arm around her mother's shoulders.

"There's so much work to be done. So many people are lost. I get you." Her mother sighed.

"Do you think Pappa will have any luck today finding work? That wasn't fair of the shipyard to cut him off. He's been there a good while and is a hard worker."

"Yes, those are the trials, I guess. Lots of new immigrants are pouring into Boston. The yards be takin' white men instead, and work for the black man getting to be slim pickin's the more folks that come from Ireland and other places," her momma explained.

"Maybe he can go back to working in one of the finer hotels. Isn't that what he was doing when I was a little girl?" Juba asked.

"That servant and hotel work was some of the first to go when more English and Irish started coming. I think as much as the abolitionists talk about helping us black folks be free, they forget about making sure we can survive and make a living."

"I pray he comes home with a job. One day at a time, I guess."

Both women sat a while longer and regarded the night sky. There was the North Star. A smile broadened on her face. All those times looking for it, and now here she was at the place she had yearned for all those years. Next to her momma. Living free.

"You know, Momma, when I was enslaved, I would find the North Star, and I knew I was looking toward where you were, up here in Boston. That gave me hope whenever I could find it." Juba's eyes filled with tears, and her heart beat hard. She'd never forget those years of worrying she'd never get back.

"Thank goodness for that, my sweet girl. I kept trying to feel where you might be, hoping that you were alive and all right. I prayed every day you would find your way. I always kept hope in my heart." Momma turned and kissed Juba on her forehead, cupping her chin in her hand for a moment. She could see the glistening of tears in her mother's eyes even in the dark, and it made a lump form in her throat. She cleared her throat so she could go on.

"When I was on my way here with all those kind people helping me along the way, I would look for it, like it was leading me back."

"It's good to have something lighting the way, giving us hope," her mother whispered and took Juba's hand, squeezing it.

Several stars shot across the sky from the west toward the sea.

"Did you see that, Momma? I've seen a lot of meteors lately."

Momma put her free arm around Juba's shoulder and pressed her tight against her side, "Seeing those shooting stars is a mysterious and beautiful thing. They are like little bits of fire crossing through the night sky and then disappearing."

They sat for a few more minutes, holding each other's warm hands tightly, and Juba watched another steady stream of shooting stars. Her heart squeezed with sadness and joy. What was that combination called?

"I think some people are like the North Star, guiding the way home. Other people are like the comets and meteors, breaking through the darkness, bright and inspiring hope, and then gone from sight but never forgotten."

Afterword

Harriet Lane

Harriet Lane left the Executive Mansion at the beginning of 1861 as her uncle's presidency ended. Reportedly, she was sad to leave Washington and the role of First Lady. A renowned hostess and style trendsetter, she must have found returning to Wheatland, Buchanan's estate near Lancaster, Pennsylvania, an anticlimax for her at the age of thirty. During the Civil War, Harriet stayed at Wheatland with her uncle and helped him manage his affairs.

Five years after leaving her role as First Lady, Harriet Lane became Harriet Johnston when she married Henry Johnston, a Baltimore banker, in a small ceremony at Wheatland on January 11, 1866. Henry was the same person her uncle had scolded her for writing letters to as a teenage girl after meeting him at Bedford Springs. The couple had two sons, James Buchanan Johnston and Henry Elliot Johnston, shortly after marriage. Tragically, both boys died in a short period at the ages of eight and nine of rheumatic fever, and within a year, her husband, Henry, died of pneumonia as well.

Even after the tragic loss of her boys, her husband, and her uncle, who died in March of 1868, Harriet's indomitable spirit carried on. She took up the cause of childhood diseases and healthcare in honor of her boys and funded the Harriet Lane Hospital for Invalid Children, which would later become Johns Hopkins Children's Hospital. She also endowed a boys' choir school in Washington, D.C., which today is known as St. Alban's School. She was also the executor and champion of James Buchanan's legacy. She worked tirelessly to get his biography published and actively tried to debunk public opinion that he was at fault for the coming of the Civil War.

Harriet moved back to Washington as a widow and was a frequent guest and active presence in the Washington social scene. Her friendship and letters with Lily Macalester lasted many years. Lily married Alfred Berghmans, the secretary of the Dutch Delegation to the U.S., in 1861.

Juba Wright

Juba Wright is a fictional character I created to embody the woman who was reportedly freed from the widow Eugenia Bass while accompanying Buchanan in the summer of 1859. Unfortunately, the newspaper stories and Buchanan's biography do not give us her real or given name or any information about her. The character I developed for her is a compilation of many narratives of enslaved persons who have written down their experiences, including Frederick Douglass, Harriet Tubman, Solomon Northup's *Twelve Years a Slave*, and *Incidents in the Life of a Slave Girl* by Harriet Jacobs. Life was not suddenly easy for freed enslaved black people arriving in the North. Jobs were sparse, and the separation of communities, employment, and services was a fact of life and did not improve after the Civil War. As we know, these are issues that America is still trying to resolve and grapple with today. I want to think that the woman liberated from Bedford Springs in the summer of 1859 went on to gain hope from her freedom from oppression, and that being free may have brought happiness to her heart and life. Perhaps she has great-grandchildren among us today who have the freedom of life, liberty, and the pursuit of happiness as laid out by our founding fathers, but with the necessary revision, for all, regardless of race, sex, or creed.

James Buchanan

James Buchanan left the Executive Mansion in the winter of 1861, telling Abraham Lincoln that he hoped he was as happy to enter it as he was to leave it. In the interim, between the summer of 1859 and the end of his presidency, the powder keg of America's division on the issue of slavery was lit on fire. After Lincoln's nomination, several southern states began secession talks. Buchanan's answer was to try to uphold the states' rights

202 ★ 𝒦𝓇𝒾𝓈 𝒮𝒸𝒽𝒶𝒶𝓁𝑒

position to decide on slavery, but in the meantime, the South was already forming what would become the Confederacy. Buchanan directed Secretary of War John Floyd to send reinforcements to Fort Sumter, but Floyd told him not to send more forces. A few months after Lincoln's inauguration, on April 12, 1861, the first shots of the Civil War were fired on U.S. (later called Union) ships in Charleston Harbor by then secessionist (Confederate) cannons.

Buchanan spent his retirement at his Wheatland estate near Lancaster, Pennsylvania. When the Battle of Gettysburg raged, he was probably close enough to hear the cannons and see the smoke rising. He did not leave. Buchanan passed away at Wheatland on June 1, 1868. Harriet was by his side.

Elias Rouse

Records show that Elias Rouse left for Canada shortly after John Brown's failed raid on Harpers Ferry but returned after the start of Lincoln's administration and the Civil War. He contributed to the building of the Zion AME Church on a gravel hill in the west end of Bedford and was an active minister in the AME Zion Church until his death. Elias's son, John, recalled his father's activism in the Underground Railroad. John became an attorney who served Bedford and the community in that capacity. Elias died in 1892 at the age of seventy at his home on Pitt Street after a long illness of "congestion of the brain," and is remembered for his renown in the Bedford community.

John Harris and James Graham

John Harris went on to volunteer for the Union troops in July 1863 and was wounded at Morris Island, South Carolina. He mustered out as a sergeant at the end of the Civil War in 1865, living a long life in Bedford before his death in 1914. His great-great-grandson, Garnell Washington, is an educator, Doctor of Sociology, and activist who works to improve race understanding and promote equality and diversity. Garnell was kind enough to take me to his family's homestead site, which is no longer standing, up near the Bedford reservoir. James Graham was Harris's neighbor, and his home still stands on Graham Avenue outside of Bedford near Wolfsburg. James was also a minister and an active member of the AME Zion Church on Gravel Hill.

Simon Cameron

Simon Cameron denied any connection to the disappearance of the widow's enslaved nursemaid. Early in 1860, Cameron was initially bent on securing the Republican nomination for president, but after much political wrangling, he did not get the bid and threw his support behind Abraham Lincoln. After much controversy, Lincoln eventually named him his Secretary of War the day after his inauguration. Their first disagreement was over Cameron's proposal to emancipate and arm enslaved black people in the south, which, at the time, Lincoln was not prepared to accept. Cameron had a long history of fiscal corruption, and under pressure from another Republican, Lincoln replaced Cameron in 1862 with another Pennsylvanian, Edward Stanton, as Secretary of War, sending Cameron to Russia as an ambassador. On his return to Pennsylvania after the Civil War, he remained a chief driver and political boss of Pennsylvania politics until his death at ninety years of age.

John Brown

John Brown was tried for his failed raid on the Federal Armory in Harpers Ferry, Virginia, now West Virginia. His raid is often credited as a primary antecedent of the Civil War. Indeed, his radicalism both inspired abolitionists and created overwhelming fear in southern slave states that played a part in the start of our nation's bloodiest war. John Brown's month-long trial, which attracted daily attention from the national press and created growing national division, ended in Brown and his four surviving accomplices being found guilty of murder, conspiracy to create insurrection, and treason. He and the other men were hanged on the morning of December 2, 1859. Walt Whitman wrote his poem "Year of Meteors," an excerpt of which serves as the epigraph at the beginning of this story, about witnessing the hanging. John Brown is buried in North Elba, New York, near the home he built as part of a planned interracial community.

Quaker Valley

Quaker Valley actively supported the Underground Railroad through the Civil War. Though Quakers are often conscientious objectors, some sons of the Valley did go to fight, given the cause. The attendance of the Quaker meeting house in Fishertown has grown relatively small in recent years, but it is an active and dedicated few. A museum has also been opened in the former meeting house in Spring Hope that is referenced in this story as Dunnings Creek Quaker Meeting. A new brick meeting house was built in the late 1800s, and meetings for worship, or First Day, as Quakers prefer to call it, are still held every Sunday. I highly recommend a visit to the museum. The active members take turns running the museum on summer weekends, and they are some of the most friendly, peaceful souls you could ever imagine meeting. I am very grateful for their time talking to me and their encouragement to tell this story.

Bedford Springs

The Bedford Springs Hotel ran on hard times during the Civil War. Southern visitors were cut off, and Northerners had a war on their hands and little time for leisure. Post-war years continued to be economically difficult for the Springs. Still, in the 1890s, there was another boom in business as the Springs competed with Saratoga Springs and other similar northeastern estates. Over the early twentieth century, the resort was used first in WWI as a training camp for communications officers and then in WWII as an internment camp for Japanese dignitaries. The beautiful buildings had many ups and downs and changes in ownership. Finally, in 2007, after being closed for nearly twenty years, the resort was restored, and new buildings were added. Today, it is owned by Omni Hotels, and it is a jewel of the Bedford Valley, bringing visitors from all over the country and the world to enjoy the mountain air and rich history of the area.

Bedford

Bedford's position near the Mason-Dixon line made it a complicated place during the Civil War. There was predominantly Union support, but some went to serve the Confederacy. McConnellsburg, a mere thirty miles away to the east, was set on fire by the Confederate Army and lost beautiful old homes and saw fighting in the streets. Though there were plans by the Confederate Army to head for Bedford, they were turned around before that could happen in the call to fight at Gettysburg. Many old buildings still stand in Bedford. Several are mentioned in this story. After the Civil War, Bedford was a quiet rural town. Its population declined as the railroads grew in Cumberland and Altoona. The Pennsylvania Turnpike routing through Bedford brought more traffic and eventually bypassed the "Great Road." Now, that road is referred to as the Lincoln Highway and circumvents Bedford. There was a housing boom after WWII, which filled in new neighborhoods in the 1950s, making Bedford a quaint bedroom community. Today, it is heavily agricultural, but it is also a tourist town catering to guests of the Springs and others who enjoy art and history, shopping, and great restaurants.

There is still a great divide in political views in Bedford County. Some families that have been here since before the Civil War claim ancestors from both the Confederate and Union armies. Brother against brother was a reality in Bedford as it was in other border states.

The black community in Bedford is much smaller today than it was at the time of this story. Over the years since the Civil War and industrialization, many people of both white and black communities left for cities like Washington, Baltimore, Pittsburgh, Philadelphia, and New York, as they are all within a day's drive and provided much greater opportunity for education and culture. Though many black residents have told me they feel welcome and an integral part of the community, there is still a great gap in how that community functions as part of the whole, but rather as a separate entity within the whole, in my observation. Today's youth seem to have a greater sense of diversity, equity, and inclusion, and I am hopeful that through our community's evolution, we can understand how we are all one with so much to share.

About the Story

Initially, I set out to write a story about Harriet Lane at the Bedford Springs. Not a lot has been written about Harriet, and the more I read about her when I began researching, the more I enjoyed getting to know her. The available letters and accounts make her out to be a woman I would have liked to have known. Learning about her time at Bedford Springs was enjoyable, as I live within a mile of the beautiful old resort, and a strong woman of that time was intriguing to me. Then I began to imagine what those summers were like for Harriet. If you are interested in Harriet, please read Milton Stern's *Harriet Lane, America's First Lady*.

Anne McCoy was my fictional vehicle for writing about Harriet. I had recently read *Carnegie's Maid* by Marie Benedict, and the idea of two women's relationships from different classes and backgrounds seemed like an excellent place to start. I live in a neighborhood in Bedford where I can walk by a house from the mid-1850s period. What is now my neighborhood was, in 1859, a cow pasture near the farmhouse I imagined was Anne's.

The Bedford Springs is an active resort that came back from the edge of obscurity and possible demolition about twenty years ago and is today a fabulous five-star resort set just outside the picturesque and quaint little town of Bedford, Pennsylvania. I highly recommend a visit to take in all of Bedford's amenities and history. Books full of history and pictures of the glory of Bedford Springs are widely available, and it is fascinating to read and look at the wonderful old pictures. Photography was becoming available during the time of this book, and many early photographs enriched my imagination and research.

Soon after starting my research, I kept coming across a brief reference to the summer of 1859, when Buchanan visited the Springs and local abolitionists freed his guest's enslaved nursemaid. I found this information in Buchanan's biography by Philip Klein, published in 1962. It was also cited in several other sources and was initially printed in the Cumberland *Civilian and Telegraph* newspaper. *"Toward the end of July, Buchanan set out for his regular fortnight at Bedford Springs, taking the widow Bass and her three young children with him. The pleasant interlude was marred by only two incidents. Buchanan found himself placed in rooms next to Simon Cameron, and the abolitionists ran away with Mrs. Bass's Negro servant girl. People at the Springs generally assumed that Cameron had arranged the episode to spite Buchanan. Apparently, some people of Bedford had persuaded the girl to leave and had given her money with which to travel farther North. But Mrs. Bass took it calmly, announcing that the girl was honest and capable, and had taken none of the money and jewels available in the rooms. She hoped only that others would care for her and treat her kindly, which she feared they would not."*

No additional information can be found about the incident. At the same time, I came across William Roy Mock's book, *The Last Station: Underground Railroad of Quaker Corner*, in my local library. That book led me to more research on the Underground Railroad and slavery in Pennsylvania. I discovered that my northern sensibilities about being a "Yankee" and my knowledge about what was really going on in the North at that time were sadly lacking and, in many cases, downright wrong. I started reading any slave narrative I could find, beginning with Frederick Douglass. Douglass's writing is excellent and vivid, and if you are interested in the first-person perspective of the horrors of slavery, I highly suggest starting with his accounts.

It was at this time that the real story began showing itself to me. I knew that I was fascinated by Harriet and Anne, but then the story of the woman who escaped from enslavement was much more critical to tell. How these women might have interacted during that incident became my work as a fiction writer and as a person interested in people. As I began to go to talks about race relations offered by the local Quaker Meeting in Fishertown, I met historians, sociologists, Quakers, and local people who all helped by encouraging me to write this story.

What I discovered was that, though Bedford and Pennsylvania were part of what was considered "the North," this area was very divided when it came to ideas about slavery. The border states were and still are full of conflict and opposing views about race, government, and morality.

Only small snippets about John Brown could be found in local Bedford histories. Still, he was at the Springs just before the president's arrival and meeting with abolitionists in the area that summer, leading up to his fateful and failed raid in October in Harpers Ferry. I suggest David Reynolds' *John Brown, Abolitionist: The Man Who Killed Slavery, Sparked the Civil War, and Seeded Civil Rights* if you want to learn more about John Brown. He was and is still a very controversial and compelling man who played a massive role in sparking the Civil War. His character was too large not to tie into the story. There are brief allusions to a potential kidnapping of Buchanan from the Springs, but whether that was John Brown or a Confederate plot post-presidency is unclear. The editor of the *Bedford Gazette* recounted his meeting a "John Smith" at the Springs while playing billiards in June of 1859. He later realized that this was John Brown with his sons. Elias Rouse's son John stated in news articles that, as a grown man, he remembered John Brown visiting his father's home when he was a boy. Still, no record of Elias's involvement in Harpers Ferry can be found besides references to his name in Brown's letters to his wife. John Brown's correspondence also mentioned Reverend Fidler and a gentleman named Joseph Crawley. Elias Rouse, John Fidler, and Joseph Crawley are cited in many sources as the primary coordinators of the Underground Railroad in Bedford.

Local experts were a tremendous help to me, and their willingness to share knowledge was nothing short of a miracle that kept me on the trail of a great story. At a presentation at the Fishertown Quaker Meeting about the black experience now and in the past in Bedford County, I met Dr. Garnell Washington and Peggy Reiman. They are principals in a company called Harris Connections, which works with groups and corporations to provide Diversity, Equity, and Inclusion education and experiences. They brought me to the land where John Harris lived (Garnell's great-great-grandfather) and showed me James Graham's house, which still stands today. Their help was also pivotal as they encouraged me and emboldened me to write from the enslaved woman's perspective.

The story took a completely different and much more impactful turn with this advice.

At the Quaker speaker series "Still Listening," I was introduced to several local historians who helped me tremendously. Kevin Mearkle was finishing his book *The Underground Railroad in Bedford County, Pennsylvania,* when I met him, and his book was invaluable to me. I cannot recommend it enough. If you think there aren't miracles, I'll also add that his wife turned out to be my new coworker (and fast friend), and they soon graced me with a copy hot off the presses. I referred to it constantly throughout the writing of this book, and it saved me many additional hours of research that I had already been searching for.

I used as much fact and research as possible and weaved it together to support the story. I had to make up some characters, like Anne and Juba, but I used real people, places, and details wherever I could. There is a lot of period-specific background information included, as I was intrigued to study the lead-up to the Civil War, and I thought readers would be interested as well. I used tragedies that I read about in slave narratives and histories of the time, as there were things that I was shocked about and sickened by. We all need to learn about or be reminded of these facts so that we never forget to treat others as anything other than people and fellow human beings. Each of the women taught me something new by imagining walking in their shoes and writing about them. I hope that by reading this story, you will walk in their shoes too, and through them, grow in your understanding of others. To me, that is the true magic of reading.

Acknowledgments

I must start out by thanking my family for their unwavering support, encouragement, and belief in me as I endeavored to write my first novel. My sons, Sam and Max's sweet words telling me they are proud of me mean more than they will ever know. My partner, John Rafter, was not only a first reader but also used his keen newsman's eye and love of adventure to be both an excellent fact checker and worthy story development advisor to question, push, and make the plot jump. Thank you love, for countless patient hours listening and reading.

My next champion that deserves thanks is my best friend of a lifetime, Megan Wahl Hegenbarth. Together we have shared fifty years of loving to read the same flavor of books, and as I wrote this novel, she was my reader that I had in mind. Megan loved the story as I wrote it, encouraged me every step of the way, and celebrated every page. She was my definitive expert on Quakers, as she is a Quaker and teacher of Quakerism at Wilmington Friends School in Delaware. She also found many beta readers for me, to whom I am so grateful! Megan, you are the wind beneath my wings. Thank you.

I would also be remiss in not thanking my other early reader, encourager, and tireless listener, all through the writing of this book, Cindy Fochtman. My friend and walking partner, Cindy, read as I wrote, gave me ideas and praise all through the process. Thank you, dear Cindy.

As I started to research and write, it seemed the more I spoke about the book, attended lectures on related topics, and sought out local subject matter experts, the more I met the right people at the right time. Through Valinda Mearkle, a work friend, I discovered her husband, Kevin

Mearkle, was about to publish "The Underground Railroad in Bedford County," which is packed with research and information that saved me countless hours of research I had been looking for. If you are interested in the Underground Railroad, you must read his book. Peggy Reiman and Dr. Garnell Washington not only were kind enough to listen to my story idea, but also to take me to the site of the Harris Homestead. While there, they encouraged me to write from the escaped slave woman's point of view, and totally changed the trajectory of the book, I believe, for the better. Through my trepidation of writing from a point of view I have never lived, Garnell gave me hope and courage that I could do Juba's voice justice. Dunnings Creek Friends were also helpers and encouragers. I am so grateful for my community.

Just as I began to write, Coltt Winter Lepley, who recently returned to the local area, MFA, writer, singer-songwriter, started the Next-door Writers Group. Coltt and all those in the group gave me my first reviews, criticisms, and encouragements, and I am grateful to all. Early beta-readers, many of my writer peers helped me grow in craft and confidence. Learning to stop being afraid to put my work out there and ask for feedback was critical to this work. Bill Fine and Dennis Williamson, who also led me to the Bedford County Historical Society board, were also pivotal reviewers who made my history sharper and provided excellent historical feedback.

Special thanks to Nancy Defibaugh Pyle and her brother Bill. Their father, William Defibaugh Sr., was the penultimate historian of Bedford Springs photos and memorabilia. They have graciously permitted me to use a photo from his collection of the Springs that inspired the cover. I do so in their dad's memory. The setting and characters of Daniel and Sophia Defibaugh at the Willows tavern in chapter fourteen are their ancestors and are based on historical details of that place and those people.

Editor Julia King was fundamental in making this story what it is. Her patience, suggestions, gracious comments, encouragement, and copy edits polished my work beautifully. Julia's expertise and thoughtful suggestions thoroughly enhanced my intentions for the story and characters.

Finally, I want to thank Sunbury Press. It was another act of serendipity that put me at the WCONA writers conference the very week I started submitting my manuscript, where I met Sunbury's President

Lawrence Knorr, who quickly decided my book was worthy of publication. Lawrence Knorr with thoughtful and thorough editor Jennifer Tedford who polished my words, have collaborated to bring this book to you today, and I am forever grateful.

About the Author

KRIS SCHAALE is a novelist interested in a wide array of genres, though her love of history and psychology always seems to find a way into her work. Having lived across the U.S., she fell in love with and now resides in Bedford Pennsylvania with her partner John and two adult sons, Sam and Max. When not living vicariously through her characters, she enjoys the outdoors, skiing, hiking, and kayaking. She uses her bachelor's and master's degrees in psychology from Pennsylvania State University to study and write about people's behavior, motivations, and life journeys. Through story, she hopes her readers will learn and be enriched in their own understanding of people and life.